W0246747

PENGUIN BOOKS
STILLBORN

Rohini Nilekani is a writer and a philanthropist. She is Founder-Chairperson of Arghyam, a charitable trust that funds initiatives in water and sanitation and Chairperson of Pratham Books, which seeks to democratize the joy of reading for children. She sits on the boards of several non-profit organizations and funds work in education, health and environment.

Earlier, as a journalist, Rohini wrote for a number of leading publications in India. She has also anchored a television show, *Uncommon Ground*, to bring leaders of the social and corporate sectors together in dialogue.

STILLBORN

a medical thriller

Rohini Nilekani

PENGUIN BOOKS

An imprint of Penguin Random House

PENGUIN BOOKS

USA | Canada | UK | Ireland | Australia
New Zealand | India | South Africa | China | Singapore

Penguin Books is part of the Penguin Random House group of companies
whose addresses can be found at global.penguinrandomhouse.com

Published by Penguin Random House India Pvt. Ltd
4th Floor, Capital Tower 1, MG Road,
Gurugram 122 002, Haryana, India

Penguin
Random House
India

First published by Penguin Books India 1998

12 11 10 9 8 7 6 5

ISBN 9780140283020

Typeset in Palatino by Eleven Arts, Keshav Puram, New Delhi

Printed at Repro India Limited

www.penguin.co.in

To my whole family,
especially Nana and Aai

FOREWORD

It has been a decade since this book was first published. And how much has changed in India since then! It has been one of the defining decades since Independence, a decade opening into a new century, witnessing unprecedented economic growth and ensuing prosperity for many and yet, a decade also of a growing disquiet for the many more left behind and waiting.

Looking back, this was a genre book, written along the lines of a familiar plot and denouement integral to English language thrillers written by Western writers of that time, yet very Indian and personal in its voice. Not too many books of the sort, if any, had been tried by Indian authors at the time I wrote it. Today, I believe, many genre books are being written by a new generation of Indian writers. This book now has much company in an expanding market.

When I re-read *Stillborn* recently, I felt that while much had changed in the world described there, quite a lot has not. And hopefully, therefore, the book's central premise remains as true as ever. Even today, millions of Indians have no access to healthcare services. And although the pharmaceutical industry has been growing in leaps and bounds, is becoming more professional by the day and has received both international attention and funding, we still cannot boast of more than a handful of new drugs that have come out of Indian laboratories and become front runners in the world of medicine. Competition is still intense; malpractices abound. And the challenge of developing a contraceptive vaccine that is safe and effective still remains open.

What has changed dramatically, however, since *Stillborn* was published in December 1998, is the role of the media. The penetration of satellite television and the 24-hour news channels have made the journalism described in this story somewhat obsolete. The internet and the culture surrounding it have changed beyond belief. Just ten years on, the methods my heroine used seem very simple and old-fashioned. However, I stand by her in her sense of conviction, her enthusiasm to reach to the bottom of the unsolved puzzle, but mostly by her sense of duty to those who do not have the means to understand and prevent their own exploitation.

Stillborn was a product of my conscience and my creativity in the period between '96–'98, when I was a stay-at-home mother to my two young children. Since this book, I have been involved less with writing and more with philanthropic and social activities in education, water and the environment.

I am happy that *Stillborn* is being re-launched. I do hope a whole new generation can enjoy it, and that it gets them thinking about the issues the book throws up.

Rohini Nilekani
Bangalore
November 2008

PROLOGUE

The moon was deserted by the clouds that night. Silver streaks picked up the shapes of huts bunched randomly along the towering hill slopes.

The Baniga tribals should have been asleep. But no one could rest in that unfamiliar air. An eerie wind had taken hold of the trees.

In a little hut, surrounded by bushes that flailed in the face of the gust, a young woman lay tossing on a woven mattress of grass. Across the light of a little kerosene lamp, her shadow splayed gigantic over the opposite wall. Her stomach protruded grotesquely above the contours of her upper and lower halves. Two children, one little boy clutching a toddler girl with luminous eyes, sat in a corner, trying not to watch. The woman was in extreme agony. She moaned, like a cow needing to be milked. The sound curved off the walls, lent itself to the unquiet wind blowing outside.

The wooden door was thrown open. A man walked in, followed by another boy. They bent carefully down to the woman, one at each end, lifting her up in their arms. The moan rose to a growl. At the door, a dozen faces had crowded in. There were questions in their eyes and on their tongues. There was no time for a debate. The man carrying the woman roughly pushed an old lady away. The rest moved aside as though connected to the old woman's limbs. Someone else came forward to help. The others watched as the group moved away. They were taking the woman to The Clinic. Where it all began.

As the night swallowed the sound of their footsteps, the crowd began to buzz. Low at first, then in a crescendo of anxiety and anger.

Meanwhile, the group reached the clinic. A team was waiting. Rather belatedly, a stretcher was proffered. The man just looked at it briefly, and then continued to carry the woman inside on his own.

The Doctor was inside, masked, gloved and ready. Steel instruments glinted evilly around her in the harsh tubelit room. Without a word, he deposited the woman on the operating table, transferring a moment of fear, a glimmer of hope to the writhing figure. And went outside.

When the cry of the baby came, it broke through the stillness of the hour, cracking it open like an eggshell. The man and the boy looked at each other, their eyes bloodied with weariness. Then they walked back in.

It was a little girl. Three and a half pounds. Her face was screwed up with the mortification of the just-born at such a graceless ejection. Otherwise, she was not much like other newborns. Her lower body was twisted up like a sari wrung out after a wash. It was wrinkled, grey. Her movements were awkward, her breathing painful. The head was elongated, her neck too short.

The mother lay next to the little one, a protective palm across the tiny, heaving chest. She glanced at the man and tried to smile. The man made no such attempt. He sat on the cold floor, gripping his wife's hand. Then he began to cry. Outside, there arose the throbbing sounds of a people in distress. Of a people who had waited too long.

2

ONE

My sane and stable existence suddenly went crazy and dangerous that April day. Since then, things have never returned to normal. We have all begun, however, to redefine normalcy. The madness started with the road accident. Some of the bones and most of the flesh on my left side were crushed and torn in the crash. I had to spend three days at St Paul's Hospital. Luckily, it is one of the most respected medical institutions in Bangalore and is located in one of the city's few remaining green patches. If I craned my neck enough, light filtered fragrant through the tall window. I could catch a glimpse of the cassias and tabebuias. Mynahs cackled and lapwings shrieked. Sunbirds and magpie-robins trilled with the joy of the mating season.

In the hospital my days went along busily, almost like being at work. Several of my journalist colleagues visited, mostly with blooms from the florist downstairs. They also brought along the inevitable poor jokes, some of which were dutifully inscribed on my leg cast. It all helped, though, as sharp and dull aches were still streaking through my body, defying giant doses of painkillers. Everyone congratulated me on having survived. On the beat, they have often seen the other side of the slim barrier between life and death.

I could so easily have died. Few people survive an

encounter with a bus, especially one belonging to the Bangalore Transport Service fleet. Statistically, I'm told, I had a 1-in-789 chance. I am going to buy lottery tickets in that series, if I ever decide to push my luck further.

I had seen the bus coming, of course I had, on that mad, hot day in the mid-morning rush hour! In spite of the ill-designed crash helmet I wore. In spite of the billowy smoke aimed at me by the vicious autorickshaw ahead. Who could miss a red, rattly monster like that? The real question was: did *he* see me? Could the bus driver see anything beyond the festoons that decorated his windshield in celebration of Ram Navami?

If he could, he certainly did not act as if he did. *'Arre, Arre!'* I remember saying as he drove into the delicately curved rear end of my trendy new scooter, knocking me off onto the potholes of Richmond Road. I'm glad I didn't die. Those would have been lousy last words.

As I hit the ground, I felt hot anger rush through me. I tried to sit up. Then, noticing a bright redness erupting from my left leg, I fell promptly into a cowardly faint. When I came to, I wished I hadn't. Dozens of sweaty faces surrounded me, ghoulish curiosity dripping from every pore. If you need to do a headcount of the under-employed in this city, you only need to stage a few spectacles.

As I had done, no doubt, in my pink malmal kameez, lying next to my bright blue scooter. A policeman was bent over me, the whistle around his neck dangling hypnotically. 'I'm a doctor,' he said, quite without reason. But by then, another man had made his way to me. He didn't look much like a doctor, though one had to take his word for it. A bright shock of golden-brown hair fell across his forehead. I can still see it glinting in the sunlight. I remember my relief, and that sudden sense of being one with the universe. I smiled beatifically and passed out again, my head probably hitting the asphalt.

There's nothing quite like the disorientation of waking

up somewhere you didn't know you had gone. Panic flared and subsided. I made myself look around me. Grey walls, white fixtures, phenyl in my nostrils. Hospital logos inscribed on each item of furnishing. Thankfully, a shock of memory was quickly retrieved from the clutter that surrounded my mind. I remembered the BTS bus and grimaced.

'Ah, you are awake!' My father rose from a chair at the foot of my bed and gripped the fingers of my good hand. My mother, I noticed, was at my head, japamala, as always, in her grip. Amma is deeply religious.

'Good job,' boomed Anna cheerfully. 'They had to scrap the bus!'

'My scooter?' I croaked, bile rushing to join my words.

'It's time to get that car you've always been promising yourself,' he replied.

My head hurt, my leg was in a cast, my left arm had bandages all over, my vehicle was beyond repair and Anna was making jokes. All was well with the world.

Someone knocked at the door and let himself in. It was the doctor with the burnished locks.

'Ah! Dr Kamath! Come in, come in. She's up!'

His slim frame moved towards me rather lazily. 'How do you feel?' he asked, grinning and waving his stethoscope. Most irritating. As he approached my bed, I couldn't help staring. His eyes matched his hair. Amber, going on brown.

'Dr Rohil Kamath here stopped you from bleeding to death, I think,' offered Anna obligingly.

'No problem. It just helped me make my daily quota,' said the good doctor, even before I could finish my prim 'thank you'. Anna and he then laughed together, almost privately. Amma just smiled, as is her wont. I frowned. Accident victims could afford not to be bound by social niceties.

Dr Kamath left soon after. But not before my parents had given him a once-over. It was clear from his name that he belonged to our Gaud Saraswat clan. Inevitably, they switched over to Konkani. Even more inevitably, they began to praise what they believe are my various accomplishments. Just before I drifted off, I suffered the visiting doctor's parting shot. 'Lucky she did not injure her "write" hand! Pun intended!' The door closed on his chuckle.

I work for a fortnightly magazine called *Deadline*. It belongs to the Heggade group of publications, the flagship of which is the number one newspaper in the state—the *Daily Tribune*. I write for the newspaper as well. Luckily, there's no competition between the two. Chandra Prasad Rao, whom we all call CP, edits my magazine. He is also consulting editor for the newspaper. I think the magazine was originally seen only as a line extension. Then we kind of surprised everybody by becoming the first successful national newsmagazine from the South. Our strength lies in incisive reporting and in-depth analysis. 'We read between the lines so that you don't have to', says our ad-blurb. I myself like to write on health issues. That's what my byline, Poorva Pandit, is best associated with.

Typically, CP was the last to pay me a visit. He started off as though it were an edit meeting.

'What's going to happen to that industry piece you were working on? Wasn't it slated for the next issue? Do you have anything else in the can?' He took a chair next to my bed as though it were an office. Before I could muster up an indignant retort, he continued.

'Never trust these bloody PROs,' he said acidly. 'That fool Bhagat told me the Dal was to file its returns this year! Now they're waffling again.'

The Dal is the ruling political party, known for its flipflopping. I made sympathetic noises. Then I said sweetly, 'Thanks for being so concerned about me, CP.'

'What? Oh! You look fine to me, considering you were foolish enough to get in the way of a bus. Still, get well soon. We're short on staff.'

We weren't, but I consoled myself with the thought that it was CP's way of saying he missed my presence at work. He is a very good friend as well as a fine editor.

'I'll put together a story on the traffic mess,' I offered. 'We could go national, arrange inputs, gory pictures, the works.'

'Good, I'll ask Amita to work with you on that,' he replied, referring to one of our new starry-eyed reporters. That's it. He was getting ready to leave.

Unfortunately, for me at least, he bumped into my father on his way out. Anna thinks the world of CP who is hardly averse to his flattery, even though my father is only 'a bloody PRO' in the pharmaceutical industry. They got talking, quite forgetting the needy patient, and started to walk towards the corridor—with the hot soup and fresh rolls I had been promised for dinner!

TWO

The accident had determined the course of the following few weeks. But what happened that night determined the course of the next few months. In some essential way, of the next few years. Of course I did not know it then. I was resting soundly, with the aid of tranquillizers. Around 10 p.m., I was awoken by the clattering sounds of people trying to be silent. If hospitals had any respect for their poor inmates, they would make their mobile trays in plastic, not in rusty metal. I jumpily opened an eye and noted that it was Dr Vitthal, the young resident doctor, with an attendant nurse. I quickly shut it again. I had no intention of being subjected to his prattle.

So I used an age-old, time-tested technique to disappear from the scene. It's called yoga nidra. Anna had recommended it to me. Anna should know. He is extremely regular with his own morning yogic exercises. 'Yoga nidra is an amazing stress reliever,' he had said. I finally learnt it from my yoga teacher last year. It works. From the outside, it looks as though you are in deep sleep when in reality, all your senses are alert and on the guard.

Dr Vitthal and the nurse went about treating my dressings as though I were an inert doll. Jab, twist, stretch, pull.

I cursed them silently. The door creaked open. Dr Vitthal urged the visitor in.

'Hi, fellow! Long time.' The intruder must have gesticulated towards me. 'Not to worry. Deep sedation.' I nearly grinned.

The newcomer, whoever he was, needed no further invitation. 'I was just going off duty,' he said in a gruff voice. Another resident doctor, I guessed.

'Are you going to the concert on Saturday?' asked the solicitous Dr Vitthal, his fingers severely testing my ability to conceal pain. I remembered Jethro Tull were to perform in Bangalore. I thought regretfully of the gold-embossed press invitations lying on my desk.

'Yes, of course, and guess who I'm going with? Remember Anshul? Anshul Hiremath? The IAS officer's son?'

'He was in med college with your brother Vivek . . .'

'Right,' said Gruff Voice excitedly. 'Only guy who would turn up in a chauffeur-driven vehicle. In ironed clothes! Remember, we went to their house once? First time we saw a CD player, right?'

'I thought the Beatles had dropped in, the sound was so sharp!'

'Yeah, well, Vivek's in town, so he looked up Anshul...'

'Dr Anshul Hiremath. Hmm. He always had all the tickets, and all the girls . . . na?' There was a bitterness in my doctor's voice. 'It helps to be handsome, with a powerful dad. My sister had this massive crush on him . . .'

'But he wasn't interested,' said the mysterious visitor meanly. 'But then, he hardly reciprocated anyone's affections, did he?'

'I thought he was in the USA?' asked Dr Vitthal, trussing me up neatly. I've seen Amma do something similar when she marinates chicken. Except I now knew how the chicken would have felt!

'He's been back for a while now. Set up his own

company. Very fancy, it seems. India Biotech. Vivek said he's trying to make a contraceptive vaccine for women.'

'Shit, that's great,' said Dr Vitthal, wiping his hands on my bedsheet. 'I was reading only recently about anti-fertility vaccines. It said the firm that delivers it first may win the biggest medical sweepstakes of the century.' He stopped for a while. He had to concentrate on the methodology of torture.

'Trust that bugger to do it first!' he said, basting a new part of my leg.

'Not so fast, wait. It's supposed to be all hush-hush. It seems they've had hajaar problems. Unwarranted pregnancies, complications, some side effects. Vivek said he knows someone on the project. Morale is low. In fact,' the gruff voice reduced in volume dramatically, making me nearly twitch in my strain to hear, 'it seems there was a miscarried foetus. Sixteen weeks. Delivered vaginally. Severely deformed. But it was stolen from the lab.'

'Crazy, man!' said my doctor. I could have thought of many other adjectives! Dr Vitthal did not sound perturbed. I guess you get immune.

'Anyway, don't worry. I have no intention of telling anyone. Still, some guys have all the luck. Girls, wealthy fathers, and then professional jackpots.' He sighed, breathing onions at me with impunity. 'Chalo, I'm all done. Off to sleep, thank God.'

He yawned, muttered something at the nurse, who had not said one word so far. Then I heard steps, and metal trolleys on their way out of my room.

I opened my eyes, thankfully freeing my body to twitch and turn. Later, I ascribed my near-perfect recall of the conversation to the fact that I was practising yoga. It both concentrates and liberates the mind.

I was wide awake now and thinking of a mysterious hunk called Anshul Hiremath. Another doctor. Who was developing a contraceptive vaccine. Who had an instant effect on girls. Who had managed to get a deformed foetus stolen from his lab.

Was it a story? I couldn't remember when I had last written anything that required brain cells upward of my hypothalamus. For lack of anything else to do, I began to type it out in my mind, thus securing, rather usefully as it turned out, the memory of the conversation. 'Returned NRI in hush-hush research on vaccine. Deformed baby found in trash can.'

There was no reason to edit it. I had reached paragraph six when I slipped off the cliff of wakefulness.

THREE

It was angry April, budding gulmohurs yearning for the promised rain. The city was dusty green on its treetops and muddy grey in its skies. The sweltering heat from two-wheelers and trucks drowned any remaining fresh air in smoke. Just another day in the boom city. I pulled up the car window and covered my nose.

Finally, they were letting me go home. My leg cast was going with me, of course. So was my irritability. Because of my sister, and to some extent my mother, I have this thing about being sick. I just cannot handle it. Luckily, I rarely even catch a cold.

Our house breathes suburban air. Thanks to a puritanical old neighbourhood of Bangalore called Basavanagudi. Amma was waiting as the car drove into the porch. I hobbled out painfully. She sprinkled auspicious water on me, mumbling a mysterious mantra. I tried not to grimace at her old-fashioned ritualism. My kid sister, fifteen years my junior, was perched just inside the door on her special chair. She squealed delightedly when she saw me.

'Akka, you look so glamorous with that cast! Trust you to spoil it with a frown,' she said cheekily. She's always quick with her tongue. It makes up for the slowness of her body. Shweta has a rare neuromuscular disorder called

Friedrich's Ataxia. It is a little like muscular dystrophy, a progressive, terminal disease. It strikes early. Muscle tissue degenerates and atrophies slowly, but inevitably. At thirteen, she was wasting away before our eyes.

'Don't just sit there, then. Come help me into my room,' I challenged her. We have this pact that we will underplay her illness. God knows the parents swing the pendulum the other way all the time. Amma does it because she has learnt that it was a hereditary, recessive gene which brought on Shweta's illness. Since it was a recessive gene, both she and Anna had to be carriers to pass it on to the next generation. One would think it would halve the burden. But no! She suffers all the guilt about passing on the defective gene. To compensate, she smothers Shweta with affection. Paradoxically, Anna does the same because he does *not* feel guilty. Or maybe because he feels a little guilty about not feeling guilty. He tries to be very sensible about it, though.

'Yashodha,' I have often heard him try to convince my mother, 'neither of us could have done a thing to prevent it. We didn't even know it was in either of our families. Accept it, ma, and let's move on.' Easier for him to say than for Amma to do. So our family runs along, wearing down the same old grooves.

Shweta and I both limped to my room. She more often than not sleeps there anyway. Settled, each in her own awkward body position, on the double bed, we heaved a simultaneous sigh of relief. I, because there is a visceral sense of security in being back in a familiar resting place. She, because she would have me to herself for the rest of the week. I'm not bragging. Shweta projects all her ideals on to me, wants to experience through me the many things she cannot do herself. She sticks as close to me as I will allow her to. This time, she was too close. She wrinkled her nose at my smell.

'God, Akka. You stink. Easier to get you out of the

hospital than to get the hospital out of you!' I laughed, quite delighted at her wit. She had cleverly paraphrased something my friend Meenal had once said. She is a journalist, and in the days before she was entitled to fly on assignments, she used to travel by rail. 'I can get out of the train,' she would say disgustedly. 'But how do I get the train out of me?'

Shweta was right. Just as the sharp smell of the train clings to mind and body long after you have disembarked, it would take days of diligent scrubbing before the combined odours of sickness and disinfectant would leave me. Other scars were going to take longer.

'So, tell me all about him,' she then commanded, without preamble.

'Who?' I said startled, but already narrowing my eyes as the suspicions formed.

They were bang on target, my misgivings. Amma and Anna were playing matchmaker for the millionth time in twenty-eight years. They, mainly Amma, want me tucked safely into matrimony especially because of Shweta, who will never be able to have a normal life.

'The handsome hero who rescued you, of course. The one you are so moony-eyed over. Dr Rohil Kamath. From our own community, no less! Amgelo Rohil! Destined, Amma says.'

Ah! Memories turned into warm honey. I caught a glimpse of myself in the mirror just as I raised the pillow to throw at my sister. The dangling earrings had been worn for the doctor's benefit, after all. I grinned, and gave in.

'Don't you dare tell Amma. But he's rather all right. And that's it.'

'Okay, but I think it's all very exciting. When will you see him again?'

The catch was, I really didn't know. I had said a meaningful goodbye to him that morning. He had contrived to come in a couple of times before I was discharged. I had discovered that he was doing his postdoctoral research in immunology. Or was it pathology? He worked at the hospital—something to do with organ transplants. I had, with little difficulty, got it from him that he lived in the bachelor staff quarters. By choice. 'I like being close to my work,' he'd said. To tell the truth, I didn't care if he had a three-hour commute. The operative word had been 'bachelor'.

Still, we had made no further plans. I had no clue if my path would ever cross his again. Not that I had much opportunity to brood over it. The next few days were taken up by the insistent demands from Shweta. To play brain games with her, sing with her the latest in Indi-pop, listen to her poems, generally cosset her madly.

I also had to prevent myself from being cosseted half to death by Amma. To say nothing of Laxmi, God's culinary compensation to my troubled family. I was overfed with every manner of South Canara delicacy. Light-as-air neer dose, sungta ghashi, fried motyala—tiny morsels of crisp fish. I was offered hot-water bags and aspirins at every involuntary ouch I uttered. I was stoically tolerated in spite of my temper. No wonder I regressed to the mental and physical state of a toddler in one short week.

It was Anna who realized that I was going stir crazy. Offering me a chilled glass of beer one muggy evening, he settled down for a chat in the patio. Our house is almost half a century old. When it was built, it had looked, I am told, like the new braggart in the block. Now, with apartment complexes shadowing every bungalow in the area, we were the respectable token reminder of the good old times.

That day, there was reason to celebrate. My cast had been removed and a heavy bandage had taken its place. At least my poor leg could breathe now. Back at the hospital with Amma, I'd kept my eyes peeled, and I suspect she had too. But there had been no sign of any interesting young doctors. Even Dr Vitthal, of the bedside conversation, had moved out to another hospital for further training.

My leg felt new, raw, itchy, awful. Mosquitoes kept wanting to taste it. 'Cheers! To your rapid recovery!' Anna said, putting down his ritual evening sip with deep satisfaction. I glugged at my glass greedily. It seemed like ages since I'd been wooed by Bacchus. Bangalore is home to many premium brands of brew. Anna had chosen Golden Glory.

I sipped regularly, swishing off the mosquitoes with my free hand. Mellowing quickly, we talked of his work. It is his one great passion in life. If Amma has turned inwards in her grief, Anna has stretched outwards. He has been with Bensen and Henicken, or B&H, one of the largest Indian pharmaceutical companies, for over twenty years. He gives it all he can. In three years, he expects to retire with full honours. Although his designation says Director, Public Relations, he is something of a miracle machine for the drug manufacturer. 'Ask Govind Pandit to handle it' is the back-up plan in any crisis at the office. Anna quite thrives on the implied compliment. And on the stress as well.

'Why don't you come with me on Friday for the BPA annual bash?' Anna said, suddenly switching topics from government price regulations. 'It'll get you out of the house a bit. It's at the Club, so there will be no climbing or anything. What do you say?'

Ever since Shweta's illness was diagnosed three years ago, Amma has withdrawn gradually but firmly from any major social appearances. She takes most of the burden of Shweta's care on her own shoulders. When Anna needs to make his family visible, he drags me with him. This time, even the Bangalore Pharmaceutical Association rigmarole seemed more attractive than the self-pitying boredom I was sinking into. So I agreed.

And that's how I met Dr Anshul Hiremath, returned NRI, hush-hush researcher and reluctant ladies' man.

16

FOUR

The Club was cool, in spite of the season. Tall, motherly trees keep its elite members protected from pollution, noise and heat. It is hard to believe that the city honks and sweats barely two hundred yards away.

Ahead of my hobble, the Mexican turf looked dry, scraggly under the lights. Bangalore's perennial water and electricity shortages have to show up somewhere in the Club! That night, rain threatened. Even the shamiana looked tentative. A few dozen people were sprinkled around the lawn.

'At last! Govind! Come, come, we were wondering what had happened to our most punctual member.' Anna was swallowed into a group of portly men, near-empty glasses in hand. It seemed as though they all wore dark suits with red ties. My father glared at me as he left my side. I had made him late.

I looked around, expecting the average age to be around my father's. I was wrong. There were men, and wonderfully, women too, not far from my own years. When I chewed that around with the uddina vadas offered by a passing waiter, it made sense. Pharmaceuticals is a sunrise industry. Like the software industry, it has made Bangalore its new capital. It attracts young talent, armed with marketing or management degrees. Or, more traditionally, with masters or doctorates in biochemistry.

I should have known. I write about the industry all the time. The mood here is upbeat, notwithstanding worries about GATT. India has been under immense international pressure to sign the General Agreement on Trade and Tariff. In the media, we've been having point and counterpoint on the issue for years! The government has succumbed. From the year 2005, we will be completely under the purview of TRIPS, the Trade Related Intellectual Property Rights agreement of the World Trade Organisation. Our economic dealings with other countries are already undergoing a subtle change. TRIPS has been implemented in stages since 1995. Still, it seems we are not too worried. The future, some say, is here. The drug industry, pegged at one thousand crore rupees, is expecting to double itself by the first decade of the new century.

Why not enjoy the party, then?

'We can beat them easily at their own game!' the voice boomed. It was Kumar Cherian, a little sloshed. I had interviewed him once. CEO, Tropic Chemic. Also current chairman of the BPA. His company has taken good advantage of the confused patent laws in India, which are designed to protect local industry, and not neccessarily local consumers. Tropic Chemic, headquartered in Bangalore, is king of the antibiotics market. The faster the multinationals come up with new products, the faster our desi company duplicates them by altering the process of manufacture.

Until 2005, almost unhindered by GATT clauses, only processes are patentable in India under the 1970 Patents Act. End products of that process cannot be patented. An Indian manufacturer can produce anything without paying patent fees, so long as the process used is legally different from that of the original manufacturer's. The result? With a bit of reverse engineering, any new and popular international drug, from Prozac to the latest generation antibiotic, can be imitated and sold in India. Usually it is sold cheaper here than in the country of origin, but at a hefty profit for the local manufacturer. After all, he need pay no patent fees, and has no major R&D investments either. Low overheads, as they say. As a consumer, I am happy that I can buy medicines cheaper here. As a journalist, I worry about the long-term hazards of not playing fair in the international game.

Looking forward to some verbal sparring on the subject, I introduced myself again to Mr Cherian. I'm not sure why I was feeling adversarial. Anyway, my best stories have come unexpectedly, from the most unprepared mouths. Especially when I'm feeling embattled.

'Yes, of course I know who you are. Govind's girl. Such a nice piece you did about us, my dear!' Not true, but who cared? I grinned sweetly, inwardly sharpening my interviewing skills, blunted for lack of use.

For the next half hour, I shamelessly extracted information from poor Mr Cherian, making sure the waiters hovered close with refills. Not that he was exactly reluctant to talk.

'You have been doing a fine job reporting on our industry, young woman,' he said, patting me on the back. 'Though not everyone agrees with what you write. I know some of my colleagues would run a mile to avoid you.' He chuckled. 'Still, anytime you need some information, come on over. I'll see what I can do for you.'

Encouraged by my murmuring, he went on. 'The heady period is getting over. It's sink-or-swim time for us all.'

He was talking about the latest game in town. The chase for the new drug, the new molecule, the new product. Something that could put an Indian drug company on the world's bulletin boards.

'By 2005, when GATT is implemented, we will finally have to pay patent fees on all the new products sold in this country. Estimatedly, sixty-eight per cent of the market. Prices will shoot up. The market will shake.' This much was common knowledge. The fear was that India would have to pull the rug out from under its indigenous drug industry. As a signatory to GATT, it would have to respect both process and product. No more mimicry.

Mr Cherian patted his pockets in a futile search for a smoke. 'And the only way to keep our bottom lines healthy,' he winked conspiratorially at me, 'is to create and patent and manufacture and sell our own products. To take on TRIPS aggressively.'

'Where will these new products come from, when most companies don't put enough money into research!' I protested.

'Too true, too true. I know some of my esteemed peers would rather bribe our enlightened politicians to ward off GATT, even now, than take on the challenges of the marketplace.' He shook his head, accepted a cigarette from a waiter, lit it and inhaled deeply.

'But you know, India has one advantage. We have thousands of years of medical know-how just waiting to be rediscovered.'

'Ah, yes,' I did sound a trifle cynical. 'Back to our glorious past. Ayurveda and all that.' So much of our pseudo-nationalism these days is dished out in little capsules of resurrected fiction.

Mr Cherian looked amused. 'Don't you dismiss it just yet, young lady. Let me tell you a secret.' He lowered his voice dramatically, causing a few people from the group nearby to look our way with interest.

'The gold rush is on right now. In our forests, on our hillsides. These new prospectors are falling all over themselves. They want to find some quick fix that sells not just here, but internationally as well. Some plant-based cure for some modern disease. One lucky strike, that's all they need.'

'But are there even a handful of Indian products out there so far? Where's the precedent?'

'It'll come, young lady, it'll come. We're all rummaging through ayurvedic textbooks, raiding medicine larders in tribal kitchens. Fishing in the deep seas. There are many leads and not enough money to chase them all.'

This, from one of India's most successful—and cash-rich—pharmaceuticals, which prided itself on setting aside good money for the development of the market. If Tropic Chemic was too strapped for cash to fish in international waters, what of the hundreds of small-scale companies eking out a living in the bulk drugs business?

There were many questions. But Mr Cherian was visibly surrendering to the aftermath of his intake of barley. He yawned loudly and apologized. 'Getting old, my dear. You need to catch one of the more energetic ones.' He looked across to the group of people which had edged considerably closer to us. '*Haan!*' he said, pleased. 'I know just the person for you. Anshul, come here a minute, will you?'

A tall young man, bespectacled, slim, but with noticeably broad shoulders, separated himself from the pack. He came forward tentatively, half-smiling at Mr Cherian.

'Anshul, this is Poorva Pandit. She's with *Deadline* magazine—writes a lot about our profession, actually. Her father is an old friend of mine. She's been grilling me dry about the industry. I thought you might handle it better. Poorva,' he gripped my hand, 'this young man has returned from the USA recently with a Ph.D in genetics. Leading edge stuff. He's set up a pioneering company here. Very, very sophisticated. Indian, er, Biotech, right, Anshul?' Mr Cherian slurred pardonably over his words.

'*India* Biotech, sir,' the young man corrected him. The name set off a slow clanging in my brain. My hand lifted to my head. The gentleman turned to me, his eyes large and dark behind rimless glasses, his eyelashes grazing the frame.

'Hi, I'm Anshul Hiremath,' he said. The 'hi' was drawn out in an American way. 'Pleased to meet you.' The hand was soft, the handshake strong and firm.

21

FIVE

Strange coincidences happen often enough in real life to put paperback writers to shame. Yet, when I thought about it afterwards, it hardly seemed like such a coincidence. Sooner or later I would surely have met Anshul. Bangalore is still small, almost parochial in some ways. The drug industry is incestuous, its members stick together, socialize, intermarry, even as they do fierce business with each other.

As I shook the hand and gazed into those startling eyes, I surfed a surge of sudden excitement. Here was a story. A story that seemed determined to follow me, instead of the other way round. Twice in one fortnight, I was being teased with tidbits about this man. I remembered the stolen, malformed foetus. It threw up a vision of little translucent creatures with long tails and big heads. I felt the beer jostling against my throat muscles. How do you keep foetuses? In a jar? In formaldehyde? Why would you keep them anyway? Like many young girls of my generation, I had refused to study the sciences so I could avoid pickled organs.

I looked at the doctor more closely. Dark green button-down shirt, light khaki Dockers. Elegant wingtips, highly polished. He looked like a youngish thirty-five. Regular features, except for the eyes. Complexion, wheatish. Black hair, cut short in the latest style. When he smiled, I understood completely why women fell hard. Anshul Hiremath's appearance suddenly became rakish. 'Have you finished inspecting me?' he asked politely, his amusement spreading to a dimple in his right cheek.

I caught myself quickly. 'Sorry! I'm not usually so rude. It must be the beer!' I raised my glass, happy to find a culprit.

'That's okay!' The American accent emerged strongly. He reached in his pocket. 'There's more information in here.' He handed me a business card printed on micro-thin plastic. I shoved it into my bag.

I was saved from further embarrassment by the arrival of Anna, accompanied by a long-lost buddy, judging from the cosy body language.

'Poorva! This is Jimmy. Jimmy Kakodia. I must have mentioned him to you. We worked together twenty years ago, in Bombay. He's now the country manager for Transpharma. Still lives in his old flat by the sea.'

Plum job, that. Transpharma is a US-based multinational with an ambitious plan for India. Recently, they had bought a sizeable stake in one of the older British companies here. Not so unusual. Buyouts and mergers are rampant in this industry.

Jimmy Kakodia was a large man with a ruddy complexion and a salt-and-pepper moustache that matched the crop on his head. He wore a tweed jacket with a broad red tie that somehow placed him in the sixties. 'Delighted, delighted,' he said to me, pumping my hand with painful vigour. It set off an echo in my leg. I winced. Anna had launched cheerfully into a story about the good old days.

'Jimmy! Remember the time we got caught with all that Scotch your sister had sent?' he asked.

'Ah, during Morarji's prohibition! We had to give half of it away to keep that officer quiet!' The two began to laugh heartily. The rest of us could only smile politely.

Jimmy noticed Anshul, who was tapping his feet distractedly.

'Ah, Anshul! You've already met Govind's daughter. Fast work!'

Anshul looked most uncomfortable. But Jimmy was oblivious. 'Govind, this young man, have you met him? He's got his own company here, something we never managed, eh? He returned recently from the US. Lots of courage,what? We used to sell him our enzymes. Then he went and found his own way of making them!' Kakodia looked most injured.

'Still, I guess he remains a client . . . in a way.' He gave an alcohol-induced conspiratorial wink.

I looked across at Anshul. He had become stock-still. I could almost feel the cold draft he emanated. He was looking across steadily at Jimmy. He made a small movement of protest. It was enough. Jimmy Kakodia faltered visibly. There was a flat silence.

I was enjoying the tension. What would happen next? Disappointingly, Anna, always the gentleman, changed the subject quickly. He herded us expertly to the dinner buffet. Jimmy walked gratefully ahead. I stayed close to Anshul. Not because he was handsome, but because of the undercurrents. I was getting very interested.

Ahead of us, the North Indian spread looked indifferent at best. Each curry was a uniform yellowish brown. Grease was floating unappetizingly above lumps of paneer, or was it chicken? Just before me, Anshul served himself sparingly, topping up his rice with generous dollops of curd. I followed his sensible example. My stomach was queasy with the vadas and the beer. Besides, we South Indians need our curd rice.

'What made you return to India, then?' I bit into a hard mango pickle, flooding my taste buds. We had moved away from the harsh lights.

He adjusted his glasses with his free hand. I noticed his

fingers were long, manicured. 'I guess we—my wife and I, we were homesick. Really. It's a bit strange there, eventually. Like a snail without its shell.'

So he had a wife. 'H'mm. Usually, though, our NRIs find it hard to actually get off their roller-coasters, even though they dream of it.'

'That's a neat way of putting it,' he remarked, his heart-stopping smile coming into brief play. Musing over events months later, I was terribly glad I had remained immune to his brand of electricity. If I had joined the ranks of his admirers, would I have been as rigorous about following up on my suspicions? Unlikely. When I fall in love, I suspend critical faculties.

'You're right, of course,' Anshul continued. 'We ourselves took a long time to make up our minds. But since I have set up my own company here . . .'

'No glass ceilings?'

'Exactly. Plus, I can continue with my research, which is very important to me. My company, is primarily into marketing enzyme-based diagnostic kits to pathological labs and to research institutes.'

'Really?' I was a bit confused. I nearly blathered the game away. Never, ever drink at work. But how could I have known? I had come to play.

His eyebrows moved up a fraction. I pulled my mouth into a smile. 'I see. Your research then, is it along the same lines?'

'Er . . . not really.' There was a definite hesitation. Then he seemed to make up his mind.

'Actually, no. We are trying something quite different.' He looked at me appraisingly. I looked back at him with innocent eyes. 'In contraception. We're far from cracking it yet. And it's all highly confidential. But I'll tell you this much . . . quite off the record . . .'

I nodded in agreement, suddenly breathless. This sort of intense physical response to the idea of a story hunt had

25

rarely overtaken me before. Was there adequate cause? Or was I just out of shape from my recent trauma?

'We are trying to develop an anti-fertility vaccine for women.'

'Wow!' I said, suitably impressed. 'How close are you?'

A shadow crossed his face. 'Very close, we think. Or very far.' He shrugged. 'It's always a gamble, a risk.'

'It sounds fascinating. Could I do a story about you?'

The hesitation again. 'Sure. On India Biotech maybe. But it's much too early to write about the vaccine.'

Show me an entrepreneur who can resist publicity and I'll show you a clean politician. I smiled brightly, modestly triumphant. The victory, or the inebriation, made me bolder.

'How was Jethro Tull?' The words frothed over, uncontrolled.

'Great! Ian Anderson at sixty-plus can still pull it off! But how?. . .'

'A good guess, that's all.' Poor recovery. 'I'll call you then. Next week, perhaps?'

He nodded, but absent-mindedly. From the corner of my eye, I saw Jimmy Kakodia hovering, obviously waiting for a word with Anshul. I excused myself and went to look for Anna. My leg was throbbing badly with all that standing. When I looked back, the two were in earnest conversation. Kakodia kept looking over his shoulder for eavesdroppers. My reporter's antennae were waving wildly. My heart was thumping as it does in the vise of a well-crafted murder mystery. Clearly, I thought, I was on to something big. Otherwise, why so much secrecy? What hold did Anshul have on Jimmy to shush him up so effectively? At that point, I was running on instinct. But I knew, right then, that I was going to find out more. I needed a meaty story to sink my mental canines into!

SIX

One more week at home. I moved up a little from infantile behaviour to teenage tantrums. I allowed myself unfamiliar luxuries. One night, Amma oiled and combed and plaited my waist-length hair. For once, I felt glad I could never get myself to cut it. Another time, Shweta went all the way to the library with Mohan the driver to borrow some laugh therapy for me. Laxmi continued to serve up miracles that passed as food. Anna called twice a day from work to check out on 'both my dear girls' as he put it. Shweta bunked several days of school. It didn't matter. That well-meaning but confused institution could hardly contain her mental energies anyway. My special sister. Puberty should have brought new hopes. It had, instead, brought the finite closer.

There was enough time to think about what I would be doing next at work. I was now itching to be back. Ironic, when I remembered how often I had longed for some free time.

There was one driver, however. I wanted to find out exactly what contraceptive vaccine Dr Hiremath was developing. If I had known of the tortuous paths down which my curiosity would take me, I would perhaps have chickened out. But in that week, I used what resources I had to find out more.

First person on my list: Dr S Gayatri, gynaecologist, also my mother's contemporary at college. It was she who had diagnosed early menopausal syndrome to account for Amma's little illnesses and depressions. I made my way to her clinic by car, using my walker in poor humour. Things returned to perspective when I saw the dozen or so women waiting patiently for their turn. At least one of them looked alarmingly pregnant.

'Sorry, sorry, Poorva. Come, come.' She has this amusing habit of repeating some words. 'How's Yashodha?' Once she'd finished fussing over my leg, Dr Gayatri asked after my mother. I was pleased to report Amma's progress, and felt obliged to mention Shweta's deterioration. The good doctor paused pensively, then shook her head. 'Pity, pity. If only I could bring some good news. I've been closely in touch with medical developments on muscular dystrophy and related neuromuscular disorders. So far, it's all at a nascent stage.' I knew that already, but had to clamp down my renewed sense of loss. I came straight to the point in deference to the women outside.

'I'm putting together a piece on the future of contraception. Implants, vaccinations, etc. I need to know, how close are we to getting the perfect contraceptive?'

'A long, long way,' Dr Gayatri was quick to respond. 'To be even good, let alone perfect, a contraceptive must be very, very safe. It must be easy to administer. It must, of course, be very effective. It must be economical. Last but not least . . . it should not need frequent visits to a health professional.' She paused. 'I say, I say, I sound like my college textbooks.'

'Just what I wanted!' I said, in my most reassuring style. As expected, she was well-informed.

'To illustrate why I believe we haven't found such a contraceptive . . . let me share a secret with you. More than half my practice consists of the termination of unwanted pregnancies. I tell you, it is not something I enjoy, but it is not something I flinch from.'

Easy to believe. Dr Gayatri is a practical woman. I waited, respectfully.

'Every method of contraception we have used so far has had an unsatisfactory success rate. Whether due to an inherent fault of the device or due to the method of using it. Or, I guess . . . I guess, the sheer inconvenience of having to use it. It is a losing battle with nature for many, many couples. And naturally, the bigger burden falls on the poor woman.'

'Someone was mentioning contraceptive vaccines, though. That is quite new, isn't it?'

'New! It's not new, but it's just nowhere near the market yet. I believe a few teams are working on both male and female vaccines. Yes, yes! One fellow right here in Bangalore. What is his name?' She jogged her memory. 'Hiremath, I think. That's it. Hiremath. Some unusual first name, I forget. It seems his research is going on in MR Hills.'

'MR Hills?' I exclaimed, trying not to sound too happy with the information. Now there was a definite location. Not too far away. The MR Hills are part of the Nilgiri mountains, about three hundred kilometres from Bangalore. They are named after the goddess Mahadevi Renuka, an incarnation of Durga.

'Why there?' I asked.

'I'm not sure . . . he seems to have set up a lab there. Together with some organization working with the tribals. God knows, God knows. Usually these researchers are very secretive till they are sure of their product.'

'Doesn't this sort of research take a very long time?'

'Oh yes, yes. It could take five to ten years, from concept to delivery. And, let me tell you, it is an expensive business, too. This fellow must be having some good financial backing.'

'Would he also have a lot of close competition?'

'Maybe, maybe. There's a team at the Institute of Science in Delhi that is at a critical stage, if I am not mistaken. But they are trying to develop a male vaccine. And then, I was reading about some other trials. In some other country . . . Brazil or somewhere.'

'How would the vaccine work, actually? Would it kill the sperms? Or destroy the egg? Or use some other method entirely?'

She hesitated, looked at her watch. Valuable time wasted on a cub reporter who had not done her homework. I felt stupid.

Then, speaking even faster than usual, Dr Gayatri filled in some of the yawning gaps in my information.

'Fertility control methods are either contraceptive or abortifacient. An anti-fertility vaccine could work in three ways, each at a different stage.' She ticked off each on her fingers. 'By preventing conception itself. By preventing implantation of the embryo in the uterus. Or, later, by not allowing the embryo to grow.

'To prevent conception, one method would be to create some . . . some block in the egg lining. So the sperm cannot reach the egg. I'm just guessing, of course.

'To prevent implantation, you would have to interfere in some way with the implantation process. Maybe raise antibodies against the trophoblast. Finally, to stop the proper growth of the embryo, you would have to create some antibodies to an essential pregnancy hormone, like hCG.'

Only doctors speak as obtusely. I've known astrophysicists who make the origin of galaxies seem easier to comprehend. I tried not to let my jaw drop.

'You understand?' Dr Gayatri asked, a little dubiously. It was too late for artifice. I shook my head. She sighed.

'See, conception and pregnancy are both very complicated processes. Unless everything works just so at all times, you cannot expect a normal human being to emerge at the end of nine months. So, an anti-fertility vaccine needs to interrupt at least one of the many vital events in the chain of fertilization, implantation and sustenance of the foetus. Right?'

I was with her thus far.

'As I said, antibodies can be created against, say, say progesterone—without which hormone the embryo cannot develop. In fact, most current research is being conducted on antiprogestins, if I am not mistaken. Then, whenever progesterone is released in the woman's body, her own cells will mount an immune response against progesterone. It will not be allowed to do its work. The embryo will be unable to survive.'

Positively hostile, I thought.

'In any case, whether you chose a contraceptive, or an abortifacient, you would have to synthesize the chosen antigen with a vector, some common immunogenic carrier like diphtheria. Or, more usually, tetanus toxoid.'

Off she went again.

'You cannot otherwise expect the body to mount an immune response against its own cells, can you? Once you decide which is your antigen—that means, to which self molecule you want to create resistance in the body—then you have to inject it along with a carrier. You know, some foreign agent which the body can immediately recognize as an enemy. Some disease causing pathogen. The two, that is, the antigen and the agent, must bind tightly together. Then the body's immune system, clubbing them as one, will generate resistance against both the agent and the antigen, even if is from the body's own cells.'

It sounded to me as if the body was pretty stupid. But I was beginning to understand. It worked on the same principle as any vaccine. Introduce the pathogen to the body in small doses; activate the resistance. Once antibodies to a particular pathogen are formed, they will mount an attack any time the pathogen is found in the body. Which is all right if the pathogen is something clearly harmful like the typhoid or cholera bacterium. But here, we were fooling the body into mounting an immune response against its own cells. It sounded like treason.

'That sounds rather unfair, somehow. Cheating the body like that. Would the enemy cells have to be violently mutilated? It sounds so gory.'

Her mouth twisted in a smile.

'It would be, if you magnified it a millionfold, I suppose. It would look like . . . look like those war movies, with lots of blasts and dripping blood. For instance, if the woman's antibodies are targeted against sperm cells, they would mount a full-scale attack on the sperm battalion. All that would be missing, then, would be the screams.'

I had not known the doctor was capable of such imagery. I thought of those funny little sperm heads and the busy tails, trying to escape a tackle of armoured policewoman cells. I had had enough.

The doctor's assistant had already peeped in twice. 'I may be back later, but thanks so much!' I shook her hand, then gave in to an impulse to hug her briefly.

In spite of the smile, she was already looking beyond me. As I hobbled out with my walker, I saw the precariously pregnant woman moving with impressive speed to the doctor's door.

SEVEN

Well, I had made a beginning. But the conversation had only yielded more puzzles. I cursed my lack of mobility. I needed to access libraries. But I didn't feel strong enough, not yet. Just that visit to the gynaecologist had tired me into a long sleep. I wished for the hundredth time that I had Internet access from my home. My computer is too outdated, a 486 SX. Not that I minded usually. My work involves mostly word processing. Just then, however, I needed information. And I wanted it right away.

That evening, I felt quite exhausted after a challenging game of chess with Shweta. The brat won. I tried to pretend I had let her. She laughed derisively. When Anna returned, we settled down in the family room. He was, as usual, in his favourite chair. The TV was on mute. Anna does not like to miss any passing spectacle, like a plane crash or a satellite launch. Now, with a whisky glass in his hand, he looked relaxed, contented. At fifty-six, he is a handsome, healthy man and attributes it all to yoga in the morning and whisky in the evening. I try to do the yoga part, at least.

'Anna, I need to pick your brains. I hope you are not too tired today?' I asked, dragging my chair close to his.

'No, no, gonu,' he said, using a familiar endearment. 'Anything bothering you?'

I brought him up to date. He listened abstractedly, as always, his eyes on the television screen. Still, I've lost count of the number of times he's helped me clarify a story idea, or given me tips on who to speak with. There is one unwritten rule, strictly observed, however. Anything that can cause a conflict of interest between his work and my job is to be avoided.

'Many things are making me curious, Anna. First of all, how does one get people to volunteer as guinea pigs for the development of something like that vaccine?'

'Arre, that's the least of the problems in a country like ours!' He sounded unusually cynical. 'If the incentives are good, if the investigators can convince the volunteers that the risks are non-existent or low, you can find the people. You know, you can play around a lot with those things. Technically, ethically, even legally, no trial can be conducted without the written, informed consent of the participants. But then, our people have so little information! They may not understand all the implications. The doctor is God here.'

I thought of our floundering GPs, overwhelmed with the stream of illnesses caused by poverty and malnutrition. I thought of their sometimes valiant and mostly self-serving dedication to the prescription of futile medication. Doctor as saviour, or doctor as shaman? I let it pass.

'It seems India Biotech has set up a centre in the Mahadevi Renuka Hills. Why in such a location, so distant from Bangalore?'

'Well, isn't that where the tribals are? Maybe they have created their volunteer base for the clinical trials there. It would be a good patient sample, I imagine. Homogenous people. Also, maybe, easy to enlist.'

'What if there are problems during the trials? Who takes the responsibility?' I was thinking of the floating foetus. Deformed. An unviable human being.

'The researchers should. The company should. But often in these trials, follow-ups are neglected. So the volunteers may not even make any connection between the problem that has developed and the clinical experiment. And then, you know how it is. Our enforcement agencies can easily turn a blind eye when they want to.'

It made me wonder exactly what organizations like the Bangalore Pharmaceutical Association do to prevent such things from happening. Anna is quite involved with its all-India parent organization as well. So I kept quiet.

'Developing a new product must be awfully expensive, na? Where do you think Anshul gets the financial backing from?'

Anna sipped at his glass and cracked a papad between his teeth.

'It is certainly expensive. Where would he get the backing? I don't know. But I guess it would, logically, have to be from an international foundation. Or through government funding. That type of research has moved, by and large, to the public sector. Liability and drug development costs have become so high that it is difficult even for large pharmaceutical companies like ours to stick our necks out. They'd rather be in an area like, say, geriatric drug development. You know, making drugs for old people to live longer, healthier. As you can imagine, growing life expectancies are making it a vast potential market. Still, family planning and population control are rather big in all these WHO-type of organizations. This Anshul's research may fit nicely into some funding niche.'

Just then, the lights went off. It was not an omen or anything. The Karnataka Electricity Board is notorious for its unscheduled power cuts. Bangaloreans take it in their stride. You can tell which children are from these parts just by observing their lack of reaction to sudden darkness. Being quite used to it, Anna and I continued amicably in the dark until Laxmi brought out the emergency lantern. Anna promised, for the hundredth time, that we would get an uninterrupted power supply system installed soon.

'Pa, could you do me a favour? Would you ask Jimmy Kakodia what he meant about Anshul being a client of Transpharma? Maybe the answer lies there?'

Anna looked long and hard at me. Or what he could see of me in the low light. The 'Pa' was my endearment, in a way. He seemed to be weighing something in his mind.

'Okay, I'll try. *No* promises! He is supposed to visit the office this week. Let's see what I can come up with.'

Amma came in then. She had been with Shweta till her special one slept. She does that sometimes, if Shweta is in pain. 'How about dinner?' she asked. Magically, the electricity came back with a surge of high voltage, nearly blinding us. Anna, smiling, went with her immediately. I followed slowly.

That night, I pored over some notes and clippings on fertility control which I found in my personal library. The latest articles were all about Depo-Provera and Norplant. They are new products, recently approved for use in India. Injectible, hormone-based contraceptives for women. Once-in-three-months contraception, if it was Depo-Provera. Or a five-year implant under the skin, if it was Norplant. I found that the development of these contraceptives has had a chequered history. Even today, many women's organizations all over the world are up in arms against the manufacturers. They remain unconvinced about the long-term safety of these products. Post-marketing surveillance is still on. In India, according to one of the articles, the injectibles are gaining popularity because doctors find them easy to administer. No more messy IUDs. No more abortions from forgotten pills.

There was other stuff on the future of birth control, including the promise of male and female contraceptive vaccines. Clinical trials on animals have shown great success. One editorial I had clipped even spoke of the huge pay-off waiting for the first past the post in the global race for a better contraceptive, and anti-fertility vaccines were the most likely contenders for the prize.

Then it all became so technical that I fell asleep. I dreamt of tall women, pygmy doctors and monstrous capsules chasing me through a green, green field.

'Akka,' said Shweta, over breakfast the next morning, 'how come there's no news from your doctor-hero? I was hoping you—and me too—could meet him soon. Amma said he's very handsome.'

I reached out to tap her, none too gently, on her head. This was all a conspiracy. And my own mother was involved!

'Sweetheart, why don't you eat your uppitu quickly and vamoose? You'll be late for school!'

Shweta cannot be put down so easily. 'Aha, Akka is blushing. Amma, come and see!' I sent her out before she could get Amma in from her morning prayers. Amma rarely allows our routine to interfere with her ceremonies.

Still, the brat's remarks had set me dreaming. With the Anshul business dominating my mind, I had almost forgotten the handsome doctor. Now the memory of his slender frame and warm eyes came rushing back. And the silly stethoscope that he liked to wave about. When was the last time I'd been in lust? At least a year ago, and that had been disastrous. Yes, I would love to meet him again. But with what excuse?

When I thought about it, though, I really had the perfect reason to go see him. Hadn't he said he was doing research in immunology . . . how to prevent the body from rejecting transplants, or something? And vaccines had everything to do with the immune system, didn't they? Who better to interview than an immunologist? Ha! I felt as pleased as a winning racehorse owner! I galloped to the telephone, my injury forgotten.

'Dr Kamath here.' The voice was soft, the modulation perfect. The memory, however, was cloudy. 'Who?' he said most insultingly, when I mentioned my name. I nearly hung up.

'Poorva Pandit. Remember? You took me to hospital after my accident on Residency Road.'

'Oh yes! Of course. The bus buster! Sorry, sorry, my mind was elsewhere. Tell me, what can I do for you?' I must admit that several unmentionable things passed through my mind then.

'Look, I'm working on a story on immuno-contraception. I wondered if you could help me with some information.' I had learnt that long word only last night. It seemed to have unexpected impact.

'Hey! You've come to the right place. I can put you on to exactly the person you should meet. My HOD. She sits in the next cabin.'

'Great,' I replied, my heart drumming. 'When can we set it up?'

'Let me see,' he said, making rustling noises in the background. 'Oh! I'll be away through this weekend. How about next week, Tuesday or Wednesday?'

I was a trifle disappointed. Maybe it was just as well. I would be officially back at work by then. Without my plaster. Certainly without the ugly walker. And since it was already Thursday, it wouldn't be long.

'Yes, fine. I'll call you back,' I said, ready to put down the receiver.

'You know what?' said the wonderful voice at the other end, just then. 'I'm glad you called.'

Outside, in the May garden, the sunbirds chirped, pecking at the beautiful red flowers of the erythrina.

EIGHT

The Tribune Tower, all glass and granite, gleamed haughtily in the pale sunlight. It has replaced the old building which used to house the press and editorial offices of the Heggade group. Like every place else, Bangalore's premier avenue, MG Road, was being totally gentrified. The few remaining ramshackle structures blushed in mute apology. I alighted gingerly from Anna's car and paid a kind of compulsory obeisance to the new skyline. I was back to work at last.

After two and a half weeks, it all seemed to have moved away from me, leaving me behind. I had a few moments of frantic resettling. The familiarity of my cluttered desk finally did it, I guess. It was so . . . mine! Poorva Pandit, special correspondent. Dust, press notes and invitations had piled up. Many of the latter were in my name, so no one had dared touch them. There were a couple of interesting ones among them: 'Restoring local health traditions. A seminar'. 'Ayurveda then and now: Pandit Bhim Natwarji'. And so on. There was a glamorous invite to a fashion show: 'Cocktails and dinner to follow. Dress: Formal Indian'. Aah! The perks of the job. I loved it all.

Still, there was an ennui clutching at me that day. The accident, the narrow escape, made real life a little dull. The weeks of work stretched ahead with the monotonous emptiness of a never-ending highway. I shook myself out of the hangover of self-pity. Looked at my papers, thought of Anshul, of mysteries and suspicious experiments. Maybe, just maybe, I could career into a little known roadway, not on a shining horse, but on a bicycle, perhaps, bell clanging madly against bovine roadblocks.

First though, I'd have to get a green signal from the boss. I looked across, stretching neck and back over my personal hump in our 'open office' to where CP sat in a glass cabin, there and yet not there, seen but not heard.

Unless he was careful to avert his face, CP's expressions read like an open centre spread. It was a standard joke in the reporter's room. RI, someone would announce, pointing at the cabin. It stood for Romantic Interest. CP's hormonal compulsions were well known. Or, Avaru, someone else would guess, watching CP frown over the phone. Avaru, meaning Him in Kannada, was the big boss, upstairs. Old man Heggade, whose grandfather had set up the newspaper group early in the century.

As I watched CP, it was definitely more RI than Avaru. The self-deprecating grins, the helpless hand movements. Strong pointers. I sighed. It was not a good time to interrupt.

I walked over to Meenal's desk instead. She is probably my only real friend at work. I have a wary relationship with most of the other journalists. It's the same at all newspaper offices. We are a suspicious, egotistical lot. And proud of it too!

Meenal is comically secretive about her work. As soon as I neared her space, she covered her notes. She is a political writer. Byline privileges come only if you get the story first. Luckily, we have no turf wars. I have always tried my best to avoid political reporting in my eight years of journalism.

'Hi!' she said chirpily. 'What's the matter with you? You look like a wounded soldier forced to return to the battlefield.'

'And getting disillusioned with the war!' I confessed.

'No, no, we can't have that. Sit, let me give you a battle bulletin. It'll cheer you up.'

Meenal has a remarkable talent for mimicry. She can impersonate not just friends and acquaintances, but also public figures. Within minutes, she had me in splits over the antics of state politicians.

'Chief minister, saar,' she whined in a PA-sort-of voice, 'it is getting very difficult for us all, you know, saar, secretaries and other, ah the, ah, officers to cross the road! So much traffic mess has become, saar, in coming to er ... office . . . they want you to do something . . . er . . . to relieve, saar! . . .'

'No problem,' boomed Meenal as CM. 'Please, er, float tenders, and get our usual friends to submit proposals. We shall begin construction of sky bridge, you know, like Laxman Jhula? Have you been to Hardwar? Yes, yes, you came with me for the chief minister's conference, yes. We went via Bhutan. So we will have one walking way without traffic to the Vidhana Soudha. It will be the first in this country, like my Indian Mickey World. After all, it is very important keeping poor government servants happy!'

More unbelievable projects have often been exposed by Meenal and her team of investigative writers. Sadly, the state has been turned into a performing circus by political expediencies.

'Thanks, dear,' I said to her, wiping tears from my eyes with my dupatta. I really needed the reality check. 'Just for that, I'll treat you to lunch at Lake District!' It was a fancy Continental restaurant that I knew she loved. She looked happy and waved me away, prying her notes loose from under the book she had kept over them.

CP's phone was down at last. He was hidden behind a newspaper. I tapped on the glass walls. He beckoned me in.

'So, so. What're you filing for the coming issue? Where's the traffic story you had promised? We need an anchor story for the middle section. Have you finished that piece on the impact of the new healthcare budgets?'

I marvelled that he rarely stopped for breath between sentences. I put my hands up in self-defence, allowing my inner weariness to show on my face. CP stopped, a question mark furrowing his brow.

'CP, I'm sorry. I have worked from home on the traffic story. It's being co-ordinated from Delhi now. You see, I don't feel upto very much yet. To tell you the truth, I've come to ask a favour.'

'H'mm!' he growled.

I outlined to him my instinctive reaction to the India Biotech story. I admitted that I was, at the moment, groping in the dark. I needed time, exclusive time, to work on this one.

'CP, I need something big, something different. A whale of an assignment to get me back in the game. I'm feeling so . . . so jaded. Could I try, CP? What do you think?'

CP is a softy somewhere deep inside. 'Not that you've done anything much since you got bus-ted up . . . get it, get it?' He can never resist his own jokes. 'But okay. I'll take you off other assignments. You will have to report back regularly to me. You have just one week, okay? To convince me that this is the national scoop we've been waiting for.'

I could have hugged him, but for the glass cabin. As it is, our easy camaraderie has led to much speculation in the newsroom. Do they or don't they? They don't, of course, because they feel no lust for each other.

Feeling much more cheerful, I went back to my desk, stuffed everything inside a drawer, took out a new notepad, and chewed on my pencil. What exactly did I have to go on?

So far, not much. I listed down whatever I had.

1. Overheard conversation: stolen foetus and other problems with contraceptive vaccine.

2. Confirmation from Anshul Hiremath that such research was on, that it was a secret.

3. Kakodia's embarrassment over the exposure of his link with Anshul.

4. Dr Gayatri's tidbit about work on tribals in MR Hills.

5. Anna's guestimates about international financial backing for Anshul.

6. My own research about contraception, the international race, the promised pot of gold.

Not enough. I needed to know more before I dared go back to CP. He could be ruthless about a sloppy idea. Why was the research being done in MR Hills? What were the complications the medics had spoken of? Who were the victims? Where did the money for the research come from? Tomorrow! Maybe I could have some answers tomorrow, when I was to meet Dr Rohil Kamath at St Paul's. Rarely, if ever, had the scent of a story turned me on quite so much. It also made me hungry.

They had an Italian buffet at Lake District. We gorged on freshly tossed pasta, made to order. Meenal always eats extremely spicy food. The red chilli peppers she added to her fettucine made my eyes water.

I told her that I was being allowed to stay invisible at work for a while. She went green in the face, to match her salad.

'You always were his blue-eyed girl,' she said, sniffing, referring to her arch-enemy CP.

'Come on, Meenal, you know he gives you your due!' I protested.

'The guy has never forgiven me for rejecting his advances,' said Meenal the beauteous, who has similar problems wherever she goes. 'He'll cut any piece of mine, given half a chance!' She slammed her fork into the plate, wrapping fierce strings of pasta around it. 'And you can get a five-page colour spread without even batting your damn eyelashes at him.'

I thought she was being unfair. I have earned my position at *Deadline*. Modesty aside, I've done some of the most difficult pieces in the magazine. It has always been CP's edict that we must not put ideological spin into our pieces and we know our readers are like us: a little cynical, a little hopeful for real change and yet, yearning for a little fun. I have catered to that reader best as I can. *Deadline* gives the number one fortnightly a sweating run for its money. That sort of success doesn't come by playing favourites.

Meenal's done her share. The problem with her kind of journalism is that you have to be really clever, insightful or just plain lucky to distinguish yourself from the pack of political reporters. Even then, it's the personalities you write about who get remembered and rarely the byline.

I soothed her very ruffled feathers by sharing the secret of Anshul and his vaccine. To trust a colleague is to give her the highest honour of friendship in this profession. Meenal promised to keep her ears and eyes open for me. I paid the bill with great flourish. We returned to work, friends again.

NINE

Tuesday threw me out of bed early and feeling much healthier. I did my entire yoga routine after a very long gap. I dressed with great care, choosing an aquamarine salwar suit that was cut to complement my thin figure. In spite of the heat, I let my hair loose, to caress my waist. My eyes sparkled with kajal. Or something else. I could hardly kid myself. I was awfully excited at the idea of meeting Rohil again.

St Paul's, like most public institutions in Bangalore, is designed to confuse the visitor. It took me precious extra legwork to find Pathology, which is the umbrella department for Immunology. I passed a door with the nameplate Dr R Shaila, HOD, Pathology. Must be the person Rohil had mentioned. I found a smaller sign for Dr Rohil Kamath next door. I knocked. The doctor was immersed in paperwork with books piled precariously high. His ever-present stethoscope sat gleaming on top.

I remember entering and sitting down. I remember telling him a bit of the truth about Dr Anshul Hiremath and that I was on special assignment to research breakthroughs in contraception. For some reason, I simply cannot recall whether or not we made small talk before my questions started. I do remember that his eyes looked bigger, more intense. That he seemed very knowledgeable, yet self-effacing. That we both smiled a lot.

'You know, you really are in luck,' he said, soon enough. 'Dr Shaila is not only an expert in the field of reproductive immunology, I think she is also related to Anshul Hiremath in some way. You know, the community is quite thick. Anyway, she used to talk very highly of him and his work.'

I noted the 'used to'. 'Would she talk to me, you think?' I asked tentatively.

'Sure, why not? Except, she's not in right now, she's attending a conference in Hyderabad, the one I just returned from.' He'd called me here, knowing I couldn't meet the person I was supposed to meet? It made me ridiculously happy.

'When you mentioned it, though, I dug out some material for you on immuno-contraception. Some of it is from a recent conference. I downloaded it just last night from the Net. I thought you could use it.'

He turned to his desk, opened each drawer without success. Dr Kamath was obviously not as efficient on home territory as he had seemed at the hospital.

'Oh shit! I've left them at my apartment! Damn!' He looked at his watch. HMT, not Titan, I noticed abstracedly. 'I'll go get them, if you'll wait. Unless? . . .'

'If it's close by, I could come.' I was calm, not at all suspicious.

'Oh, great. I usually walk down for lunch, anyway.'

I guess that's how Rohil and I became a team. At his apartment, a sudden but natural beginning was made. Usually, I fall in lust a little after I fall in love. But this time, it happened simultaneously. And so easily, without any awkwardness. We touched accidentally, trying to reach the same book from his oversized bookshelf. It felt so good, so *neccessary*. We then touched on purpose. I remember registering the heat generated by his caress. It was almost debilitating. I had to keep reminding myself of my real reason for meeting him. I left before I had a chance to turn wanton.

That evening, I told Shweta about meeting Rohil again. For a person who had almost egged me on, she became surprisingly quiet. Quiet soon turned to sulky. For the first time Shweta seemed jealous of my many romantic escapades. Jealous that Rohil may take me away from her. Or so I guessed. Her insecurity was palpable. Her lips trembled, her eyes pooled. That got me worried. For years, I have been, I suppose, presenting myself as the bedrock for her emotions, the one person to whom she could turn anytime. In whom she could confide totally, who would always be there.

I did not know why Shweta felt that way, that day. What had happened between Rohil and myself to make her feel threatened? Precious little. Shweta, it seemed to me, was going way ahead, too fast. But nothing I said or did that evening would calm her down. She wouldn't look at me, wouldn't talk to me. In desperation, I spoke once more to the figure all scrunched up in bed. 'I love you, gonu. I will always love you.'

'*Always* is a luxury I don't have.' Shweta, always brutal, occasionally manipulative.

I cringed, but held firm. Shweta's doctor has often warned us not to make her feel too special. Stuffing my mixed emotions under my pillow, I resolutely turned off the light.

But I could not sleep, even after gentle snoring came from her unhappy bed. The sheaf of papers Rohil had finally remembered to give me proved very useful. It was like a beginner's guide to the origin and future of contraception. The prevention of procreation was high on the list of world priorities. I found dozens of references to research on vaccines using antiprogestins. That's what Dr Gayatri had been trying to explain to me. Antiprogestins, quite simply, are progesterone blockers. And progesterone is very important in the process after conception. A vital part of the endocrine response. Antiprogestins deprive the conceptus—another term for the embryo—of the crucial hormone required to sustain pregnancy. When the sperm and egg have finished the mating dance, these antiprogestins play party-pooper. They make sure the band shuts down.

By now, researchers have pretty much figured out how to keep the laboratory animal in check. As I had read before, possums, marmosets and other mammals have had their reproductive systems subjected to every form of interference and control. Eventually, the goal is to control human fertility. Researchers are trying many ways to stop the unguarded process that leads to the birth of an unwanted human being. But nature, it seems, resists control. If you stop something in one place, it sets off a reaction somewhere else. I gathered from Rohil's papers that it is very, very frustrating and very, very expensive to develop the better contraceptive we are all waiting for.

It occurred to me that Anshul must have already overcome all these initial impediments. If he had the backing to continue his research in the face of worldwide competition, then, surely he must be close to a solution? Half-obsessed with Anshul, half-hypnotized by Rohil, I fell into an uneasy sleep, listening, as always, to any sounds of distress from my young sister in the next bed.

TEN

The morning rays had cleared Shweta's mind. The night's inner struggles showed up as dark rings under her melting eyes. She came up to where I sat with my newspaper and coffee. 'Sorry,' she whispered. My tension was released all in one whoosh. I nearly lifted her off her feet, till my ankle screamed. I breathed a 'Forget it, sweets, it's okay.'

'Can you call him home this weekend?' she asked, when she'd stopped wincing at the way I'd dropped her down. Perfect solution. 'Rohil? Great idea. I'll ask him,' I replied, glad about the early truce.

I brought up my favourite subject for discourse again in the evening, with Anna. Not Rohil—I don't need to talk about that subject, merely to dream. No, it was Dr Anshul.

'Yes, yes, that reminds me. Jimmy came over today. Funnily enough, he himself brought up the topic of India Biotech. He asked me to keep the relationship between Transpharma and Anshul to myself. Naturally, I asked him why.'

Anna peered into his empty glass, walked over to his well-stocked bar for a refill. He was being very careful with his words, I noticed. Tonight's poison was Cardhu, a Highland single malt. I tried to be patient. He brought me a glass too.

'Jimmy says it's no longer an official relationship. Apparently, there are some negotiations going on between the parent company in the US and this, er, Hiremath's company here. I believe there is some sort of major disagreement. In any case, he suggested that it was not a direct link. Some foundation that Transpharma supports in the US has been partially funding India Biotech's vaccine research.'

I swirled the ice-cold Scotch around my tongue. Something did not seem right.

'If it is the foundation that is supporting Anshul, then what has Transpharma got to do with him?'

'I don't know. Jimmy himself seemed very vague. Perhaps deliberately. He was uncomfortable talking about Anshul at all. It would have been very rude of me to push further.'

'Maybe I should just ask Anshul directly. After all, I was there when Kakodia mentioned all this. Do you think he'll come out with very much, Anna?

'Oh, he may tell you about his sponsor, if it's a straight deal. But don't expect too much else, gonu. Secrecy is completely vital in the development of a new product.'

'How come so many people already know about it then?'

'Well, you can't keep the idea itself quiet for too long. He must have filed intermediate patents to protect his work. That's the standard practice on a new molecule or application. It's mere self-defence so that another developer on the same track can be stalled. But it is such a long haul from there to project completion that word leaks out, sooner or later. Still, the medical community can close ranks very quickly on these things.'

'The ivory tower syndrome.'

'Can't blame them, or should I say "us"? With people like you prying around, one can't be too careful. Which brings me to the point I wanted to make. Since Jimmy, who is an old friend of mine, has specifically requested confidentiality, I would expect you to respect that. No mention of Transpharma.'

'But Anna!' I protested. 'What if I find out about it from some independent source? What if it is a vital link in the story?'

Anna looked at me in that thoughtful way of his. 'We'll cross that bridge when we come to it.' And that was the best deal I could get.

Over dinner, I spoke of MR Hills. I had been toying with the idea of going down there. It's not too far from Bangalore, and it promised a pleasant break, even if there was nothing to be discovered on the story. Amma raised her head at that. She so rarely intervenes in our conversations that I was pleased. It was she who yielded the best resource person for this yarn I was spinning so giddily.

'Arre, doesn't Vikram live there? In MR Hills? Some work he's doing with the tribals? The other day, Manju, his aunt, Mother's cousin . . .' she explained for the benefit of Anna, who could rarely remember relationships. 'She had come over with Usha. It seems he's taken a vow of brahmacharya. Manju did not know whether to be impressed or to feel cheated out of a matchmaking prospect.'

We laughed. Coming from Amma, who has been throwing young men in my path for ever, it was especially rich.

'You're right, Yasho,' said Anna. He too seemed pleased that she was more animated today. He'd been a bit nervous about Amma's reclusive behaviour. 'Dr Vikram Gopinath. I had quite forgotten. His father, Gopinath Sridhar, was our neighbour a long time ago. Haven't you met Vikram, Poorva?'

I couldn't remember. 'She has, once. He had come here,' said Amma pointedly. 'But she thought I was up to something, and excused herself.'

Oh well. Now that the gentleman had chosen celibacy, it didn't matter!

'Vikram was with the Communist Party for a while,' Anna reminisced. 'Sridhar never could figure out what made his son go radical. He has set up a tribal development centre among the Banigas and is something of a cult figure there, I believe. Wait. I remember reading about him some time ago. Where was it? Ah! In the *Hindu*. I guess you can look it up.'

'Great, thanks, both of you,' I said. 'Amma, do you think I could take Shweta with me, if I were to go to the hills?'

The rest of dinner was spent discussing the pros and cons of an outing for Shweta, who was not present for our late meal. The debate remained inconclusive. We retired, yawning, to the stifling heat of our summer beds.

ELEVEN

I had enough background on Dr Anshul Hiremath now. It was time to call on India Biotech Pvt Ltd. Back at my desk, I pulled out his card from the new file I had created. There were several numbers listed. I had to cross three barriers before his clipped voice came on the line. In the background, I had heard raised voices which fell silent as he picked up the link. He was very quick to identify who I was.

'You'd promised me an interview. Is tomorrow convenient?'

'Actually, we've become terribly busy suddenly. Maybe sometime later?'

But I had not been in the profession for eight years for nothing. With a little charm, a little deceit about the kind of piece I was doing and a lot of pressure, I made Anshul yield reluctantly to my request for an interview. His secretary gave me the address and directions to the facility. It was, of course, all the way across town. But I would have gladly gone to the other side of the country. I felt strangely elated.

I had the rest of the day to myself, thanks to CP's generous sabbatical offer. I could have easily whiled it away anticipating my next meeting with Rohil. In deference to Shweta, it had been set up for Saturday. We had decided to start out at home and then have a quiet dinner by ourselves. He had chosen Afghan, a new restaurant with an eponymous cuisine.

But there was Dr Vikram Gopinath to follow up on. I switched off my amorous thoughts and took the lift up to the library. Normally, I would have bounded up the stairs. Now the ankle hurt if I overdid things.

Mrs Guntur, the librarian, greeted me noisily. She is a plump, short, bespectacled lady given to a raucous laugh most unsuitable to her profession. It shakes the silence and brings all the studious heads whipping up to see what the matter could be.

'Poorva! I heard all about the poor bus.'

She became, I think, the seventy-fifth person to make the same joke. Her laugh followed inevitably, making me the cynosure of all eyes there. I quickly fielded my request. Mrs Guntur is far more capable than she looks, with her flouncy walk and her bold sari prints. Within seconds, I was looking at a clipping on the Baniga Kalyan Kendra, MR Hills.

Anna had been right about Dr Vikram Gopinath. There was a box item devoted to him. I peered at the photograph. Mid-thirties. Lean. Prominent nose. Apparently the Banigas, who live about fifteen thousand strong in the mountains, are split up into four or five groups. Each group has a loyalty to a certain camp. Apart from the Kendra, there is the inevitable government intervention centre, one missionary effort, at least one extreme left wing group, and a couple of other NGOs. It sounded like a volatile mix. Still, the Kendra claimed to have about five thousand Banigas under its influence. It had set up a healthcare centre, a school, and a vocational training centre. The article gave a Bangalore address where Vikram Gopinath conducted local business once a fortnight. I copied it down, thanked Mrs Guntur, and returned downstairs.

I encountered a few suspicious, envious glances on the way. Obviously word had got around. Poorva Pandit is on an assignment. She need not file regular—read boring—stuff. I kept a small smile on my face, kept my eyes focussed at a middle distance and made my way to my cubby hole.

Good old Jayamma, the office aide, had left a cup of coffee on my desk. She'd covered it to keep it warm—with the rag I use to wipe my desk with. I smiled at the courtesy. She considers herself a den mother to the editorial staff.

We do seem to need one. Sometimes, we squabble like siblings. At other times, we ignore each other like strangers. While working long hours on a story, we resent every colleague who has a light load. In our own free time, we head off to the table tennis room at the end of the hallway. The decrepit green table is probably the only hangover from the old office. With the renovation, the Tribune Tower has left its traditions behind. No more clacking typewriters. No more metal stands overflowing with old newspapers. Computer screens blink quietly all over the building. The telex machines, the operators, have all been replaced. New telephones, even new coffee machines on each floor. Polished granite flooring. Air-conditioners. It's lucky they did not find new, improved models of the staff.

I grinned to myself at the thought. I could handle some of my colleagues being replaced. Or upgraded! I gulped down my coffee. Strong, double sugar. Then I dialled the local office of the Baniga Kalyan Kendra. My luck held. I didn't know then that misfortune was simply piling up. The 'once a fortnight' turned out to be that very day, a blazing hot Thursday in the third week of May. I took a rickshaw to the Chamrajpet office, suffering the potholes, the unauthorized road humps and the erratic drivers with poor grace. I think my temporary chauffeur was glad to eject me at my destination. I missed my scooter. Not that I could have ridden it yet. That reminded me. A couple of weeks before, Anna had booked a Maruti 800 for me. He'd said it was a soft loan, negotiable terms. It would be so great to have my own car.

The Kendra was lodged in a nondescript little bungalow. Dr Gopinath himself was right outside. He was a total caricature of the social activist. RK Laxman would have found him disappointingly perfect. Tall, emaciated, wearing the predictable khadi kurta-pyjama, his nose even more prominent in real life. But he had a sweet smile. And the most disarming manner. With a mild namaskara, he drew me in from the small lobby to an ante-room that was ten feet square, spartan except for woven grass mats that covered most of the red oxide floor.

'Banni, please sit down,' he said, and I squatted, automatically assuming the padmasana posture. He noticed, and smiled. Without realizing it, I had made a friend.

Once he started to talk about the Banigas, 'please call me Vikram' became increasingly animated. He described the unique character of the community, their intense efforts to retain their identity and still swaddle the intruding culture. It was impossible to get a word in for the first fifteen minutes. Finally, I managed to mention Anshul Hiremath's alleged work with the Banigas. 'I hear there were some problems with his research. Do you know anything about it?'

Even as I uttered the words, an enormous fear rose in me. Vikram Gopinath could easily be a partner in Anshul's work. Maybe tribals from his own centre were part of the research. I gave myself a mental slap. I had not considered that possibility.

'Houdu, houdu, India Biotech. You know, we have long been suspicious about it. Dr Hiremath is using the Shakti Sanghatana people in his team. There is too little information coming from there. Recently, though, some stories did come my way. It is a little disturbing.'

Relief flooded through me. 'What kind of stories?'

'I heard, and nodamma, I have no proof, that one woman nearly died from complications in her pregnancy. I know that they are developing a contraceptive. People are too quiet. Something must not be working right, alva?'

So my information was accurate.

'Can I come see for myself? Maybe I could visit the research centre?'

'You are welcome to try. Though if you come through my organization, you may encounter some antipathy. The Shakti Sanghatana people keep to themselves. I am sad about that, but that's the way it is.'

I decided to take my chances with Vikram. I left with the tentative plan of going up to the hills the following weekend. I had quite forgotten to mention our family connections. But there would be time later.

TWELVE

I could have taken the bus to Anshul's office the next day. Anna's car was not available. But recent events had left in me an aversion, if not a fear, for the red road hogs. So I bumped the twenty kilometres to Yelahanka, the extreme north of the city, in a rickshaw.

Get caught in a traffic jam in the morning rush hour, and you'd know instantly why Bangalore would never make it to the league of the Big Four metros. Permanent potholes, a keen disregard for pedestrians, a chaotic cocktail of vehicles. All competing for fifty feet or less of carriageway. And one hapless policeman, hardly visible through the exhaust fumes of idling vehicles, warding off cancer with an imitation gas mask or a handkerchief. Here, everybody believes in the dictum *'solpa adjust madi'*. It means 'please adjust a little'. I fear we Bangaloreans are soon going to 'adjust' ourselves into oblivion.

With such thoughts bouncing around in my head, I was quite taken aback by the vision that suddenly came up to my left. High walls in white draped with a curtain creeper in dark green. A satellite receiver mounted on a mast indicating a dedicated communication link. A brass-and-black board announcing India Biotech Pvt Ltd. A security guard's cabin in glass, with the inevitable grills.

Past the visitor's book, I seemed to have floated into a miniature America. An expanse of trim lawn dotted with hybrid flowers threw into relief a low-slung sleek white building. The granite columns in front harked to a colonial architecture. But the rest of the complex was a gleaming high-tech oasis away from the muddy megalopolis outside the gate.

I was ushered through sanitized corridors which suddenly opened onto a vast atrium. Greenery and light brought the outdoors inside in a beautiful showcase of interior design. Then more corridors. I clip-clopped hurriedly behind my guide into the second one from the left. We reached a door that was surely a vanity piece. Quite different from the rest. Carved rosewood in geometric designs. A feminine touch. As the thought touched the shores of my mind, a female voice floated out.

'Come in.'

I entered a large room, well lit, deeply carpeted. The woman walking towards me was jaw-droppingly glamorous. Never mind that the skirt suit she wore looked out of place in this hot season. She had on cool blue accessories that localized the flavour well enough.

A long-fingered, unpainted hand stretched out.

'I'm Surabhi. Anshul's wife. He has spoken to me about you.'

There was a touch, an undercurrent of something I could not catch. As a single woman, I am used to such coolness from wives. So I said the appropriate things. But I had not expected to find the spouse there. Where was Anshul?

She read my mind. 'My husband will be with you in a minute. Can I get you something to drink?'

I asked for water. She walked to the desk and buzzed someone. It gave me a chance to look around.

Anshul's office was exactly as it should be. An NRI trying to recreate an American environment. An outsize desk in pastel wood. Computers, an array of telephones, an electronic diary, open. Pine cabinets, bookshelves with titles like *Microsoft Secrets*. Paintings and etchings and haunting photographs reminiscent of Ansel Adams.

Anshul strode in just then, a file of some sort in his hand. 'Surabhi, why on earth does . . .' He saw me. Stopped and cleared his face. 'Well, hello! Poorva, of course. You are very punctual.' Maybe too much so? I stood up to shake hands. 'Have you met Surabhi here? She's one of our directors. And my wife.' A simple explanation. Anshul's eyes crinkled nicely. I sat in a straight-backed chair. Husband and wife took the opposite sofa, looking earnest. What do the Americans call a sofa? While I tried to remember, quite unneccessarily, they were both waiting for me to say something. I felt a little lost, though I had been through it all in my mind. Finally, it was Anshul who interjected, not unsympathetically.

'I was speaking to you about our business the other day. Our core competency is in enzymes. Marketing. We sell diagnostic kits to laboratories. And to research institutions.'

Yes, of course. The journalist in me surfaced belatedly. I asked competent questions about the distribution of enzyme kits, the niche market, the competition. It turned out the enzyme division was doing extremely well for a recent startup. They had started by importing the enzymes from Transpharma to assemble kits. But they had soon developed indigenous substitutes that reduced costs considerably. Which explained why Jimmy Kakodia had expressed comic disappointment, that day at the Club. There did not seem to be too much competition yet. Clients were in both public and private sectors. Turnover was an impressive, three crore rupees in just over a year. There was an adequate business story here.

I guess we all knew that there was something else I was after. 'What's really interesting though, is the vaccine research you were talking about that day. I know you said it is too early to write about it. Maybe you could just give me some background, some basics?'

They exchanged glances. Anshul seemed to be asking his wife a question. Surabhi looked instantly wary.

'Ah, yes, the vaccine. It's my favourite subject, of course.' Anshul sounded almost apologetic. He had nothing to apologize to me for. So he must have been worried about Surabhi. Theirs seemed to be an intriguing relationship. 'It's hard for me to know when to stop once I'm started, I warn you.'

'Oh, I'm really interested. Imagine, a vaccine that can prevent pregnancies, as it prevents typhoid or cholera. How did you start on it?' I was all eagerness and innocence. Surabhi was still watchful.

'I had worked on it for many years, back in the US. When I was doing my Ph.D in genetics. My subject was the zona pellucida . . .' Seeing my look of ignorance, he added, 'That's the sort of shell on the human egg. I had some accidental breakthrough then. But you know, the approach to research is different there. Exhorbitantly expensive, high liability costs. The industry, and the government, are too cautious. I guess they've burnt their fingers once too often! It's a continuous battle getting support—even for genuine research. At least in some fields.'

I didn't understand his point too clearly. I would have thought all research originated from there! Still, I knew better than to interrupt.

'In any case, seven years was long enough. We,' and he looked to Surabhi, confident of her assent this time, 'were homesick. I told you that, I guess. So I worked pretty hard to get myself this grant to support my research right here. We chose Bangalore because of my links here. I studied at the Institute of Science. And the weather's right, you know.' The low-watt, high-impact smile flashed. Fascinating.

'Your vaccine, does it actually prevent fertilization? Or does it abort the conceptus?' I must admit I was using techy words to sound less ill-informed. 'Conceptus' is just another word for the embryonic cell cluster.

'Ah! You must have done a backgrounder.' Anshul was surprised, on his guard. Surabhi gave him a piercing look, then looked calculatingly at me. Luckily, her husband continued.

'That's the beauty of this one. Unlike other vaccines under research, it is not an abortifacient. It does not destroy the embryo, but prevents conception itself. You see,' Anshul, glancing at Surabhi, faltered briefly. 'Er, well, not to get too technical, but the idea is to create antibodies that prevent the sperm from entering the egg to fertilize it. No hormonal roulette involved, nothing harmful. Until now, people have tied themselves up in knots trying to stop pregnancies after fertilization, through hormonal interventions. You know, by blocking progesterone or something. Risky stuff. We are working only with the zona pellucida. We have succeeded in raising an antigen from the glycoproteins on the zona receptors. It's simple, and beautiful.' Anshul's entire body was speaking. He was leaning forward, his eyes gleaming, his hands agitated. I was mesmerized.

'For decades, people have been looking for the perfect contraceptive. Safe, effective, cheap and convenient. What better way than through a vaccine? It is cost effective, reliable, easy to administer even at a mass level, safe, no pain, no mess, no invasive intervention. Perfect.'

Dr Gayatri, I remembered, had used almost the same parameters. 'You have already developed the prototypes? Have you tested them on women?' I tried hard to underplay my interest.

'Yes, we are at an advanced stage of our trials. We're in phase two. Our field team is working in MR Hills. Actually, our sponsors are quite happy with our progress. We have the requisite permissions from the government, it's all going well.' I caught Surabhi crossing her fingers at that. Anshul touched her hand briefly.

'Who are your sponsors? I believe research of this sort can be prohibitively expensive?'

'Luckily, I was able to convince the Biogene Research Foundation, a venture capital fund sponsoring genetic research all over the world, that my product was viable. By relocating in India we wanted to shatter the myth that it is—as you put it—prohibitively expensive to do such research. Our budgets are very reasonable by worldwide standards.'

Bridges began to connect all the fuzz in my mind. This was the link Kakodia had spoken of. I could see evidence of the Biogene grant all around. Obviously, worldwide standards were way above local ones! Everything looked spanking new, the paint, the pictures, the greenery, the computers. No dust, no poverty, no India, even. This could be anywhere in the world.

Anshul and Surabhi began to walk me around the complex. Anshul's long strides were hard to keep up with. My leg was throbbing already. I bit back a request to go slow.

Closest to the CEO's wing was the research and development section. Obviously Anshul's pride and joy. A white womb. Rows of tubes and vials and machines that looked like nothing else on earth. A strange pervasive smell that hung like a hospital memory, making my nose twitch. And angular technicians scattered about, measuring things or staring at computer monitors.

The sanctum sanctorum, where the vaccine research was on, yielded itself abruptly, as though it now had no choice but to do so. It was the last door of the wing. It had 'Authorized Personnel Only' etched on it to warn intruders off, but no locks or special security, I noticed.

Soon, my head was full of serums and gas chromatographs and various other gadgetry that fed rows of computers with information at different stages of vaccine development. Much of it remained vague, though I tried hard to piece it together intelligently. Finally, Anshul, perhaps sensing my inadequacy, offered to give me some material to leaf through later. I accepted rather gratefully.

Then we moved on to the other, more public side of India Biotech. The research wing was not just physically separate from the enzyme marketing and distribution end of the business. It was like another company altogether. Here, things looked more casual and the employees were obviously younger. There was talk and laughter. The noticeboard displayed the date of the next marketing group picnic. Happy Birthday messages were pinned up on computer stationery. The India Biotech family. Americans believe in high bonding and tight-knit groups. Anshul had brought the culture home. At least to half his company. Maybe he's a Gemini.

Several people stopped to speak to Anshul or Surabhi, casting curious but not unfriendly glances at me. One face looked familiar.

'Is that Tushar?' I asked.

'Yes,' said Surabhi, smiling across at the lanky man speaking to someone across the room.'Our financial whiz-kid. You know him?'

'We were at school together.' Tushar, a whiz-kid? He had been the most laid-back of guys, at least during the board exams. Must have changed. Surabhi called out to him, he turned and looked at me properly. 'Poorva Pandit, no less.' He smiled almost shyly, reminding me of his post-puberty awkwardness. 'We see the byline all the time. But what are you doing here?' Tushar took my hand and pumped it. 'Are you writing about Anshul? It's time someone did.' Ignoring the great hope in Tushar's voice, Anshul merely refuted the idea. 'No, no. She wants to write about the vaccine. I keep telling her it's too early.'

The conversation drifted along, till a musical gong signified the lunch break. India Biotech had its own little canteen, to which I was now invited. We retraced our steps to the atrium and walked towards an arrow saying 'Garden Cafe'.

We took a table towards the centre, Surabhi stopping often to chat with employees. From the fragments of conversation I caught, I gauged that she handled personnel. Surabhi herself confirmed that later when she joined us. 'Sorry. Being head of HRD has its own demands here.' She smiled, eased herself into an empty chair, looking more like Ms India than an HRD manager. She checked, almost automatically, what Anshul was eating, and ordered a sparse lunch of greens and cheese from an over-attentive waiter.

Tushar seemed very much part of the inner circle. And he must have had a personality makeover. The ease with which he spoke to his bosses clearly proved the respect he commanded and suggested his indispensability. I wondered if he would share any sensitive information. For old times' sake. It was worth a try, later.

When I finally left India Biotech, it was on the assurance that I would do a general piece on Anshul and his company, with minimum reference to the vaccine.

'Of course, as things fall into place better, you will give me first chance at the story, won't you?' I had to ask.

A relieved Anshul promised heartily. Surabhi insisted on organizing a car to escort me safely out of the premises, back to my office. I took a couple of painkillers, and dozed off in the air-conditioned vehicle.

THIRTEEN

Returning to my fourth-floor office, I encountered the bossman on his way out. He was dressed very snazzily. A deep blue shirt open to his hairy chest, khaki trousers, a designer belt. RI in the middle of the afternoon? 'I'm going to the chief minister's,' he said testily, as if interrupting my thoughts. 'Why have you been avoiding me?'

Not true, but with CP, you have to give up on the little things. 'I need a little more time, CP,' I begged. 'I'll get back to you in a couple of days.'

'Well, hurry up.' He was growling. He hates the present chief minister. 'This whole thing of yours is irregular. Most irregular.' The elevator swallowed up the rest of his misgivings.

My desk looked empty, forlorn. I'd just been throwing all my papers into a drawer. I sat down, did some breathing exercises to focus my mind. Then I decided to get a perspective on my current story obsession.

Q1: What is driving me on this story? Motivation?

A1 : Some force I have not felt before is driving me on this story. I feel plateaued in my career. I need something to shake it up.

Q2 : Why am I so convinced that there are dark secrets at India Biotech?

A2 : It's a gut feeling about Anshul. Maybe because of the conversation I overheard. Something's going on that needs to be exposed, written about. In any case, the development of a new product like that can rocket India into a new orbit. So it's a story anyway.

Q3 : What will I do if I am absolutely wrong in my suppositions?

A3 : If I'm wrong, I'll apologize. Or I'll quit. What the hell!!

That felt good. So good that I hopped out of office to go to the cybercafe down the road. I go there occasionally to access the Internet and cruise on the Web. Not just for my work, but also to find out, almost gluttonously, about the latest research on neuromuscular disorders.

Pranay was there. Familiar, but funky, with the long hair, the earrings and tight jeans. He manages the place. I doubt if he ever goes home. I wouldn't be surprised if he just turned into a cursor and slept on the monitor at night! He settled me in front of a PC and personally brought me a cup of steaming hot coffee. 'For you, beautiful, anything,' he said, when I thanked him.

I just love the idea of a giant, anarchical, interdependent system that snakes through tens of millions of computers and at least twice as many lives. The Internet. Irritating, time-wasting, mind-expanding ocean of information. Maybe our first alien contact will come as a message on the World Wide Web. 'HI THERE, HUMANS! Are you interested in intergalactic trade? Please click here for more information.'

I called up a search engine, looked up 'anti-fertility+ vaccine'. I got fifty-six entries, most of which seemed irrelevant. I did find out that at least two other teams, one in Brazil and one in the USA were conducting advanced clinical trials on a vaccine which seemed similar to Anshul's in its efficacy. However, both used antiprogestins, as Dr Gayatri had suggested, to interfere with the production of progesterone. They started acting only *after* fertilization had taken place.

A revulsion snaked through me. I had just, quite suddenly, grasped what it meant. This was the silent scream. The killing of a birth at its moment of origin. I remembered Sharada, a friend who would not use IUDs in spite of her gynaecologist's advice against the pill. 'I refuse to participate in a process that unknowingly but consciously destroys a potential life, month after month.' I had scoffed at her then. She sounded like some of my radical feminist friends who think family planning is a Western conspiracy to destabilize India.

Both the vaccines under development were using tetanus toxoid as the immunogenic carrier. When injected with it, the body begins to mount an attack against progesterone-producing cells. Poor, confused body. I wondered just how effectively scientists would be able to control all the unknown processes that together make up the body's simplest functions. They are not boasting yet. It has not been easy, after all.

The problem with the vaccines under research was that the power to prevent pregnancy was shortlived. The antibodies could not be sustained in sufficient numbers to stop the pregnancy, month after month. So the antigen had to be administered much too often. The article also suggested that the antigen, raised from human tissue, was very unstable. It required careful handling and storage. Research was on to create a synthetic version. So far, no success had been claimed. Many years of research work accumulated steadily as the perfect contraceptive vaccine remained elusive.

To me the other day, Anshul had seemed quite confident of success. Could it be that he had already found a way around the problem? The answer lay, perhaps, in the research station at MR Hills. I would have to go there without informing Anshul. It was most unlikely that he would permit me to snoop around in the very womb of his research project! I decided I would go there first and inform him later. Such journalistic privileges are allowed.

By the time I left the café, my brain was filled with tremendous bytes of information on other vaccines as well. Vaccine research is apparently very, very big. Recent successes include the hepatitis-B vaccine. At least thirty more are on the anvil. The biggest newsmakers? Anti-AIDS and anti-cancer vaccines. But they are not exactly imminent. So close and yet so far, as Anshul Hiremath would have surely said.

FOURTEEN

Saturday evening at last. By the time I emerged from my room, dressed in bottle-green and cream, Dr Rohil Kamath, whom I had heard arriving, on the dot, had settled down in the living room with my family. Muted laughter floated across as I tried to glide gracefully into the room. I had on a high fashion ensemble halfway between a pant suit and a salwar kameez in the latest Indo-Western style. I kind of felt neither here nor there myself.

There was the sort of pause that could be attributed to either embarrassment or appreciation. I looked at Shweta first. She had a bemused look on her face. All around her was evidence of bribery. Flowers, chocolates, a board game of some kind. It had worked. She greeted me cheerfully.

'Hi Akka, you're looking great! Why didn't you put on my jade earrings? Let me get them for you.' She got up, carefully, slowly, and began to walk away with her awkward gait. Unusually, no one offered at once to go in her stead.

Rohil had stood up, looking—well—dashing. Molten copper T-shirt tucked into slim denims. Shweta is the family poet, but just then, I could have written a poem about my melting heart.

'You're still limping,' said lover-boy. It hardly set the

kind of tone I was expecting. I returned to earth and turned
to alcohol. Soon, the ice-cold beer had warmed everybody.
Even Amma agreed to a shandy. I call it the 'Rohil Effect'.
It has stayed with us ever since.

When we finally got up to leave for the restaurant,
Shweta bid us goodbye rather reluctantly. I'm glad I did
not give in to my immediate instinct to ask her along! Still,
her jade earrings hung from my ears, glowing softly green
against my hair.

Over mounds of saffron-flavoured rice peaked with
tender kebabs and a minty yogurt flowing alongside, we
settled into a delicious dinner at the Afghan.

'What is the prognosis for Shweta?' Rohil asked. It had
obviously been bothering him all along.

'Not that great, as you probably know. She has
Friedreich's Ataxia. It's crippling. What worries us most is
possible heart disease. Or diabetes. We can have her with
us for another five years or, if we are lucky, ten. But it will
always be tense. Unless . . . do you think a miraculous
breakthrough will come along?'

'There is always hope, Poorva. They are looking into
genetic reprogramming, neurological alterations, just so
many unbelievable things. I know there is worldwide
research into NMDs, neuromuscular disorders. She has time.
No need to despair.' His voice was gentler than I had heard
it so far. Even when I was trussed up like a country fowl
at the hospital, this doctor had been thinking up lousy one-
liners. But by then, my mind was on the subject of Shweta's
condition.

Of the forty types of neuromuscular disorders, which
include muscular dystrophy, not many are benign. Most of
them are fatal. Even though they may be slow to kill. At
least, in Shweta's type of NMD, the brain remains
unaffected. For us, it is a great blessing.

'She is such a spark, though, isn't she?' It was as if I had
spoken aloud.

71

'A big brat,' I said. The discomfort in my throat slid down slowly with the beer.

'Is Shweta the reason why you write so much about medicine and health?'

I nodded, struggling for complete control. 'Of course, Anna's in the industry too. It all came together somehow.'

'You know what? I looked up our library clippings a couple of days ago. A couple of your stories . . . about panic disorder, about the patient's right to information . . . were very well written. Erudite. I'm impressed.'

So was I, when he reached out to caress my forearm. Conversation became less coherent for a while after that. I returned to a safe subject before we could become a public nuisance.

Rohil quite surprised me then, by turning very serious. His casual, humorous posture had had me fooled, I guess. He began to talk, with a quiet passion, about his work.

'As I was telling you the other day, my interest is in organ transplants. One of the areas I work in is tissue typing, matching organ donors with recipients. It is crucial, otherwise the new organ will be rejected. There is so little time we get to find the right person for the transplant. A few hours is all. And there fits my dream. I want to help set up a nationwide network of information on available organs and needy patients. Online.'

I admit I was overawed. It sounded like a foreign tongue. HL-A typing. Lymphocyte cross-matches. Strange terminology for an unusual branch of medicine.

'They are just beginning on that sort of networking elsewhere in the world. I think . . .' He paused to order more beer from a turbaned Pathan waiter, 'I think that here we have one more opportunity for India to get in on it. Right at the top. Leapfrog over all the other stages. Especially now that the Internet has established itself in the mindset of our administrators. Still, it all needs money. And, I guess, a higher value—a premium on life!'

We pondered over that a little. His current work brought him to the brink of new life in the time of death. My current research had revealed a kind of death at the brink of new life. We felt sombre.

I remembered recent scandals that had blown across the country over organ bazaars.

To CP's disgust, it had been our rival newsmagazine that had ripped the cover on an organized racket to harvest organs from poor or unsuspecting people. Especially kidneys. There had been many crackdowns later. Knee-jerk government responses. Doctor witch-hunts.

'We always seem to throw the baby out with the bathwater,' said Rohil, speaking of the kidney scam. He waved an imaginary stethoscope. 'Now even legitimate patients are deprived of their donor kidneys because of all the damn legislative hotchpotch. As usual, the very rich and the very corrupt will still find a way around. That's like bringing back the bathwater and leaving out the baby! Crazy situation!' He shook his head rather violently, spilt some froth over the tablecloth and wiped at it ineffectually with a napkin.

I reached out and stilled his hand. I too had written about the medical and ethical issues involved. I had interviewed a young man named Hamid. Construction worker. Twenty-three years old. Startling grey eyes. He had gone into a small-town hospital near Bangalore for an emergency operation and had returned home minus two organs instead of one. His appendix, and one kidney. His father, a fifty-five-year-old drunken lout, whom I also met, had been compensated with five thousand rupees.

I had turned the story around a little. Gimmicky. But I did not want it to seem like just another horror inflicted upon an unknown in a sea of similar disasters. So I had personified Hamid's kidney. Recorded its fictional trail, ending, finally, inside the body of a wealthy Arab gentleman of sixty-eight years, with acute renal failure. I had been livid when CP had called it 'cute'. He'd swallowed his words later, when we got good reader response.

Rohil did not want to get too deeply into the ethics bit, I could tell. He was squirming. And I hadn't even done my self-conscious, indignant act.

'Look, you can't really eliminate malpractice. But I'll tell you something. Organ transplants are going to become very common in the future. Each day, we learn more about preventing organ rejects. In India, we have so many healthy organs being wasted! If they were harvested on time, we could save so many, lives.'

It was funny, I thought. Some dying people could put life into other dying people! But do nothing for themselves.

'Take road accident victims,' continued Rohil earnestly, now jabbing at his kebabs with a toothpick. 'Sixty thousand deaths each year! Highest in the world. Yet, if we could get there on time, some of those deaths could be redeemed by transplanting organs into other bodies. That's what I want to be able to do!' He watched my jaw muscles clench, my eyes glaze over. He probably realized that the subject of roadway deaths was not my current favourite. Like some macabre music video, my mind was throwing up images of various organs floating in the air. Liver, pancreas, intestines. Problem was, they were mine. Leaving my body as I lay somewhere bleeding. I concentrated instead on feeling angry with him for being so inconsiderate. He backtracked rather hastily.

'You know what? I just remembered. I'm presenting a paper at a conference on 'Advances in Immunology' in June. There will be many experts on immunology there! You'll probably find out all you'll ever need to know about immuno-contraception right there!'

'Sounds okay,' I said, readily switching moods. 'Where is it going to be?'

A crafty look came over his face. 'It's in Goa,' he said, almost innocently. 'Will you come?'

'I'd love to.' Rain, research, resort and Rohil. Resisting would be ridiculous. 'Let me check with my editor.' CP would need careful treatment over this one, I thought.

We just made it to his quarters before we actually began to undress each other. I guess we had underestimated our thirst. We quenched it a little more that night. Then Rohil put in some cork-stoppers. He said, later, that he wanted our first time to be memorable. 'More in Goa,' he promised, before he dropped me at my door, leaving me heady with the combined fragrances of raat ki rani and jasmine from the garden.

FIFTEEN

It was a fine Saturday morning. Shweta and I set off close to dawn, even before the milkman and the bulbuls could announce themselves. I had won two rounds. Amma had agreed to Shweta making the trip to MR Hills with me. CP had promised to pay expenses. I had filled him in on all that had been happening. Except the bit about Rohil . . .

Our driver, Mohan, was at the wheel. He has been with us for many years. Amma and Anna certainly have more faith in him than in their own offspring. Still, Amma hovered about anxiously while our weekend bags were loaded. Laxmi ran out at the last minute with a tiffin box of hot idlis, her world-famous chutney and a huge canteen of water. 'Don't drink the water there,' she warned us. She touched the top of Shweta's head briefly, before returning to her kitchen. Shweta's eyes were bright with an unaccustomed excitement. Two whole days with Akka to herself. And a picnic at MR Hills. It was lucky she'd been feeling well. Otherwise Amma would never have let her go.

Leaving Shweta to her Hindi pop music, I spent much of the entire five-hour journey to the hills planning my interviews. Dr Vikram would be there, of course. I had to, somehow, also get to the India Biotech camp and meet the researchers. I was not sure they would speak to me about their work, or even let me past the door.

I had deliberately refrained from telling Anshul that we were going to the hills. I had even warned Anna not to mention it to anybody. I have never indulged in such cloak-and-dagger journalism before. It was getting exciting. Of course, there might be less of a story if there was nothing illegal or, at least, unethical going on. Ah! The contrary plight of the media! We must feast on rot.

I had forty-eight hours to get to know the Banigas and little to go by. All the information I had gathered so far was from Vikram or from what I'd read in the article. It was amazing how reclusive they appeared to be even in these days of globalizing the village.

The car began to ascend the Ghats, just past the little town of Maddur. We had stopped there for the spicy, unforgettable vadas the place is so famous for. Shweta seemed hungry in spite of the demolished idlis! A good sign, I thought.

Then the landscape began to alter noticeably. From dry deciduous shrubbery, we moved to moist deciduous forest, and finally into the semi-evergreen range. It was a stunning change of vista in a mere twenty-five kilometres. Later, I found out that it was a unique biosphere, home to many species of valuable timber trees like the honne, the surhonne, the sandalwood, the teak, and the precious rosewood.

Finally, we were almost at the top of the hills, with thick evergreen patches of forest on the ridges across. These mountains form a chain that link them to the Nilgiris. The forests here are barely navigable in parts. They have long been home to sandalwood smugglers. The most notorious is moustachioed Murugan, known locally as 'Yajmanru' which means 'the Boss'. He's been evading forest rangers for many years. The papers are full of the exploits of special snoop teams dispatched in droves to smoke him out. We had suffered witticisms from Anna about that, enough to worry Amma further. 'If you two are held hostage by this Murugan, I'm not paying any ransom. The poor fellow will probably pay me to take the pair of you back!' Anna had said. Amma, of course, had quickly made sure he regretted his little joke.

There we were, as high as one could go by this trail. Up here, the air was cooler; the colours of the birds brighter; their song unpolluted. No cars, not even the ubiquitous trucks, anywhere. The tinkling of bullocks' bells mingled with the crunch of their carts over the gravelly road. At Shweta's request, Mohan pulled over at a particularly picturesque spot. I stopped writing, jumped out of the vehicle and breathed in deeply. My lungs, unaccustomed to such clean air, ached with the effort. Surrounding us were plains and hills. Even so late into the summer, there was still some green, though interspersed with thirsty yellows.

When we set off again, there was little change in the scenery to prepare us for what lay round the next bend. Villages do not have suburbs. Or subvilles. Suddenly, we were at the Baniga Kalyan Kendra. Behind the wrought-iron gate was a cluster of semi-thatched huts around a central courtyard bordered with bright flowers. Dr Vikram Gopinath came out almost immediately to greet us, with a humble namaskara. Shweta was limping from being cramped up in the car. Gently, he helped her into his room which was close by.

'We grow our own coffee,' said Vikram as our nostrils registered the flavour of steaming hot cups coming at us. 'And collect our own honey. Everything we need is right here, all around us.'

There was not that much around us, when I scanned his room, which was as spartan as his Bangalore office. But needs can expand if you let them. From what I had read, from what I could see, Dr Vikram didn't allow these runaway needs to break personal, philosophical barriers. I felt a rush of gratefulness for people like him.

He escorted me around the Kendra. It was a sprawling settlement, and yet it did not overwhelm. Spaces between buildings seemed more alive than the structures themselves. At least they were more populated. I looked around, my mind wide open. The Banigas have distinctive features. Flat noses, high cheekbones. Obviously, the blood has not mixed much. As we walked past people doing their jobs, many turned to glance curiously at me. Every other person had a smile for the doctor. 'We try to train people in sensible vocations,' he said, taking me around what he called the 'life skills centre'. A place where young people could re-equip themselves with basic learning. 'Sadly, even the traditional skills have had to be institutionalized so that they can be preserved. This is an era when packaged bread is sold even in the smallest hamlet shops. Old skills now have to be perpetuated with new markets.'

So the students were taught to make coffee and candles. There was formal training in honey collecting and bottling, weaving, herbal cosmetics and carpentry. It seemed directed at outside markets, probably urban. That disturbed me a little. This was not the happy ending of a Gandhi-inspired 'small is beautiful' effort. But then, I had no *locus standi*. So I did not speak up.

New aspirations tried valiantly to blend with the old at the Kendra, but remained disparate. Like the rudimentary printing press now in operation. The tribals printed all the stationery they needed for their growing interaction with the outside world. I glanced at some information booklets. They were in rudimentary 'Indish', most articles like 'the' deleted or unnecessarily crowded into sentences. Quaint. But they did not stand a chance in the sophisticated word bazaar operating beyond these hills.

'Nodamma, you must understand,' Vikram stopped his tour under the spreading shelter of a Singapore cherry. Obviously not indigenous, but graceful as ever in its new home. 'We are not trying to overrun their culture at all.

They have retained many of their ways. Yet, it is not fair to deny them access to modern benefits under the guise of preserving their heritage. It is a tightrope walk most of the time.' I could imagine some of the pitfalls. Is satellite TV bad for a sheltered tribal people? Is detergent evil? Must antibiotics be kept away?

I asked about the source of funding for all these ventures.

'Oh, it comes,' he smiled, his face breaking into appealing wrinkles. 'I started out in one second-hand van, using it as a mobile dispensary. All this,' he arced his arm across the expanse in front, 'came with the support of well-wishers. We try to sustain ourselves with our own enterprises now.'

The most insidious, and most inescapable, of the influences that assaulted the tribal community was television. A black and white community set had recently been replaced with half a dozen colour TVs in each of the housing settlements. Baniga children were now singing the latest Kannada film songs along with their harvest-time rhymes.

'It would be foolish to say it was all bad,' admitted Vikram. 'At the same time, one can see how the youngsters are succumbing to the dominant culture. They will soon forget that they had one of their own, forget even to retain the best of their own. That's the real tragedy.'

To counter this, the doctor had set up a little pilot project to gather information on local health traditions. Thanks to a grant from a Dutch agency, he was soon to get a computer that would help him maintain his databases on medicinal plants and their uses.

'Some people feel, I know, that I have sold out by accepting this grant. Maybe, maybe.' He smiled sadly to himself. 'But there was no way we could do it manually for very much longer.' To each his own devils.

Vikram left me, then, to attend to his work. I continued on my tour with the help of a couple of very young male volunteers. I met the sole researcher at the makeshift lab where the medicinal plants were collected, processed, stored.

'Research and Development Manager', said the placard on his desk. Charudatta had studied ayurvedic medicine, then he had come under the influence of the Vivekananda movement, and finally made his home here. He was busy labelling and bottling some black seeds. 'It's Krishna tulsi,' he explained. 'Quite common. But we used to say that about so many plants and yet they have disappeared. So we want to preserve this genetic line.'

I looked around the spacious hall. Dozens of shelves housed hundreds of glass bottles; each neatly labelled in Charudatta's handwriting. Posters stuck to the whitewashed walls reinforced the visitor's interest in the preservation of local biodiversity. Somebody here was dedicated to the cause.

'We have identified six hundred useful plants indigenous to this region,' he proffered his information eagerly, like a schoolboy showing off his project work. 'There is tremendous potential here to document the uses of each one. But,' and his shoulders drooped visibly at the thought, 'we need a lot of resources, and a lot of money for that.'

The competition, too, was intense. Many other Indian and international companies had set their sights on the same data. Suddenly, the hills had become a veritable hot spot of tourists from the scientific community, fishing around for opportunities, mining for information from the tribals, offering huge amounts of money to anyone willing to share his inherited knowledge.

Many among the tribals had seized the opportunities offered. Who would not? Young men began to work for fancily named companies with even more fancy salaries, at least by local standards. They traded information; they collected plants. The cleverer ones set up independent consultancies, offering herbal information on a freelance basis. It was amusing and distressing at the same time.

'Soon, some multinational will file a patent for a very commonly used remedy. They tried with neem, then with turmeric. For God's sake! The US authorities, not knowing any better, may easily accord them patents. And then they will be laughing all the way to the bank, while the people here won't know what hit them.'

I thought of the local people having to use haldi and neem wrapped in a multinational label, in a disposable plastic tube. 'Surely, they are not that naïve?' I asked. I find it hard to buy such fears. I can't believe any multinational could possibly uphold its patents in remote locations, anyway. Even if the law allowed it. God knows many American corporations have not succeeded in stopping copyright violations of music and film material, even in well-known urban areas.

'No, you are right, they are not.' Charudatta cheered up with some distant memory.

'I have a sneaking suspicion that the tribals are not yet telling all they know. You see, even among them, there has always been a system of intellectual property rights, even though there was no fancy name for it. The local healers zealously guarded their knowledge of native medicines. And it is no different today.'

Good for them. I remembered Kumar Cherian's words at the Club. Maybe we can beat *them* at their own game, yet.

Back in Vikram's room, Shweta, who had been resting, was called in for a rejuvenating, thick drink of ragi porridge. It was flavourful, but sat heavy in the stomach. Chatting alongside, I told Vikram about our family connections. 'Ah, *that's* why you seemed familiar,' he said, perhaps being polite. We shared some amusement about his Aunt Manju.

Later, in the intense late morning heat, poignant with a forest quietness, we sat outdoors under the shade of a sprawling old tree that I could not recognize. I veered Vikram round to the subject of Anshul's research station.

'Houdu, houdu, of course you want to know about that. See, India Biotech has set up out there,' and he pointed towards the north. Unlike in the city, where such directions could never be enough, up in the hills it made sense. Here is here and there is there. 'About ten to fifteen kilometres by road.' Where he pointed, there was little to see. Shimmers of heat made mirages of the mountains beyond. A barbet started his monotonous call, toc, toc, toc: near and yet so far.

Vikram told me, or rather, he *warned* me that the Banigas there owed allegiance to another NGO. That they were led by the Baniga Shakti Sanghatana, the BSS, which was considered quite militant in its views. I did remember a little from the clippings at the office library. The BSS was linked to the Shakti Dal, a political party based in Bangalore. It believed the tribals should be mainstreamed quickly, through government handouts, if necessary. At the moment, they were agitating for a hydel power station in the hills. They wanted industries to come up here in the backyards of modern civilization; they clamoured for local employment. Obviously, the BKK and the BSS were on a bit of a warpath. I gathered that Vikram's world-view was dismissed as effete, even regressive.

For the BSS, India Biotech offered a plum opportunity to reign in the technological might of the outside world. The company had hired volunteers and helpers among the locals, who were being paid city rates for their work. At first, everything had seemed just fine. It had all been kept quite secret. The BSS, perhaps, had not wanted other Baniga settlements to muscle in. Recently, though, there had been a few murmurings. Information about the vaccine trials had begun to leak out. There was some gossip about a deformed foetus. People from the BSS camp had been coming to the Kalyan Kendra, asking innocent medical questions.

I watched Vikram as he spoke. He seemed to be stepping outside his image. He was pulling at the rough grass beside him. It seemed a gesture of stress, not of habit.

'I fished around a little, tried to find out if the women had given informed consent. Whether they knew exactly, that as in all experiments, there were unknown risk factors.'

I had done my background work. 'Informed consent' is a cornerstone of international policies on drug research. It implies that any volunteer must be shown, with signature or thumb impression, to have completely understood what he or she is letting himself or herself in for. India, predictably, has stringent laws on informed consent—in the books. Ethical review committees have been set up. We are good at that sort of thing.

Vikram looked up at me. I wondered if he was not a waste of manhood, with his long eyelashes, his unusual trimness. His hands, now pulled away from the grass, were crossed tightly in his lap. 'From what little I could gather, nobody seemed aware that there was a genuine risk. The men were happy because of the compensations. The women were getting free contraception. One social worker, who later visited us at the Kendra as well, spoke of "new freedoms" for Baniga women. She sounded like a publicist for India Biotech!'

The doctor's voice was louder. Shweta, sitting lazily next to me, looked up. 'I was not too convinced,' he said. 'At one point, I had threatened to sue India Biotech. But I held back, thinking of how much of my time would have to be spent on it.'

He looked a little ashamed, perhaps at his retreat. But I could sympathize. Legal backlogs in India are genuinely fearsome. Even if one does, finally, get a judgement in one's favour, getting it implemented may involve a tamasha of events. I've seen it so often on the beat. Frustration sets in like a disease, even if the petitioner's intentions are honest.

'I have just heard,' continued the good doctor, 'that a woman there has delivered a stillborn child. She was a volunteer, Madhamma. One of our boys is engaged to her oldest daughter. It seems she conceived in spite of the contraception. They say the child was badly deformed. Thank God it was dead.'

At last! Here was real, concrete evidence. I began to sweat a little with greedy anxiety.

Vikram was getting agitated. He twisted his hands. It looked odd on a man who otherwise appeared composed. 'I have sent word to find out more. If necessary, I have decided to visit the station myself. The problem is, in this case, the research coincides with the government programme on population control.' He seemed bitter. 'Nobody wants poor tribals to proliferate. So the government is quite happy to look the other way. The DCAI, that is the Drug Control Authority of India, has many officers who are pliable on these things. Like every public institution in *Bharat desh hamara*.'

He offered to send someone with me, in our vehicle, to the BSS settlement where I could find India Biotech. 'Chamla has some relatives there,' he said, calling out to a young man hovering nearby. He was dressed simply but very neatly in checked shirt and trousers. His complexion reminded me of perfectly ripened chikoos from my grandfather's farm—smooth, brown, with a warm blush on the surface. 'He helps me in my medical work, like the wonderful compounders in the old days,' Vikram said. Chamla smiled at that, straightened himself further. 'I hope you are able to find out the truth. Maybe we could take some action then.'

I felt quiet, purposeful. I called for Shweta, who, in her inimitable style had started to chatter with a gaggle of schoolgirls. 'Let's go to the battlefront, girl,' I said.

SIXTEEN

It was close to high noon. I had forced Shweta to put on a cap in deference to the brilliance outdoors. Chamla entered the Maruti Esteem gingerly, as though he could hurt himself in the process. Once inside, however, he quickly began to direct Mohan. He switched on the music. He rolled the window first up, then down again. My sister was quite amused. But Mohan was not. Eventually, after forty minutes of bumping through unpaved, snaking pathways, we came upon a settlement quite unlike the Baniga Kalyan Kendra.

There were clusters of bedraggled huts; thatched roofs patched here and there with bits of plastic and cloth. The sun was high in the sky and washed everything with a harsh light. I noticed dozens of homes, each one small and self-contained with little front yards fenced with thorny hedges. Together, they spread a dark patch over the hillside.

As soon as our car came into view, the children appeared. A gleaming car in these parts is too rare a sight for them to not go through at least some motions of excitement. Somehow, it seemed to me, rather unfairly I suppose, like a charade. A battery of kids, poorly dressed, bellies distended, laughing, some holding up younger siblings, running towards the car, shouting. It happens every time, out there in the rural underside of the country. And I hate it.

I hate it because it makes me feel like an unwilling oppressor. Earlier, in innocent days, I used to smile graciously and wave when the cherubs came. I used to ready my purse. Even to me, then, it had seemed patronizing. A friend had acidly remarked that it was distinctly 'colonial'. So I had stopped. After all, the idea had not been to hurt, or to take pleasure. But nowadays I am rethinking the issue. I try to do what comes naturally to me at that point in time.

I quickly got down from the car, to reduce the distance between myself and the kids. I squatted, started to talk to the group huddled before me, with its inevitable stragglers. 'Hello, Akka,' they chorused, no doubt in rehearsal. Then they returned, cheerfully, to a slight variation of Kannada. It was obvious that they, like myself, had been through this before. Visitors from the big cities, asking the same kind of questions over and over again. Then, when the children had said the things that seemed to satisfy them, the strangers inevitably distributed all manner of goodies. Not very useful things, maybe. But pretty looking ones, no doubt. I, stupidly enough, had come empty-handed.

Following excited directions, we moved towards the first cluster of huts. A few old men were sitting outside in the shade and watching. Some women were freeze-framed in routine work. Obviously, they all belonged to the same genetic pool as the BKK residents. But for how many generations more? I had a sudden insight into what 'browns' must feel when confronted with 'whites'. Not a new feeling, but shameful and powerful nevertheless. I felt a rush of extreme shyness, an inability to cope with what lay ahead. I quelled that emotion and waited for Shweta to catch up. The children were egging her on. The women watched her slow stride and spoke to each other. Somebody went into a hut and brought a mat which she then spread in the common courtyard that linked half a dozen dwellings.

Introductions were awkward. I was not white-skinned.

I had no curiosity value. Nor had I an apparent purpose in coming there. Plus, I had brought nothing, not even praise.

Shweta broke the ice. 'Have you all eaten yet?' she asked a woman who appeared to be sun-drying her long hair. A babble, a chorus ensued. Clearly, it was lunchtime. It was only then that I felt, almost simultaneously, the pounding of my hunger pangs and the aroma of masala that hung in the sultry air. In spite of our patent uselessness, we were very cordially invited to the meal. I looked around for our escort. But Chamla had already disappeared.

The lunch was eaten in community style, possibly in our honour. It was piping hot, served from darkened earthen pots. Ragi mudde, red hot beans saaru, pickle, watery curds and plain rice. Perfect. Shweta, poor baby, ate like a starving child. The women fussed more over her than over me. I am used to it.

I began to talk. Of myself. I explained, vaguely, that I was writing a story about government help to the tribals. Shweta's eyes registered disbelief. I returned a 'don't you dare!' flame from mine. I am practised in the art of getting people to speak. I'm not particularly proud of it. But it is useful in my profession. The women gathered around me and began, slowly, to talk.

At first, much to her discomfiture, we discussed Shweta's health. I looked at her pleadingly. She nodded, almost imperceptibly. They spoke of poultices and medicines that could help. I took copious notes, determined to ask Amma to try some of the remedies they suggested.

Soon, the meal was over. Some women had walked away, obviously for kitchen chores. The older women sat close to me. Young mothers clutching children at their waist remained a little further. The teenage girls gathered directly in front of us, in an excited semicircle. A few male children swung round and round the poles, noticeably more active than the girls.

I found myself observing—as an outsider. A writer, a

harvester of sound bytes and pithy phrases. I did not know how else to be. So I tried to postpone the harsh self-judgements.

From Shweta's health to the community's health was an easy jump. 'I was told there are special doctors who have come from Bangalore to help the women here?'

'Help?' snorted a wrinkled mass of woman with grey eyes. Cataract, maybe. 'Did you say help?' But a younger woman interrupted. 'Now, Amma, don't start. They did come here to help. And they did help. Look how many women have benefitted.' The old woman cackled, but lapsed into a muttering silence. The stories tumbled out soon after that.

When 'Indiya-biatec' first set up shop here, 'two cold seasons ago', the men in the tribe had welcomed them with open arms. The women had taken some time. They did not want such personal scrutiny. 'Then Rita Madam explained many things to us,' said the woman who had shushed her Amma. '*Dr* Rita Madam,' said someone else. The woman silenced her. 'Running Doctor,' said a chit of a girl, from the irrepressible sidelines. But she was subdued as well. 'Our girls,' said the shushing woman, 'have been using old medicines to stop babies. But these people have more modern methods. Their way has worked, mostly, I believe. Only recently there have been some problems.'

An old woman started an incoherent argument over that. I asked, hastily, about Madhamma. There was a silence. The oldest among the women—others, I had noticed, seemed to defer to her—edged forward in her squatting position. She squeezed my hand excruciatingly tight and pinched my cheek. A gesture that was perhaps meant to be a reprimand. Her voice was strong for her age. 'You already know about that, is it? Nobody can keep secrets anymore.' She shook her head, half left to right, half up and down. 'Always you people who come, you want everything. Then you want more.' I cringed. 'Still, we will show you. Come.'

Not very far away stood a hut, much like the others. Podus, I was told the dwellings were called. A handkerchief-sized yard around it was fenced with low, scraggly bushes. Chickens scurried about, irritated with the interruptions. But the hut was seemed isolated from the noise around it. Our group halted outside. Madhamma, the women informed me in hushed tones, was still recovering from her delivery. 'She is bitter and angry. She will not talk.' Someone told me not to waste my time with her. I stood there, quite confused.

Just then, Madhamma emerged, almost without moving. Someone made her sit down. She sat. They formed a small circle. I sat at the rim. Shweta stretched out her stiff, bent legs. Madhamma would not talk. That did not stop the others. From what I could gather, one of the women, painfully thin, with the standard unruly hair and an innocent smile was taunting her about her husband. 'He caused all your problems. To make money off you.' Silence amid exchanged glances. Then a visible wave of anger flitted across the newcomer's face. I felt Shweta recoil from it, move closer.

Madhamma then let open the floodgates of her emotions. She stood up, swaying a little, and began to talk in a low voice that was powerful in its reach. She cursed everyone, made obscene gestures at the tormentor who had so calculatedly provoked her. Then she addressed herself solely to Shweta and me. I had to strain to understand what she was saying. Her language was slipping into a dialect.

'Whatever that bitch may say, I was not the only one. There were fifty women. Fifty. We all took injections. Happily. None of us wanted babies. Not one of us! Our men don't use the cap properly. Those government doctors . . . they put things inside you if you don't want babies. It hurts. But Rita Madam only gave injections. A tika.'

Tika . . . It was the name given to vaccinations. Against DPT. Measles. Tetanus. For women and children. Massive

90

blitzkrieg of government advertising all over the country. Take the tika for yourself. Protect your child. It had worked. Polio was down, diphtheria on the decline. All over India, people trusted the tika as an injection against illness. Why not believe Dr Madam?

I pieced together the story as Madhamma continued to speak, almost unable to stop. She had taken the contraceptive vaccine twice. The 'doctors' had promised rations and clothes for the little ones. They had delivered. Everything had been all right for a while after that. She had some routine checks on her urine and blood. Then she had quit going to the research centre. Her man had 'jumped camps' and had gone to work in another tribal area where the government people had their agencies. She had followed. But neither of them had been able to settle down there. Even the four children had been unhappy.

Meanwhile, Madhamma had developed all the symptoms of pregnancy. Vomiting, weakness, amenorrhea. She had thought it was something else, because the research station Dr Amma had shut her womb opening with an injection. So two or three months had gone by. Then they had come back here. The station's social worker had made her go back to the centre. They had found she was pregnant—in her second trimester. The other doctor, who comes from Maddur, was unwilling to try out a risky abortion. They took her for an ultrasound test into the town. 'It was my first time in a jeep. It was painful. It hurt my baby.' The woman rubbed her hand over the memory. I vividly remember the gesture.

Madhamma's voice gave away little of her feelings. It was monotonous, with little inflection. Even her words were ordinary. It was her body language that told the story. Her fingers had clenched themselves. The veins in her neck protruded as if she had been shouting. Her eyes were smouldering. 'They said he was not growing properly. He was not regular, not like my other children.' Madhamma was suddenly ready to talk. 'Everyone, the midwives . . . my man, they decided they would allow the child to be born and strangle it. I agreed.' She sat down suddenly, swirling the dust around her.

Shweta winced. I reached out to touch her. But I understood, dimly. If you live under the laws of nature, you cannot be sentimental. Deformed babies should not be made to live out a life sentence. Even if black points accrue to the parents. Luckily, Madhamma had not needed to consent to such a barbaric act after all. Three weeks ago, she had delivered a premature child. Two weeks early. Stillborn.

It occurred to me then, that Dr Anshul Hiremath, who had seemed so confident of the progress of his trials, must surely have known about Madhamma. I would have to keep in mind that he was consummate at deception.

'Dead. He was already dead. He would have been my second boy if he had lived. And if his brain was not so small. And if his legs . . .' Madhamma stopped, getting up abruptly. I got up too. Involuntarily. But she disappeared into her hut. Someone followed. Nobody wanted to talk. Then a woman came and stood directly in my path. She wore a light-coloured sari. I noticed because all the other colours around me were darker, brighter. She looked authoritative.

'I saw the little thing. I delivered it. It was not human. Only stubs for legs. The face was screwed up.' She made an ugly face. My heart started to beat faster. I looked at Shweta. There were ancient tears on her cheeks. For every living soul that had ever felt abnormal. Ever felt unwanted. I felt a terror grip me. Why was I doing this to her?

A young girl piped up, obviously out of turn. 'Tell Bangalore Akka about Ketamma.' Her mother glared at her, brusquely told her to be quiet. But the topic had been laid out in the open.

And so I met the woman who changed the course of my

work. And my thinking. I did not know that, of course. I gently asked about Ketamma. Without a word, one of the middle-aged women beckoned to me. I asked Shweta whether she wanted to stay back, to rest a bit. 'No way!' said my girl, bravely.

Ketamma was perhaps in her late twenties. Or early thirties. She lived not far from where we were then. Her eyes were fiery, almost bloodshot. Her hair seemed unruly in spite of being generously oiled. I shivered with a kind of premonition.

'Keti, this girl and her sister have come from Bangalore. They wanted to meet you.' One of the women spoke to her. She nodded and looked us over assessingly. She was thin, almost emaciated. I thought I could see the beginnings of a baby in her belly. She was sitting apart from the other women, busy stoking the open-air fire which engulfed a darkened aluminum pot. The women who had come with me started to talk quite openly to the ones who were already there. They spoke about Keti. I glanced across at her. Could she not hear? She continued her work, unconcerned by the concentration of focus on her. I could not decide whether to speak directly to her or not.

'Is she pregnant?' I asked the woman who had brought me here. She nodded, and the other women automatically lowered their voices. I began to fear the worst. But I held my tongue, not wanting to disturb the silent process that was going on.

Finally, the old woman who had clutched at me so hard, spoke up. 'She has three children already. Two boys. So when her man told her to take the injection, she did not mind. It seems they gave her rice . . . and two saris. Clothes for the children. School fees for Raghav. Maybe because her man works with those BSS people, she got special treatment. I don't know. People say that.' The woman trailed off. I held my breath, not daring to speak out the questions in my eyes.

'She went into hysterics,' the old woman continued, quite

disconnectedly. 'She frightened everyone.' One of the boys, listening nearby, went into an imitation, shouting meaninglessly, jerking his body. His mother shushed him violently. The old woman continued, no longer looking at me, speaking almost exclusively to her neighbour. It was as though everyone was tackling the subject for the first time. Again.

'How did she get pregnant even with the injection? Those doctors say she was already pregnant. But it cannot be. I have seen a hundred babies being born. This one is in her fifth month, at best.'

'At the most sixth,' another woman agreed. 'My Radha looked like that even in the seventh, though.' Silence all around. The bird calls sounded eerily loud. A hornbill. Some mynahs.

'Why didn't she have an abortion?' I risked, gingerly.

'That's what I asked,' retorted the old woman. 'How much we all begged her. The lady doctor was almost in tears. Her man, I know he also told her, threatened her even. But no, she would not move from her position . . . All the women in her family were stubborn like that.' She looked at Keti accusingly, clamping on her the sins of her ancestry. '"I will have the baby," she said. "It is a gift of God." Hmph!'

Several people started talking at once after that. I tried to harvest whatever sounds I could. Ketamma had stumped everyone with her refusal to have the baby aborted. Even when the researchers had warned her that the baby could be severely deformed. They had even given her gory descriptions to make her change her mind. But she had become, if anything, even more obstinate. If God had wanted her to have the baby—even if she had not wanted it—there must be a good reason. So why throw away the baby before giving it a chance?

The weeks turned into months. It became too late to do anything about the pregnancy. Finally, they had all left her alone. But the idea of her foetus hung amidst them all, someone said, colouring the mood, interfering with the festivals, with the conversations. An unborn baby already larger than life.

The doctors had offered to conduct various tests. They did just one. In Maddur. They wanted to take her to Bangalore for some more treatment. Imagine! At their cost. But she said no to everyone and to everything. 'Look at her,' said the old woman in disgust, 'she doesn't talk much anymore. Even to her husband.'

I listened quietly. I was fascinated, horrified, irritated. All at once. Surely Keti must know they were discussing her. I looked over to where she sat. A stillness had come over her. I could not help staring. This then, was the heart of the story I was chasing. Suddenly, like an illumination, I understood what my activist friend Anuja keeps trying to convince me of. Population policies or family planning methods, she says, cannot be imposed from above. The social and psychological costs, especially for women, can never be factored into a government programme. Nor, it seemed, into a research project.

I had to write it down; record the abrupt shaft of understanding that pierced through me. My notepad lay before me, turning dusty with the dry breeze that picked up the soil. I dribbled out some words. They made little sense to me later, though I always flash back to that moment in times of sudden conviction.

From the corner of my eye, I saw Keti call out, just then, to someone inside her hut. A boy came out nimbly in response. He must have been seven or eight. I realized these children probably looked younger than they were. Malnourishment does that to you when you are young. It does the reverse when you are old. The boy came and sat cheerfully by his mother. He said something that made her throw back her head and laugh, showing big yellow-white, ripe corn teeth. The duo got up, went inside, swinging the door shut behind them.

SEVENTEEN

Shweta had been doodling in the sand. When I looked across, her pictures were of little stick figures, some with limbs missing, some disproportionate. Shweta, Shweta, Shweta was written under them. My eyes filled with tears. For her. For Madhamma. For Keti. For myself too. All our tears are, in a way, for ourselves. Usually, I do not let the waters leave my eyes. I have taken it upon myself to be strong. To be unlike Shweta and Amma. To be there for them. But that day, I let the tears fall.

Much later, Shweta and I stood outside Ketamma's hut again. I tapped gently, nervous of the response. I kept Shweta deliberately close. For the first and last time, I was using her disability as a shield. Or as a weapon, maybe. And I hated myself fiercely for it.

Another little boy, even younger than the one we'd seen before, opened the door.

'Is your mother there? I want to show my sister your house. It is pretty.' The face grinned, disappeared briefly, then returned. The wooden door yielded. We stepped in. Shweta, quite exhausted by now, was excruciatingly slow.

'My friend lost her baby recently. The doctors took it out. She is very unhappy. But she would be proud of you.' I spoke to Keti, who had not uttered one syllable since we came in. We were sitting on the cool earthen floor. Two steel glasses of coffee, or was it tea, had been proffered by the boy. A stunningly pretty baby girl, probably just under two years, all brown eyes, brown hair and plump brown skin was playing with odds and ends.

Keti looked up sharply at my words. 'Yes, you have to lose many babies before the men and the women understand.' Keti's first words to an outsider warmed my heart with a husky grip.

'Are you eating well? For the baby?' I asked. I wanted, desperately, to keep the conversation going.

'I manage fine. My man does good work. He collects medicinal plants for the station.'

'I see. Where will you have the baby? At the doctor's hospital?'

'No, I'll be here. Three children were born here. Why should this one be different?'

'Do you think they . . . er . . . the station people who treated you are doing their job properly, Ketamma?' I was obviously losing direction, flailing.

She thought for a minute, motionless. 'It's what you make of it. You cannot escape your destiny. But you must try. I tried.'

'Please don't be angry with me, Ketamma. I really do understand about you, about why you want to keep your baby. This friend of mine, Revati. She used to cry everyday. She used to say, "So what if my baby had no hands or legs, she would still have been mine." They made her take out the baby anyway. And now here, they say your baby will be abnormal because of the vaccine, the injection. I think you know that. How do you not get scared? I need to know. For myself. For my sister. For my friend.'

'God gives you as much strength as you need to deal with your, how to say it?. . . Your lot in life. No more and no less. I'm not worried. I can manage.'

I thought, then, about Ketamma's God. Here among the

Banigas, God was primarily pagan. Nature, in all her manifestations, was the spirit of the universe. Trees, water, fire were all revered. Somewhere down the line, Shaivism had become mixed up with the original belief systems. So now the rituals were hybridized: with the lingam representing equally all the forces of life. The faith, though, had it remained the same?

'What about your husband?'

'He was angry. Now he is sad. But what can I do, ma?'

What indeed? Nobody can do anything in the face of such an unjust dilemma.

'I don't know why I am talking to you,' Keti looked up piercingly at Shweta, then at me. She hoisted the baby girl playing on the floor onto her lap, rocking her absently. 'Many people came before. I could not speak to them.'

She fell quiet. I had nothing to say.

'I think it is because I wanted to be like you. Beautiful and school-going. I wanted long earrings and I wanted pretty clothes, like the television ladies. But it does not happen for everyone.'

I had not felt so inadequate in a long time. Not since Shweta's incurable illness was explained to me for the first time. Mumbling a thank you, I said we would be back. I kissed the boy on top of his head. He was surprised, even shocked. Maybe it was an inappropriate gesture. I helped Shweta out. It had been a numbing experience. I tried not to think anymore.

Much later, under starlight that left no place for the sky, we were escorted to our bedroom back at the Kendra. I tried to soothe away Shweta's tiredness, her depression, by massaging her curling legs with a gel. I gave her extra painkillers. Then I started on a story I'd heard. A story of the moon and the stars.

The Sun had become jealous, one day, that the Moon had so many friends in the night sky. He, meanwhile, had to blaze away all day, and all alone. The Moon, a gentle creature so dependent on the Sun, got very upset. One of the stars soothed him down. 'The Sun is so strong, his light so powerful, he cannot see beyond himself. Otherwise, if he would only look, the Stars, the Moon, why, the whole Universe is right there beside him.'

I sat there by her pillow, soothing her forehead, her hair, till I heard her breathing settle. Then I sat up late into the insect-filled night, making notes, thinking hard. There was so much more work ahead on the story. Here I was, an artificial urban transplant in this rural stage setting. How could I delineate the ground, set the markers? How could I tell a tale that I had never heard, never lived? I agonized over my thoughts until my head began to throb. Then I recited my prayers, chanted the Ramraksha stotra. I would just go ahead and work anyway, I decided. And now, I had a reason, not just a hunch, to do so. And to do it right.

EIGHTEEN

A high-tech island in this sea of poverty. A stock phrase, perfect to describe the sight it made. The 'India Biotech Pvt Ltd' nameplate was diminutive; the sloped roof of the building was designed to blend with the environment; its whitewashed walls were politically correct. Still, its spanking newness, its air-conditioning equipment, the generators humming in the background, the sleek lighting fixtures: they quite gave the game away. I made a mental note to check out electricity availability in the area.

It was Sunday morning. After a long chat with Dr Vikram over a soul-satisfying breakfast of akki roti and fruit, I had made the trip to the research station without Shweta. She had been too tired. I myself felt equally drained mentally. Today I would have to pretend I was innocent of all that I knew, if I wanted anything out of the staff at the research station. Dr Rita Madam. The 'Running Doctor'. I was already feeling negative about her. After yesterday, I needed to ascribe immediate blame. So I seethed. It took a forty-five minute session of yoga: asanas, pranayama and meditation to calm my mind and energize my body. I bent my head and prayed that I would have the strength for all that lay ahead.

My escort, Chamla of the chikoo cheeks had come

willingly with me again. He now spoke quietly to some people standing under a champak tree, close to the low-slung buildings. There was a lot of head-nodding and pointing. Chamla beckoned to us. We walked to the main door. I rang a tinny bell that shrieked through an inner hallway.

It took half an hour to get past two men and one woman, each in an ascending order of clinical garb. Finally, we were granted audience with Dr Rita George, MD, Clinical Pharmacology. As if that was not a nameplateful, 'Manager, Research Station', was also added at the bottom. I looked at the slim woman in front of me. Pink cotton sari, white overcoat, curly, well-groomed hair. Broad forehead, straight nose, high cheekbones, thick lips. Spectacles in the latest fashion, gold-rimmed, low-glare, expensive. Thankfully, a warm smile on her face. I put her age at forty-five.

'Hello,' she said, with only a hint of a coastal accent. Her outstretched hand was soft, rubbery. Maybe from the constant use of gloves, I thought. But her grip was surprisingly strong. Like a confident man's. 'I am told you know Dr Hiremath. What can I do for you?'

I handed over my card. She read it carefully. 'I read *Deadline* occasionally. I like it,' she said. Measured words. Not at all hasty. I began to change my opinion of her already.

'Thank you. Actually, I was here to interview Dr Vikram Gopinath, at the Baniga Kalyan Kendra.' Lies will get you everywhere in journalism. 'When I visited Anshul's office last week, he had mentioned the India Biotech facility here. To tell the truth, I was so impressed with what Anshul explained to me about the vaccine you are developing, I couldn't resist coming to see the set-up for myself.' It was a set-up all right.

It worked. The 'Anshul' opened any remaining door of doubt. Dr Rita offered to show me around. 'Give me just a moment,' she said, neatly putting away the papers she had been working on. From where I sat, the papers looked like bunches of statistics interspersed with summaries. She put them away in a file cabinet next to her desk and clicked it shut. Not one paper lay about on her desk. I used the opportunity to scrunitize her working space. Not much to see. A photograph hung on the wall opposite her desk, black and white, of some family at a beach. Hers, I presumed. Father, mother, three girls and one . . . maybe a boy? All similar looking, all smiling similarly. On her desk, I noticed a paperweight with some DNA helix hologram inside its glass. The base said 'Biogene Research Foundation'. She got up, smoothed her clothes and led me out of her neat, clean office. Her body movements were like the room. Neat, tidy. Circumspect was the *mot juste*, I thought.

We began a ceremonious tour of the facility. Although the research station was adequately equipped, it was nowhere near as sophisticated as India Biotech, Bangalore. I wondered why. Maybe it was not necessary. Maybe it would be too flamboyant. Out of place in these ancient habitats where poverty and wealth took on such different meanings.

There was only one computer, taking pride of place in a small room. A door led right into the doctor's office. The little rectangular space was lined with cupboards, file cabinets and desks. There was one prominent telephone.

'Is it working yet?' Dr Rita asked a passing white-coat. He shrugged, shook his head, made an improper gesture at the medieval-looking black instrument on the table.

'We have a real problem with the telephones here. More often than not, the lines are down. I don't know how we are supposed to keep in constant touch with Bangalore!'

'Don't you have a computer connection to Bangalore?' I looked around for a modem.

'Oh, you see, Anshul—the Dr Hiremath bit was over, it seemed—has been working on it ever since we came here a year ago! Finally, he has got the clearances, I believe. We are hopefully going to have a dedicated line between the two offices soon.'

'Does Anshul come here often?' I asked.

An expression of anger, or perhaps resentment, flitted across her face. 'He did come once. When we had completed the arrangements here. Then he said he would like to come once in three months. But he's been so busy, you see. And this . . .' she pointed generally at the outdoors, 'is not very comfortable for him. Or for his wife.'

Yes, it would be hard to picture sophisticated Surabhi here, in the mud and the poverty. For that matter, Anshul too would seem, somehow, wrong. They belonged to more air-conditioned—or rather—'view-conditioned'—climates.

'I guess he must be quite comfortable leaving it all to you,' I said soothingly. Dr Rita did smile at that, but not from the heart.

Next, we entered a laboratory. It looked like the pathology clinics one goes to, where they extract unmentionable fluids from one's body. God knows Shweta visits such places regularly.

Looking around, I saw lots of equipment for biochemical analysis that sat around giving off those typical laboratory smells. It appeared that Dr Rita, a highly qualified clinical pharmacologist, was the only senior-level person there. She had a technical staff of five people under her. A gangly microbiologist, Sadanand, a petite pathologist, Ragini, and a staff helper, Damodar, were introduced to me. They were all rather young. Therefore, I thought, inexperienced. I wondered if I could meet any one of them separately, later. Sadanand, with his long, loose limbs, looked quite friendly.

Apparently, the others had already been here for one and a half years, setting up the volunteer base, laying the ground here in this remote location, creating the all-important goodwill. The research station job was not the world's most exciting, at least for them. From what I could gather, it largely consisted of collecting and analysing blood and urine samples, compiling information and keeping track of volunteers. A visiting gynaecologist, Dr Padma, came in once a month from Maddur. Or sooner, if called upon.

So, the 'vision' element, the big picture, it seemed, was restricted to Dr Rita. It was she who showed maximum pride in her work, she who had the ring of authority. The others, I noticed, seemed to defer to her, even in their body language. I watched a lot of bending and nodding and 'yessing'.

There was not much else to see. A couple of wards with beds and all the paraphernalia to go with medical establishments. There were no human beings around, only medicines, vials, bedpans, gloves, sterilizers, the inevitable posters on family planning. And several cartons of disposal syringes. Disconnectedly, I wondered how they disposed of their medical waste. It has become a gargantuan problem in Bangalore. But then, there was no worry about AIDS here. Not yet.

Back in her office, over strong, hot coffee, Dr Rita relaxed into a conversation.

'If things go according to schedule, and I am sure they will, we should be able to go into phase three very soon.'

'What does that mean? Is it the final stage?'

'Yes. It is the final pre-registration phase. During phase three, new drugs are tried out on a larger sample of selected patients from the general population. Basically, it means the drug is out in a limited market with those doctors who have enlisted for the trials.'

'What is phase four then?'

'You see, once the drug is approved and in the market, company representatives keep in touch with the physicians who dispense the drug, in order to watch out for any rare adverse reaction which they might have missed during the trials. They also try to understand patterns of drug utilization. Then reports are compiled about the efficacy. This phase is also known as post-marketing surveillance.'

Yes, I already knew about that. A thought occurred. 'What is the average lead time between research and sale?'

'I would say, even today, it is a good ten years. You see, they are trying desperately to crunch time. But with all the problems that insufficiently tested drugs have caused in the past, many national drug administrations are getting even tougher.'

I thought of Thalidomide, the sleeping pill prescribed to pregnant women in the seventies, that had led to the birth of so many abnormal babies. I thought of other medical disasters. I thought of AIDS.

'But haven't AIDS medicines come out rather quickly into the market? Has it been ten years since they began researching them? It seems like just a couple of years or so.'

'It is very interesting that you should ask me that,' said Dr Rita, looking at me in surprise. She had obviously not expected me to be so well prepared. 'Actually, yes, the US FDA has given priority to AIDS-related drugs. It's because, you know, of the fatal nature of the illness. Little to lose, and not much time in which to lose it!'

She paused, but was encouraged, I guess, by the eager expression on my face. 'You see,' she said, and I realized it was her most favourite phrase in the language, 'I was reading about it only recently. This AIDS research has put doctors in a very peculiar situation. They are facing a moral dilemma.'

'How?' I asked, just to keep the flow.

'You see, they develop these new drugs which appear to work very well. So, hundreds of AIDS patients line up eager to be volunteers for the trials. They hear about it on the Internet, I am told. And they have nothing to lose, you know. They are going to die soon anyway.'

I waited for the moral dilemma to emerge.

'But the doctors and researchers in the Western world, you see, they are bound by law. They have to do double blind tests for a new drug. So they have to keep some patients on the old drugs in order to understand the efficacy of the new drug. So those patients cannot get the benefit of the new drug in prolonging their lives. It's a difficult decision. Here are these patients dying . . .' She paused again, considering her words. 'Or rather, I should say, they are wanting to live . . . to try out the new drugs. So, you see, it is peculiar you brought up the same topic today.'

I decided to be more low key. No point attracting too much of her speculation. She had mentioned Western laws as if they were a breed apart from ours. I filed away a reminder to speak to my lawyer friends about international law, and pursued a new direction.

'Do you have any competition to the vaccine being developed by you here?'

She took a long time to answer that one. I think she was still thinking about my precocious question earlier.

'No,' she said. 'Not really. But to keep it that way, we have to maintain secrecy. We cannot afford to have a competitor discover our formulae, our antigen, or our dosages.'

I thought about that. Of spies and moles and business espionage. It seemed a little far-fetched. In any case, I guessed all the important documents would be in Bangalore. Naturally, most tabulations would be done on computers, and there were precious few of them here. Not that it made any difference to me in my personal research on this ever-expanding story. I wouldn't be able to recognize a formula if you smashed it into my face. That's what comes of being a liberal arts graduate in this country.

Sadanand came in just then, his shaggy eyebrows knitted in anxious query. 'Madam,' he said diffidently, towering over her at her desk. 'See, these tabulations do not seem to match my earlier blood samples . . . here the antigen availability is quite different . . .'

Dr Rita smiled gently up at him. 'Let me see,' she said. She took the sheaf of papers from him, studied them acutely for a few seconds. Her brow cleared. 'You see,' she said, 'this! . . .' Jab-jab with her pen, and 'this, here . . .' has been placed wrongly. She made some markings and fired off some explanations about something called a peptide PCR, whatever that was. It seemed to satisfy him, at any rate. He gathered up the papers, beamed first at the 'Madam', then at me. He departed, his long arms swinging slightly out of sync with his gait.

Dr Rita seemed to gather herself. She made an imaginary tick mark in the air. Then, looking at the clock on a nearby wall, she offered to share her lunch. I agreed without fuss. For the next ten minutes, we quietly and amicably ate from a steel tiffin brought in by a tribal boy at the dot of one p.m. Dryish rotis, beans palya, red rice and saaru, curds and pickle. Quite adequate. We washed up, drank water, and settled down again.

'Do you know why they call you the "Running Doctor"?

She laughed spontaneously, her white teeth and red gums showing up nicely. 'Oh! You see, they find it very amusing that I go for a jog every morning. Earlier, they used to line up to watch me.' She gurgled at the memory. 'Now they are used to it, I suppose.'

I looked more carefully at the woman sitting across me. Now that I knew she was a runner, I noticed how compact and taut her body was. How her brown skin glistened with good health. I decided to take a gamble. I decided to assume that her fitness was a special crusade.

'What a coincidence,' I chirped. 'I love jogging too!' I could swear my hurting leg kicked me in some corner of my mind. I ignored it. 'Maybe I could join you, then, tomorrow?'

I had half hoped she would cop out, so that I would not have to change my return travel plans. She didn't.

'Oh, sure,' she said, apparently pleased. 'I try to leave at five-fifteen in the morning. But if you are coming, I could wait? . . .'

I cringed mentally. Since the accident, since the invasion

of so many unfamiliar chemicals to stop the aches in my body, it had become hard to keep any early-bird routine.

'Great,' I heard myself saying, 'I'll be with you at six . . . But where?'

She gave me directions to her home. I thanked her and prepared to leave. Belatedly, I realized I had asked almost nothing about the problems with the stillborn foetus of Madhamma and the troubled baby inside Ketamma.

Emerging into the late afternoon sunshine, I found a gaggle of children waiting for me, their faces full of curiosity. I felt that same cringing feeling as before. Next time, I thought to myself, I would definitely bring sweets, umbrellas, books, whatever. I smiled in a watery fashion at my scraggly audience, hailed Chamla, and drove off in my chariot with an unusually grim Mohan curving his way into the approaching half-light.

NINETEEN

'Here so soon!' said the sibling sarcastically as I found my way to our makeshift quarters. The sun, dipping down below the mountains, was etching a fiery goodbye on a sliver of wall. Birds had cautiously begun to chirp. An evening breeze travelled through the verdure, sighing at our little window pane. Shweta was sprawled on the bed, with papers and some sort of clay jewellery around her, looking picture perfect under the glow of a tungsten bulb. She seemed to be at work on 'A Project'.

'That's pretty, did you make these?' I asked, picking up a pair of earrings with orange beads and terracotta swirls.

'Yes, Jeema taught me to make them. These girls here are so clever, Akka, they know all sorts of things that would take me a lifetime to learn.'

'I'm sure they are saying the same about you, brat, at this very moment,' I smiled maternally at the wistful look on her face, and flopped down on the bed. 'God, I'm tired,' My words sank into the pillow. 'But it was worth every moment.'

I proceeded to fill Shweta in, further distilling my thoughts and ideas. She was happy to resolve the mystery of the running doctor and groaned when I set the little travel alarm for 5 a.m.

A knock at the door heralded room service. Vikram had very kindly, and surely as an exception on account of Shweta, had our meal sent to us. We gratefully ate off sparkling steel plates, a meal of rice with spicy dal and vegetables, and shortly after, collapsed into our mothball-scented bed.

I must have slept soundly in the blessed peace of that night. I woke up a few seconds before the alarm could jangle Shweta's nerves. Feeling surprisingly fresh, I got into jeans and a T-shirt, and went outside into the dawn.

Like me, the avian life was stirring. A string of unfamiliar bird calls blended with the songs of the bulbuls and mynahs. A cold mist clutched at the trees, and a shiver passed by my heart. I wondered at Dr Rita's commitment to her morning run, and her research. It was an unlikely combination in her, somehow. Still, loneliness can find astonishing outlets. I knew an old man, Somaiah, who spent hours talking to trees. He would tell them jokes, mundane anecdotes, even read aloud to them. They did neither better nor worse than trees with less loquacious company. I remember feeling disappointed that they did not grow taller, or faster, or turn blue. Somaiah himself expected nothing in return from his silent listeners.

Mohan was ready to set off when I reached the car. Except for a morning stubble, there was nothing to show for his early start. I, however, had to suppress a couple of yawns as my body's sleep system protested at the disturbance in its pattern.

Dr Rita was waiting, limbering up outside a pretty little cottage draped with pink and white bougainvillea. She wore dark blue sweats, running shoes—Nike, I noticed—and a hairband pulling back her curls, broadening her forehead further. She looked at her sports watch and smiled, fresh as a morning jasmine.

'Right on time. Excellent,' she remarked, her accent sharper, as I joined her in jump-starting my limbs, gingerly testing the bad leg for sit-ups. We took off soon after, at a warm-up pace. The Running Doctor had chosen a little track that led into tall trees, delicately backlit with the stretching rays of the sun.

The sheer joy of using my body to its fullest capacity, to allow it to take in unadulterated lungfuls of crisp air gave me a delicious intoxication. I felt I could go on forever; sweat gathering lightly on my forearms; shoes crunching past summer leaves; suddening upon feathered fowl. But Dr Rita's watch was programmed to beep at regular intervals and we kept to her schedule, winding down after half an hour, coming into a clearing not far behind her house. There we allowed ourselves to catch our breath, to let our heartbeats return to normal, using gentle movements of neck and shoulders to cool down. Then we each took a sip of water from a little bottle belted around her waist and sat down on the grass, perfect companions for the moment.

The workout seemed to have loosened some of her reservations. 'You see, when I run, I feel free and powerful at the same time. I hate to miss a day.' The doctor was perspiring unashamedly. She gave me an uncertain look, perhaps not sure whether I understood.

'Is it important, to be powerful?' I asked gently, not looking up at her.

'I don't know. I grew up as the third of four girls.' So the fourth in the photo, I recalled, was not a boy. 'In Kerala. Trissur, you know. I wasn't anybody's favourite. I was too short, too dark, too quiet, too stubborn. Then I used to wish for some kind of powers. Now of course, there is the power of my work.' A dazzling smile replaced the earlier uncertainty. 'I shall always be grateful to Anshul for the opportunity to work on this project.' There was a look on her face just then, something soft, which made me wonder if she had a crush on her handsome employer.

'Of course, it was hell at first. Being here, so alone . . . in this rudimentary place. I would get scared. Of the tribal men, of wild animals. But I got over it. I found a way to protect myself.' She made a trigger with her fingers and went 'Dishum! Dishum!' her head cocked to one side, one eye closed in mock aim at me. She looked very professional, down to the gleam in her open eye. We laughed.

The talk turned quite naturally to Anshul. The dream doctor. It turned out she had met Anshul in Maryland, at a conference of some sort, about four years earlier. After her MD in clinical pharmacology, she had been working at a biotechnology firm, where the pay was great but the research had become boring. Anshul and she confessed to a common ennui. They shared a common vision. Anshul soon offered her a job. When the chance to return to India to work on a new molecule fell into her lap, she was delighted.

'Anshul was so persuasive, his vision so convincing, I would have done anything,' she said, her neck curved down, her face almost hidden. '*Almost* anything.' That came out softer, as though it was said to herself. 'And I have never regretted my decision,' she added, looking up in slow motion.

I could understand that easily. Anshul's charisma was effortless. Now that I had seen him, I could just about visualize the legion of women who had drooled over him, and would no doubt continue to do so. To be fair to the woman in front of me, I could also appreciate the power of his hard-sell in the business department. Anshul himself was so convinced about his dream, it was natural to be carried away.

I wondered if Dr Rita was in cahoots with Dr Anshul to suppress information about the problem pregnancies. She was not about to enlighten me on that. Just as new questions began to bubble up, Dr Rita gathered herself and drew me to my feet with the same surprising strength I'd noticed earlier. 'Time's up,' she said. The tone did not brook argument. I did not want to break the fragile thread that was now binding us. I followed her back to her cottage, my leg sparking off memories of old pains. The conspicuous silence from her became hard to break. I just kept pace, my mind a jumble.

At her door, there was no invitation to come in. It was a pity. I would have loved to observe the amazing Dr Rita in her own home. As she opened up the painted wooden shutter to let herself in, I got an impression of a room lined neatly with books, stationery and writing material. More like an office. More like *her* office. I thanked her profusely for all her help, and expressed the hope that I would meet her in Bangalore soon.

'That would have been very nice,' she said, formally, as though we had never sweated together. 'But unfortunately, I will be out of the country for the next few weeks.'

Since I had absolutely no desire to face Anshul and Rita together, I was rather relieved. 'Oh, dear, too bad!' I breathed, followed by a 'maybe some other time. Thank you so much, Dr Rita. Bye.' And left, limping only a bit.

TWENTY

Back at work. It was Monday afternoon. We had left the Mahadevi Hills right after my morning run, without stopping for breakfast at the Kendra. All my 'thank yous' to Vikram had been waved away with a 'come back any time'. Silent rain clouds and a noisy crowd of children had gathered to see us off. There had been monsoon drops in Shweta's eyes when she said her farewell to Jeema.

By the time we reached Maddur, pangs of hunger and shafts of pain from my angry leg were demanding equal attention. Both Shweta and I gorged on crisp masala paper dosas, accompanied by strong Mysore coffee. I had aspirin for dessert.

On my way to see the boss, I waved to Meenal, but moved on before she could hide her papers. Straight to CP's glass house. And bother his privacy.

'Yes?' His hand was over the mouthpiece.

'It's urgent, CP.'

He ended the conversation quickly and waved me into the chair opposite. 'Okay, sweetheart, tell me all. Why are you looking so washed out?'

I told him. Everything. He can be a very good listener. He sort of murmurs encouragement now and again. At the end of it, he said 'H'mm' and knocked his fingers meditatively on the table.

'Okay. We'll go with a cover. I'll pull out all the stops. It's a big story. And,' he added meanly, 'there's nothing else happening anyway. We'll use a backgrounder on medical ethics in India. Court cases, human interest stories. The works. You concentrate on writing your piece.'

I just looked at him. I had done a lot of soul-searching the previous night and had arrived at an unconventional decision. Now I had to break it to him.

'CP,' I said, very quietly. 'I don't want to write it. Not yet.'

'What the hell? . . .' he started. I made a pleading gesture, stopping him midway.

'I have never encountered anything like this before. Yes, I could easily write it up. It'll make a great story. Everyone will be shocked. If we get it right, people will agitate, Parliament will consider new bills. If we get it wrong, it'll move to page seven of all the newspapers in one week.' I paused.

'So?' he prompted. 'What's wrong with that?'

I just looked at him. 'That's not enough, CP. I think there's more to this story yet. I have not found out the details. To be fair to Keti, to Madhamma, maybe, God knows, also to Dr Rita, I need to continue looking, asking. Get Anshul to talk. It'll take time.'

'Great,' CP was at his most sarcastic. 'You want a story that changes the world. Meanwhile, some jumpy journalist will catch on and splash the scoop. There goes your big chance at fame.'

I was not really worried. In the information supermarket, unbranded information goes quite unnoticed. None of the players involved in my story were exactly looking for publicity. Quite the opposite, in fact. Besides, I realized just then that I had gone beyond the need for small-time fame. But CP had a job to do. He harangued me some more. I held firm. He dismissed me angrily, saying he would let me know his decision later.

I passed Meenal again, quite forgetting to look at her. She must have noticed my expression. Within seconds, she was at my desk.

'What the hell happened in there?' she asked.

I gave her a very abbreviated version. She looked surprised.

'This is most unlike you, Poo. What do you hope to achieve exactly?'

I looked miserable, I guess. Because I didn't know either. I just wanted to wrap it all up properly before I went on an accusing spree, sensationalizing the plight of the two tribal women who had become, for me, the centrepiece of my article.

'CP just doesn't understand. This is not a national story or anything,' I protested, on the defensive at once. If only I had known. 'No one is on my trail yet. Surely I deserve more time?'

'Okay, but you will not be filing any articles in the meanwhile. If your byline remains scarce, you're certainly going to raise a few eyebrows around here.' Big deal, I thought. It showed on my face. Just then, CP called me on the phone. I went back to his office.

'All right. I spoke to Avaru. He gave the nod. But that's only because I convinced him. I'm putting myself on the line for you. Don't forget that. All your expenses will have to be cleared with me first. I am giving you two more weeks. That's all.' Dumb relief began to flood my guts. I looked at my calendar. We were nearing the end of the second week of June. I made a thumbs up signal to Meenal.

What was left of the overcast day was spent looking up the source material Anshul had given me. Details of the vaccine, and of the mysterious Dr Hiremath, emerged more clearly. Five years ago, while still doing his Ph.D in genetics at the University of Maryland, Baltimore, USA, Anshul had decided to go it alone. Interesting, I thought, that Transpharma headquarters are also in Baltimore. Had

Anshul made contact with Jimmy Kakodia back then? Maybe he had impressed someone else in Transpharma, who'd become a sort of godfather. Someone who saw, perhaps, a business proposition in his work.

And how he had worked! In his spare time, Anshul had concentrated totally on his obsession: to isolate a peptide. He needed to find exactly the right protein molecule to help him build his vaccine. And his dream.

Naturally, he began to look for the right antigen in the zona pellucida, the subject for his doctoral thesis. Naturally, that's where he found his magic peptide. A glycoprotein in the receptors of the zona.

It took years. Days and nights of relentless work yielded one protein molecule that appeared perfect to raise an antigen for his vaccine. He named it FRP-41. It was an inexplicable name. Did the initials signify anything personal? I would have to ask Dr Anshul.

That particular peptide or protein molecule, FRP-41, is site specific. It does not appear anywhere else in the human body. So any impact by it or on it is strictly restricted. This made it relatively safe for Anshul to experiment with, since it would not cause adverse reactions in an unknown part of the body. Combining FRP-41 with a common immunogenic carrier—tetanus toxoid—Anshul experimented successfully with animals and in-vitro tests till he had standarized some human dosage efficacies.

When FRP-41 was injected into the body along with tetanus toxoid, the female's immune system was deceived into recognizing both as enemy cells, even though FRP-41 cells were kin cells. The immune system could not separately identify its own cells, so tightly bound were they to the disease-causing cells of the tetanus toxoid.

The simplicity of it was stunning. It was the ultimate kurukshetra. Flesh against flesh, past against future.

The zona pellucida is not made up of a simple cell structure.

The cell has a lot of receptors. Each receptor plays an important, if little understood role in allowing the penetration of the sperm cells. Similarly, sperm cells also have receptors on them. The sperm cell receptors must fit perfectly into the zona cell receptors for proper penetration. FRP-41 cells on the zona pellucida, are completely exposed only during the most fertile period of a woman's menstrual cycle, when the egg is ready to receive the sperm. This is also the time when the zona cells get ready to facilitate the entry of the sperm into the egg lining.

That is precisely when the antibodies raised by Anshul's vaccine prepare for swift action. Ready against the perceived threat of the FRP-41 cells, the female's warrior cells do not even need to destroy the sperm cells. All they need to do is to block the entry of the sperm by creating an impermeable wall along the receptors of the zona.

Receptor to receptor interaction is exactly like a lock and key mechanism. Without the right key, the sperm cells cannot fit into and unlock the zona cells. The antibodies come in the way.

If all went according to Dr Anshul Hiremath's plan, these antibodies would line up in numbers ferocious enough to simply prevent any fertilization of the egg. Defeated, the sperm would no doubt recede. Till the next menstrual cycle. Then the trick was to make sure antibodies were still thriving in the body in adequate numbers to repeat the blocking game.

There was an extract from a WHO report along with the papers. It said an important prerequisite for the acceptance of a contraceptive should be its reversibility:

'A vaccine for fertility regulation should be capable of inducing an immune response designed to inhibit fertility. However, it should wane and become ineffective after a defined period, say one or two years.'

I tried hard to understand the anxiety behind that mandate. Sure, circumstances could make you change your mind about not having a baby. Personally, I could visualize few possibilities. Still, everyone needs reversible contraception, to be on the safe side. In Anshul's case, that was not a problem. If anything, he had the reverse problem. He had to make sure his vaccine did not lose its potency too quickly. He wanted to arrive at a one-year efficacy. Women who took his vaccine should not fear impregnation for at least twelve menstrual cycles. So far, he had succeeded in giving only six months of immunity.

Anshul was nearing the end of phase two in his clinical trials. Phase one trials had been conducted the previous year in Andhra Pradesh. Normal, healthy women volunteers not particularly in need of contraception had been enlisted to sign on for the first part of the project. In any drug trial, phase one must be conducted on people from the general population and not on the patient population at whom the drug is targetted. This is to verify proper human dosages and to determine safety from side effects. It made sense. You do not directly want to try out your miracle medicine on the dying—in case it is not a miracle. Before that, of course, upto and until phase one, trials are usually conducted on animals or in-vitro in the laboratory. Once the tests on animal or human tissue give glimpses of positive potential, permission is obtained for further testing. Phase one begins the in-vivo testing, which is on live human beings.

The corridors of medical research are littered with the refuse from investigations that had to stop right there. More often than not, medical science has found that real human beings are not predictable enough to respond like cells in a lab dish. If Anshul Hiremath had gone that crucial step forward, he had reason to be optimistic.

There was mention of small side effects on the women in phase one. Hives, rashes, some excess bleeding. These adverse reactions were acceptable, the papers seemed to suggest, and could be overcome by tinkering with dosages of the antigen. I tried to visualize a fieldworker explaining that to the women who had to endure these 'adverse reactions'. But I was outwitted. The paper made a self-righteous disclaimer that no known drug is without any side effects:

'Adverse reactions are an inescapable cost of modern medical therapy. It is all a question of balancing the safety requirements with the society's need for useful medication.'

An edifying little postscript.

There was also some information on pending patents. Apparently, India Biotech had already filed investigation patents with the DCAI. They had supplied all information relating to clinical trials in phase one and had received permission to go into phase two which was almost over now.

From what I could gather, Anshul's phase two trials were carried out on about seventy-five women. These were carefully selected, sexually active women between twenty-eight and forty years who were in need of contraception—an internationally acceptable target patient population. They were given the vaccine every three months, at first. The most recent version of the vaccine was administered after a six-month gap. Anshul was hoping, before going into phase three, to increase the efficacy of the vaccine to a one-year time period. I guessed it would be a question of fine-tuning the potency of the antigen.

Plenty of information. There was, not surprisingly, no mention of unwanted conceptions, miscarriages, deformed foetuses and advanced pregnancies. Still, I had promised Anshul, foolishly, that I would not publish anything about his vaccine yet.

TWENTY-ONE

I set out on an evening walk, in spite of the threatening rain. It was more of an amble, really, just to keep my bad leg exercised. All that MR Hills bonhomie with Dr Rita was costing me. That's when it hit me. It was at least three days since I had thought of a particular doctor with honey-coloured eyes. Or was it somewhere between amber and topaz? I couldn't remember. My God. Why hadn't he called me? Of course, he knew I was to be away. I cut short my stroll. In any case, my leg was not pleased with the insult added to its injury. I called Rohil. He was still at work.

'*Itne dinon se khabar nahin, dil ko hamare sabar nahin . . .*' His voice had an edge I had not heard before. The impromptu verse explained the row of Urdu poetry titles I had noticed on his shelves. Okay, so it was not Ghalib. But there were so many facets to the man. Later, I often felt guilty at how much I had sidelined Rohil throughout my obsession with the vaccine trials. Just then, however, a smile threatened to split my face.

Our conversation meandered romantically until he brought up Goa again. Goodness, I had quite forgotten. The conference was slated for June 20-22, Friday through Sunday. It was under the auspices of the International Immunology Association (IIA), India chapter. Rohil said he could easily get me an invitation as a reporter. There were some other press people invited, too. It would be a junket. Until then, I'd curled my lip at those.

'I'll clear it with CP,' I promised. 'But did you speak to Dr Shaila?' The mysterious Dr Shaila, Rohil's boss. When would I meet her?

His voice took on a puzzled note. 'Yes, I did. She says she would rather not talk about it. She says all her information about it is confidential. I can't help feeling she knows something uncomfortable.'

I sighed. Not much to be done there. Not now anyway. Still, I filed away the information. You never know.

An idea flashed by, in spite of Rohil's return to sweet everythings. 'Hey, do you think Anshul will be there in Goa? It makes eminent sense, doesn't it?' Rohil promised to find out, and we signed off over noisy telephone kisses. Small comfort.

Shweta joined us for an early dinner that night. Sevai, small onion sambar, fish fry. The menu helped me swallow my sorrows. I had suffered many rebukes from my mother for wearing down my poor sister. She did look pale, but cheerful.

'I've written down my experiences at MR Hills, Akka. I'm submitting it to the school magazine.'

'Nothing about my story, I hope?' I asked, alarmed. I am a journalist first.

'I knew you would ask that. I won't tell you!' said the brat.

I threw a soft ball of sevai at her. She caught it and gobbled it up. My parents looked surprised, then disapproving. Nobody said anything. Shweta winked.

The next morning I went in to work petrified at the prospect of facing the boss about Goa. Sure, he made me squirm. But to be fair, CP, having gone an inch, was relatively easy to pull along for the yard. He actually agreed to the trip without calling on his calculator. I kept a very straight face, which made him extremely suspicious. 'Anything up?' he asked.

'You mean outside my story?' I asked back, innocently.

'You had said this fellow is very good-looking. You don't, er, feel anything for Dr Anshul Hiremath, by any chance?'

'Like what, CP?' I asked.

'Nothing,' he said, quite in retreat. I was sure his concern was only that I should not bias myself in the doctor's favour. I grinned to myself. Wrong number, CP.

I had three days before I would be off. Rohil had the conference material, invitations and hotel confirmations delivered at my office. All delegates would be staying at the Goa Paradise. Pictures of heaven were prominent on the brochures. An excitement began somewhere around my navel, and used it as home base till I returned to Bangalore, early the following week.

That evening, I took Anna away from his television for a chat. He drank Glenmorangie, I drank kokam sherbet. His was golden warm, mine burgundy cold. I brought him up to date. He was disturbed by my gory descriptions of what I had heard about Madhamma's stillborn child. Anna likes to keep his world sterilized. Maybe that's why he takes Shweta's illness with so much equanimity. He purifies it somewhere in his mind before dealing with it.

'I need to meet Anshul again, Anna. Confront him directly with all the information I have. Let's see how he reacts.'

'You need a wedge. Some tool to worry him with.' Anna himself worried with the idea for a minute. 'And you know what, I think I have just the thing for you.'

Anna loves nothing better than dramatic suspense. He's a great fan of detective novels. From Agatha Christie and John MacDonald to Elmore Leonard, Jack Higgins, he's read them all. He's been reading Lawrence Block and Mike Ripley of late, if that's any clue. He made me wait, most impatiently.

'Jimmy called me today for some work.' Aha, the Transpharma connection again. 'He mentioned, finally, that BRF was reluctant to extend Anshul's grant money. Apparently, they have found "some problems with his methods". Those were the words he used.'

That was a significant development. I thought of the BRF paperweight in Dr Rita's office. If Anna's information was correct, where would India Biotech go, at this crucial stage in the research, without the infusion of capital from BRF?

'I couldn't get him to say more. But in the light of what you are saying about the abnormal pregnancies, it does fall into place.'

'BRF wants to get away while the going is good, huh?'

'Maybe, but more than that, if they have found something irregular in his work, even a trace of it, they will dissociate themselves completely. You know how high liability costs can be. You know what happens to pharmaceutical companies, especially multinational ones, that get dragged through the courts over some real or imagined drug-related problem. Certainly, Transpharma would put tremendous pressure on BRF to pull out if it's one of the big donors.'

'You surprise me, Anna. Are you saying that BRF will refuse to dirty its hands even a little bit? That too in a Third World country, where graft and malpractice is only to be expected? Imagine the rewards, though. A new molecule, with exclusive marketing rights or something for its doting donor, Transpharma!'

Anna sat upright in surprise. 'Don't be so cynical, child. Journalists can hardly afford to be. In any case, if it makes you feel any more satisfied, I was not defending their sense of honour. It's just that drug administrations everywhere are getting very finicky. There has been too much public outcry about failed drug experiments. These companies just don't want to be in the dock. Their eyes are on the bottom-most of bottom lines.'

I felt a bit silly, jumping in like that. Knee-jerk, immature, that's me. I had read too much, though, seen too much about the way drug companies worldwide operate, to feel particularly apologetic. Maybe it's more fiction than truth. I'll give it that. The bad guys are very worried about their image now. Maybe things are changing. I know Anna's company tries really hard to be ethical. Even so, it does have to deal with the bureaucrats. And there's no way to do business in India without yielding a pound of flesh.

I kept Anna awake late into the night, asking him what it would entail for India Biotech once BRF pulled out. Citing numerous examples, Anna said BRF could hardly demand the money it had already invested in Anshul, however tight the contract. It would have to be content to make some sort of sweet deal where its money could be treated as a soft loan, payable with interest if and when Anshul collected royalties on his product. Or, said my wonderfully knowledgeable Anna, Anshul could replace BRF with another sponsor, who would take on the full burden of the BRF funding commitment. Ha! I thought. Fat chance.

TWENTY-TWO

Rohil called early the next morning. 'Hi, Sunshine! You were right. Anshul is participating in the conference. His wife is coming with him, I believe. He's presenting a paper: Zona Pellucida—The Final Frontier.'

'Great!' I said, rather excitedly, quite ignoring the new moniker. 'Almost three days of a captive Anshul, almost to myself.'

'Hey,' he growled, possessively. 'I'm going to pretend I did not hear that.'

I had to emulate a lot of Party Line telephone operators to make up for my gaffe.

I then called Vikram's centre in Bangalore. They said he would be coming the next day. I called Dr Gayatri and made an appointment to see her. I dialled India Biotech as well, but something in me decided to bang down the phone. I would just confront Anshul in Goa. Then I got ready to meet Praful Shah, retired Drug Controller, with whom Anna had fixed me an appointment. I noted down everything I needed to know. I had to ask him about the processes that go into the approval of a drug. I also wanted to find out if the tarnished image of the Drug Controller's office was accurate. Whether someone like Anshul could push his agenda all the way to the market through dubious means.

Stillborn

Praful Shah, Drug Controller (Retd), as the nameplate offered, lived in a quiet bungalow in Jayanagar. It was designed as the largest suburb in Bangalore, but has now become almost a city centre. His was a stone house with a sloping roof. And a vicious Doberman tied to the gate. No bell on the outside.

I shouted out. After some louder attempts a slip of a girl came running out from the rear. She took away the dog. It looked most disappointed. I waved at it triumphantly. I am not a dog lover.

In the living room, Mr Shah was reclining on a settee with lots of colourful, bulky cushions. He wore a white kurta pyjama, casual but crisply ironed. He was plump, with bulky cheeks, and sported old-fashioned spectacles over a large, bulbous nose. He smiled at me.

'Please don't mind. I cannot get up too easily. Sit down, sit down.'

I guessed at rheumatism. Maybe just arthritis. Maybe rheumatoid arthritis. Very painful.

I thought of Shweta and smiled sympathetically.

'Govind called me yesterday. Wonderful man. We always got along well.'

Anyone who likes Anna gets reciprocity from me. I smiled some more. The slip of a girl slid in with two glasses of water, and what looked like lemon juice. She also kept a bowl of some dark liquid in front of Mr Shah. 'It's juice from the leaves of the guava tree. Very healing.' I believed him because of the conviction in his voice.

Mr Shah had been briefed admirably by my dear father. 'I believe you want to grill me about drug regulation! But remember, I have been retired many years now.'

'Anna said you were just the right person. That you had a unique perspective on the issue of new drugs.'

'Ah, he must be referring to the Hyperthine business. You see, I had intervened, in my younger and more foolish days, to stop a drug against hypertension. It was showing

127

nasty side effects in some rare cases. The company was trying to suppress information.'

'Yes, Anna told me. He said it was touch and go for you. That you had offered to resign. But the subject set me thinking. What if some adverse reaction is noticed only after a drug has been approved for the market?'

'Yes, of course that happens. You know about the classic case of Thalidomide. They did not realize what effect it would have on the foetus of a pregnant woman who used it. You see,' Mr Shah made a dreadful face as he sipped a bit of the lethal looking potion. Then he covered up with a wan smile. 'Unknown, unusual reactions cannot be prevented completely. That is the limitation of regulation.'

I briefly explained what I needed from him. I tried to create a hypothetical scenario about a vaccine for a common disease. Pregnancy can be a sickness for those who don't want it, I figured. I asked how much control the DCAI actually has over the development of such a drug.

Mr Shah was either very sharp, or just very well informed by my father. 'Are you talking about that Hiremath fellow's vaccine? I know he's making a contraceptive vaccine.'

I spluttered a yes. 'A colleague of mine spoke about it the other day. They are all quite excited by the potential of this product.'

'Did your colleague say anything about adverse reactions? Are the clinical trials going on as expected?'

'No, he did not say anything major. In fact, I had actually asked. He didn't seem to have the details. He said it was reasonably well tolerated in phase one. Phase two results should be going for clearance any day now.'

I had to take a decision quickly. Could I trust him? Anna had indicated so. But then, he was a retired Drug Controller, for heaven's sake. CP's glowering face smoked across my mind. Two weeks, he'd said. I guessed I had little time. And no choice.

'I believe there have been some conceptions in spite of the vaccine being administered. And some spontaneous abortions. I even overheard someone speak of deformed babies.'

'Really? Then surely the DC's office will know something . . . I can find out. See, they are supposed to do periodical checks during the trials. Contact the target patients, make sure there is no ill-treatment . . .'

'Does it always work out that way?'

'Well, quite frankly, no. They just do not have the resources to keep to the letter of the requirements in such cases. They are short on funds, short on staff. They have to rely on random checks. Things can and do . . . *slip* through.'

'People say that the DC's office can also be quite accommodating. Could I bribe my way through to the end of a product cycle?' I spoke haltingly, on unsure ground.

Mr Shah laughed as though I had presented a quaint idea. His kurta actually jiggled over his belly.

'I won't deny that there must be several corrupt drug inspectors. They may hasten some approval or confirm the quality of some batch of drugs. But it would require a really large-scale conspiracy to keep sailing through so many levels of clearances on an unsuccessful product. So, even if this Dr Hiremath manages to stay in the game very long, he will have to be stumped in the end. There is no way, in today's environment, that a drug can be so obviously dangerous . . . if what you say is true . . . and still make it to the market.'

I felt a little deflated, I must admit. The fictional construct which had built itself up in my mind, quite unnoticed, was shattered. I had assumed that Anshul was involved in suppressing information about his problems. That he hoped to push his product through anyway. According to Mr Shah, that was impossible. Which meant that Anshul would have to make the product work better. How would he manage? Especially if BRF walked out on him?

I told him a little about the tribal women I had met and I asked him about the requirements of informed consent.

'Yes, those rules, at least on paper, are very strict. In all these trials, volunteers must sign a form saying "I am willing to take this treatment. The risks have been explained to me." In the kind of scenario you mention, there is also a clause where the woman must agree to terminate pregnancy in case of conception.'

I wondered if Keti had signed such a form. Whether it could actually be used against her.

'But let me tell you,' Mr Shah continued, 'there are many ways around it. Especially when the people are illiterate. The person who takes this informed consent is the key. If he or she is sincere, fine. Otherwise, I have known of cases where, instead of consent for anesthesia, people are asked, "Are you a vegetarian? If so, sign here!" After fifty years of Independence, not even fifty per cent of our people are functionally literate enough to tell the difference anyway. So what consent? What information?'

Maybe Mr Shah was hypertensive as well. His breathing had become shallower, his cheeks had reddened. He was very disturbed. Careers in government, especially when you are trying to stem a rotten tide, can be very stressful. I have written a couple of obits for honest officers who died young.

From nowhere, just then, a wifely figure materialized. She carried a steel bowl and water. And a worried expression. Could she have been listening through a screen? She gave the bowl to Mr Shah. 'Juice of white pumpkin. Very good for high BP.' He swallowed it briskly, chased it down with water. The presumed wife looked at me enquiringly. I got the hint, made a few excuses, and got up. He promised to let me know if he heard anything more about India Biotech's clinical trials. I gave him my card, scribbled my residence number on it, thanked him very genuinely, and exited the room. Outside, I heard the dog snarling as I firmly latched the rusty metal gate.

TWENTY-THREE

Early morning phone calls are always scary. Dr Vikram's call the next day only confirmed my theory.

'Poorva,' he said, the static on the line giving his voice an alien tone. 'Something terrible has happened. A deformed foetus was found here last night. It must be from the India Biotech camp . . . I've informed the police.'

It was the strangest news. Deformed foetuses seemed to be everywhere. Where had normal babies gone? Vikram told me more. The foetus they had found was not fully intact, certainly not normal. It was in a bottle, preserved in formaldehyde and had been left on his table. The bottle had some marks of scratched-off labels on it, suggesting that the foetus had been forensically or pathologically examined. Not knowing what to make of it, Vikram had handed it over to the local police.

The wheels in my mind were spinning even as my body registered nausea, panic and disgust. An unidentified foetus! Maybe it was the same one, stolen from the India Biotech lab. The words of Gruff Voice—the doctor in my hospital—wafted back to me. After all, how many of them could be floating around in the hills, anyway? I winced at my own choice of words. Still, why had it appeared now? Why at Dr Gopinath's? Someone, obviously, was trying to warn the doctor. Or to warn him off. But who? Perhaps I should just ask Dr Anshul Hiremath about it directly. But if I did, he might block me off all further information.

I was uneasy. I exchanged some more information with Vikram. I told him I would probably need to come back to the hills. He said I was welcome to use his camp as my base. He also said he himself was going to now send in some spies to find out what on earth was going on at India Biotech. He promised to keep me informed. We signed off, both of us worried and disturbed. I couldn't figure out whether I was chasing the story or the story was chasing me.

As it turned out, Anshul called me before I could call him. 'Ms Poorva, I thought you had promised you would not write about my vaccine till I gave you the signal.' No preliminaries. He sounded like a refrigerator. Freezing. 'Then, behind my back, you go to my research centre, get all the information you can from Rita, who should have known better. The gall!' I heard an ice cube tinkle. 'And you don't have the . . . the decency to tell me—to *ask* me.' Certainly it was no time to speak of planted foetuses.

I made soothing noises about how I had gone to interview Dr Vikram Gopinath, how the story about his Baniga Kalyan Kendra would be out soon, how I had no intention of writing about his vaccine, how I would keep my promise, how I would be able to tell him more in Goa.

'Goa? You are going to be in Goa? Did that Rita tell you I was going? How did you? . . .'

'No, no,' I said, pouring sweetness into the receiver. 'My friend Rohil is going to present a paper at the immunology conference. I'm just there for a joyride.'

What could he say? He put down the phone. I think I was off *his* list of friends.

Then, I met Dr Gayatri briefly. There were even more pregnant women and babies in her waiting room than before. Maybe Anshul was on the correct path after all. Somehow, I managed to edge in. Wasting no time, I explained the anatomy of Anshul's vaccine to her.

'Very clever, very clever,' she said, scrubbing up at the small basin. With the mask on her face, it sounded like an echo. I asked whether it was really so special.

'You must be joking,' she said severely. 'For years, researchers have been looking at the zona pellucida as a perfect site to develop a contraceptive. In spite of all the money and time they have put in, no one has succeeded yet. It is very tricky . . . not to mention exorbitantly expensive . . . to isolate one glycoprotein molecule that works for you in a stable, predictable manner. On top of that, you would have to find a way to mass produce it for trials and field use.'

I was impressed. Both by her savvy and the apparent difficulty of Anshul's task.

'How expensive would it be?' I asked. It seemed the only technical question I could put forward, anyway.

'Oh, it would cost crores and crores of rupees. At least two hundred million US dollars to develop a new molecule. They use the thumb rule that it costs about five thousand dollars per patient. I was reading about Depo-Provera and Norplant just recently. You know? The injectible contraceptives?'

I nodded vigorously. Something I knew at last.

'Well, their manufacturers are still, still putting in money for post-marketing surveillance.'

'Post-marketing surveillance?' I repeated, involuntarily. Then, immediately, I remembered the term from my recent research.

'Yes, yes. After all, unless you monitor a drug's performance in real field conditions, you can never really judge its total, total, er . . . safety. Its efficacy. Post-marketing surveys are long-term monitoring studies that are absolutely crucial with any new drug.'

I remembered one thing more, just in time.

'If the contraceptive vaccine has to be injected quarterly, or six-monthly, then you would have to administer tetanus toxoid equally frequently. Is it safe to do that?' My last tryst with a tetanus shot had been right after the accident. But I couldn't remember when I'd had the one before that. At least ten years ago?

'I'm glad you asked me that,' said Dr Gayatri with a 'thank God' expression on her face. Obviously, she clearly recollected my last visit, when I had appeared quite ignorant. 'Actually, and they have done a fair amount of research on this, there is no known adverse reaction to tetanus toxoid, even with high dosages. So yes, there should be no problem with using it as a carrier.'

Finally, I ventured to mention, extremely casually, that a deformed foetus had been found. In a bottle. At an unlikely place.

'Is it routine to preserve human, er, babies like that?'

She looked at me, surprised at the question.

'Naturally, naturally,' she said, 'or chemically, actually.' She allowed a brief smile at the joke. 'Students and teachers need to understand the processes in pregnancy. It is still one of the biggest medical mysteries! Since we cannot work with a pregnant woman's live foetus, it is very, very important for clinical research to preserve a miscarried embryo.' Visions of a tiny morgue filled with unborn babies rose biliously in my mind. Feeling decidedly queasy, I left quickly, squeezing past a mother-to-be with aggressive intentions. Trying hard to push aside the gory images, I began to think of Anshul's financiers. BRF had been really generous to Anshul. Surely they must have expected quick results. Maybe a quid pro quo for Transpharma. It is quite common in the West, I believe. Research organizations are often funded by corporations that have a commercial interest in the direction of the research. Still, I wanted to know what the deal could have been. Why did they sever it so quickly? I would soon have to call upon Mr Jimmy Kakodia. Jimmy Uncle. He obviously knew a great deal. But he would have to wait. Until after Goa.

TWENTY-FOUR

Friday evening. There were, I counted, at least ten shades of blue in the sky. And a few of pink. I stood in delight at the balcony of my hotel room. Swaying masses of monsoon palms swished outside. They kept my view of the sea tantalizingly elusive. The Goa Paradise was one of the newer hotels. Recent zoning regulations had forced them to build away from the shoreline. I could catch a glimpse of froth now and again, taste the idea of water but not own it. I immediately planned a long walk in the morning. And a deep swim.

I looked at the expanse of sky. It promised wetness. Apologetic lightning skimmed over cloud gathers. A reciprocal gleam from an aeroplane taunted the night. Thank God there were no traffic jams, yet, in the air.

I had reached Goa late in the morning. Rohil had been on my flight. But so had many others of his fraternity. He could not spend any time with me, but restricted himself to dropping eyefuls of promise over various parts of my body.

The conference had started right after pre-lunch introductions. Each delegate wore a designer name-tag in green and blue. From the speeches made by the chairperson and others, the main focus of the conference seemed to be AIDS. I should have known. The medico-scientific community has really outdone itself in garnering attention and 'aid' for humanity's latest paranoia. Lesser subjects like Rohil's—organ transplants—were not given prime-time slots. Just as well for us, I realized.

Searching through the crowd, I had caught a glimpse of Anshul and Surabhi. She was quite dazzling in an off-white sleeveless kameez with matching palazzos. Her arms looked sleek, muscular, waxed and tanned. Arms are always a giveaway. I thought of mine, well hidden under my shirt. They had slipped a bit. But then, I had the accident as an excuse. I looked again. Anshul was wearing a dark, formal suit. In the daytime. In Goa. Luckily, the season was wet rather than hot. Before I could decide whether to speak to him, he was swept away on a tide of white skins in dark suits. There were plenty of those. Chartered flight from New York, I had heard. Who could resist tax breaks and balmy weather?

For the promised festivities, I was all dressed up. What's a conference without a little glamour? I had chosen a midnight-blue silk shirt with delicate cutwork embroidery on the yoke and sleeves. It allowed skin to show through the design. Subtle, I hoped. My black skirt was slit, but not too immodestly, at the back. I had actually dared to put on my Indo-roman sandals. I brushed my hair till my arm ached. It was left loose and slithered down my back. Since there was no static in the weather, I assumed it crackled with the sexual energy building up inside me. I was extra careful with my eyeliner. A touch of lipstick. And I was ready. My mouth curved upwards all by itself as I walked down to the dinner lounge. '*Piya milan ko jaana*,' I hugged the song to myself.

Weeks later, I realized that Goa had been the only hiatus since the accident when I had truly relaxed.

Disappointingly, he, too, was in a suit. Indian men will never change. Still tied to a colonial dress, when kurta-churidars, even dhotis, suit them so much better! He had already picked up two glasses as he walked across to greet me. He moved in the relaxed, lazy style that made my internal movements quicken. I caught myself writing moony lines about his sex appeal in my mind. Maybe it was the repressed romantic in me. Maybe I could take up writing romance novels after this damn story was done.

'You look edible,' he said ferociously, as he handed me my wine. He made sure no one was watching. Then he nibbled at my ear. My hair came in the way. Pure keratin. Pangs of hunger rode through me.

It was going to be cocktails, dinner and dancing. Perfect. The hundred-odd people were obviously ready to party. Only about two or three dozen belonged to the female persuasion, from what I could see. The ratio was on my side.

I came face to face with Anshul. Inevitably. He had an orange juice in his hand. He looked terribly distinguished in a blazer. His eyes glittered coldly.

'Ah, Anshul, I'm so glad I've met you,' I started.

'Really?'

'Please,' I said hastily, 'let me clarify a few things. I did not intend to go behind your back or anything. Why should I? You yourself gave me adequate information about your vaccine, remember? I read through all the material. It is simply stunning. On paper, it seems foolproof!' Lies, flattery and deception are the permitted tools of my trade.

However brilliant and crooked he might be, Anshul was also vulnerable. I told him I was looking forward to his presentation the next day. Especially now that I knew what the zona pellucida was. He laughed. Reluctantly. I sensed an opening. Sluicing through, I talked about what I had learnt about India Biotech's chase for the perfect contraceptive. About Anshul's mission. I tried to be witty. I tried to be charming. He mellowed a bit eventually.

'You know,' he looked ruminative and twirled his glass. Maybe it had vodka in it after all. 'If I, no, if *we* can swing it, we can really put India on the global map. I'm not boasting. At least not much.' He shrugged self-deprecatingly. I forced myself not to melt towards him. This was a man who, probably since childhood, was used to having things . . . and women, no doubt, his own way. A man who had lied about his vaccine. Who did not seem perturbed that women were conceiving deformed babies because, or rather, in spite of it.

He looked up at me, his eyes sharp. 'Nobody else has come this close. Nobody! Though they are barking at my heels. I was told so before. I can hear them now.' He looked behind him. So did I. I imagined a pack of snarling dogs.

'We sort of lost it, you know. Otherwise, medicine, preventive medicine, therapeutic medicine, it was nurtured here, on this soil.' I guessed he was referring to India. NRIs are usually born-again nationalists. So long as they can stay in San Jose.

Anshul then launched into an erudite account of the Sushruta and Charaka groups who lived in the hillsides around 200 BC. I had not known that. He seemed to assume it was common knowledge. 'They were our first social scientists, really. It is believed they were young Brahmin boys who had studied in the ancient north-western universities at Taxila . . . you know about that?'

Years of experience at nodding wisely during interviews came to my rescue. I even smiled.

'Anyway,' he continued, looking a little dubious. 'When they returned, they applied what they had learnt. They experimented with herbs, roots, all manner of available plants. The Charakas excelled with medicine, the Sushrutas with surgery. They kept meticulous records, marvellously enough. Do you know, some of their surgical instruments still survive in the museums in London? We've lost most of the original literature. But we know this much—they brought in the tradition of healing.' He looked deep into my eyes. But his heart wasn't with me. Just as well for mine. 'I guess,' he added, 'I just thought of it . . . they also helped build up a world-view.'

'I thought Sushruta was a person who wrote one of the Upanishads on medicine.'

I had given up any pretense. He looked at me sympathetically. Poor ignoramus.

'Well, yes and no. As I said, it is believed that a few students grouped themselves . . . you cannot even call them a tribe, it was more of a loose organization really. Somehow, the names they took on have long been used as singular pronouns. But the point is, the Sushrutas and Charakas were a people who revolutionized the idea of healthcare. Returning from their long years of study, they could no longer relate to the dichotomy in society, where certain castes of people did not have access to healing. So they changed that. They became roving doctors, healing anyone who needed to be healed. They made medicine proactive. And they were systematically annihilated by the orthodoxy, which felt threatened with so much social empowerment! By 200 AD, they had been decimated.'

Anshul looked pensive. I resisted the urge to soothe him. I thought there were some similarities, some pointers for him in the poignant tale. 'After that, nothing much happened in Indian medicine for many centuries. Sad, isn't it?'

So, did Anshul see himself as a shining warrior for Indian science? Was it 'return to the roots' patriotism? He seemed so knowledgeable. I was fascinated. I could feel my pupils dilate, my body language change.

My personal shining warrior seemed to sense something too. In a trice he was next to me, asking to be introduced. Slightly bemused, I did the necessary, and before I could protest, I was skilfully removed from the scene. It was simply a matter of pressing my pulse points. But I had made progress with Anshul. I didn't want to upset the equilibrium by asking him any awkward questions about pickled foetuses. Not yet. I gave up the rest of the evening to my own idea of paradise.

The band was in fine fettle. Rohil and I were not too bad ourselves. We danced wildly together, working off a sinful Italian dinner of pasta and salads. We gyrated wackily to the sounds of techno and rock, Goan melody and Hindi pop. Most unexpectedly, Hindi pop had taken hold of the young generation in the past five years, some of it sung by the resurgent, sixty-five-year-old Asha Bhosle.

'Who would have thought *O mere sona re* would return to the charts thirty years later in a new avatar?' Rohil laughed, as he made new moves to an old sound. 'Just proves we can co-opt any cultural trend from anywhere!' He banged me at my hip, making me wince with an almost forgotten pain from the nearly good-as-new leg.

Eventually, the music changed. Now it was slow, drowsy. 'Come and be my love . . .,' the female singer crooned. Way back from the seventies. But most welcome just then. Our bodies fused. The promise of the night began to enfold us in its magic . . . sweet and slow, like the agonized music.

'That's it. Let's get out of here.' Rohil's voice was low, disturbing. I nodded. Together, we left the hall now vibrating to the sounds of the next song: 'When I'm sixty-four'. Up the flight of stairs and breathless outside my room. In a conspiracy of delight, we let ourselves into the room, firmly shutting the door.

It had begun to rain with the wild insistence of the Goan monsoon. The wind blew in eerily through the doors of the balcony. I walked across, threw open the heavy curtains. Pale light filtered past the greenery. I returned to the door, leaned on the master switch. All the bulbs switched themselves off. Rohil froze next to me. As I moved, smooth and languorous, I could sense the lightning intermittently outlining my silhouette. I crossed over to the little fridge, which backlit me briefly as I reached for the bottle of white wine, chilled, compliments of the manager. The glasses clinked like anklets. I was definitely playing some role. I came back to Rohil, who was still as a statue.

Unable to bear the anticipation, I stood still, my body drumming silently. The vibrations seemed to release Rohil. Slowly, he came up to my trembling frame. Reaching with an unexpected firmness, he took the goblets out of my hands, rested them on a nearby stool. I could not see his face, he could not see mine. The darkness liberated our insecurities. His touch got bolder, his fingers confident. He awakened nerves, melted me with a flaming tongue. He licked away sudden tears, let me taste his own.

Releasing his hold briefly, he picked up a wine glass, took a long sip and transferred the cool liquid to my surprised lips. I sucked Savignon Blanc off his mouth. 'Liked that?' he asked. 'Mmmm,' I murmured, unwilling to talk.

He laughed then. Flexing his muscles, he picked me up off the floor. His arms were locked tight across my back, his chin at my waist. I felt dizzy. 'I'm impressed already,' I think I gurgled. 'You can put me down.' He did. On the sofa, which was barely wide enough for the two of us.

Kneeling alongside, he ran his fingers across the length of my body, peeling away barriers of silk and lace. Sight, smell, touch. Taste and sound . . . Time became space.

The lightning had stopped. Rain fell more gently. The lawns were already saturated. 'Rohil,' I whispered urgently.

He understood immediately. 'Are you sure? I can easily wait, you know,' he offered, only a little half-heartedly.

'Are you kidding? I can't.' I was growling. He laughed delightedly.

'Here we go, then. Vrooomm.' A motorcade of kisses down my neck. He took out some shiny packets from his pocket. 'Weapons,' he said in mock ferocity.

I hoped we had time to run through his stockpile. 'I'm armed too,' I chuckled. He touched my lips with cool fingers. The chuckle became a purr. I nipped at his thumb. He stepped up the pace of our lovemaking then. The rain stopped, eventually.

TWENTY-FIVE

Over a late continental buffet, the next morning, I was introduced to Dr Kerring. Tall, lean, bearded and with receding blonde hair, he looked the epitome of a tenured professor. He turned out to be the Director of the Institute for Reproductive Immunology in Washington, USA. Actually, we met because his wife oohed and aahed over my breakfast attire. Handspun khadi in the colour of winter sunshine. A few moonshine accessories. Plus a flush from the previous night. Anyway, Dr Kerring, as it happened, was bang on target for my story. His job was pretty much to direct research on immuno-contraception. I could not have chosen better if I had tried.

Elated, I quickly put on my very best journalistic manners. At the risk of them clashing with my dress.

'Are you researching male or female contraception at your institute, Dr Kerring?'

'Both, actually. Though most of our work has been concentrated on raising sperm antigen. We believe it is time the male of the species took on some of the responsibility for controlling runaway population growth.' His eyes twinkled.

'Bravo,' I said. Americans do have an easy humour about them. It's almost a *sine qua non* of social interaction.

'But we are also developing contraceptive vaccines for women.'

Someone must have written his lines for me. I was so surprised, I said the first thing that came to my mind. 'Er . . . do you know one of the people present here is also . . .'

Dr Kerring stroked his beard. 'Of course. Dr Anshooll. Yes, I have read his papers. He's done some excellent work.'

'Are you in direct competition with him, then?' I can be quite direct, too.

'Yes, of course. But the market is rather big, you know. About three billion strong worldwide. And growing, if we don't do something about it.' There he went again. I would have to crack a jokelet soon.

'Are you very near breakthrough point?' I had to persist. I knew that the product which made it to the market first would have tremendous competitive advantage.

'Yes, one of our teams in New York is just about ready. But that's all I'm going to tell you now, young lady,' he said, spearing a piece of papaya with his fork. He looked me straight in the eye, his pale blue ones quite determined. I hastily scooped up some kiwi fruit. His wife was quite happy to fill in the silences after that.

Pity. I had not got enough out of the man. From what he had said, there was a team neck to neck with Anshul in the race. Well, I would have to find someone else to continue talking to. Then I could return to the redoubtable Dr Kerring, better prepared. What I badly needed just then was an international expert in immunology, preferably a gynaecologist, someone who was not directly involved in contraception research. I was only asking for the moon. In my rather ebullient mood that day, I told myself that nothing ventured was nothing gained. I got hold of a list of delegates. There were one hundred and fifty. Benign descriptions accompanied each name. I shortlisted three, then selected one. Dr Judith Ferraro. Consultant, Assisted

Reproduction Centre, Boston. She had a string of alphabetical additions to her name. If she was attending this conference, she might also have some interest in the field of immuno-contraception.

I found her, finally, in the swimming pool. In the afternoon when all the papers had been read, all of us had a couple of hours to ourselves. I left Rohil with admiring colleagues who had liked his presentation, and headed outdoors.

I dived into the deep end of the clover-shaped pool, the nip in the water exciting my skin. The swimsuit I was wearing was cut high at the thigh, low at the bust. A promotional gift from the new swimwear companies diving into our modest markets. Not something to wear at the Club in Bangalore. Here, it did not matter. I swam lazily, looking around. All four pool petals were crowded. I gave up the idea of the laps I was planning. I like floating on the water in various yoga postures. So I practised my internal cleansing in what I hoped was a quiet corner of tiled blue.

That's when Dr Judith floated by. Luckily, she did not sport a swimming cap. I recognized her face from the photos I had pored over. I tried to uncoil my legs suddenly from their padmasana posture. I went under. When I came up, spluttering, she was looking in my direction with some concern.

'Hello,' I said, coughing a little. 'Aren't you Dr Judith Ferraro?'

'Yes, I am. And no, I am not related to Geraldine.'

We became friends soon after. Being in the sauna, steam bath and jacuzzi can do that to you. I don't particularly enjoy being dried out of all my waters, or steamed like an idli either, but I wasn't complaining. We talked.

Dr Judith's Italian blood was there for all to see. Dark, flashing blue eyes. Very dark hair. In her early fifties, perhaps. Trim. Burn going on tan. And very jovial.

'I have no very good reason to be here,' she confided,

'but I just could not resist the invitation.' It was her second trip to India. She had done the northern tours, she wanted to taste South India this time. When we finished with the cocktail conversation, we began to talk of her work.

'I help infertile couples conceive. I have patients who've delayed their babies too long. Women between thirty-five and forty-five, pioneers, in a sense, because they hauled women's privileges up to standards of decency. Now, they are not sure if it was worth it. They don't regret it, exactly. But they do want babies. It's sad, sometimes, to see how *much* they want babies. But nature is horribly stubborn. I make a lot of money. And I get a few babies.'

She spoke of single women who also wanted to conceive, highly successful corporate women who needed the status of motherhood as well. Even without men. Women who went through every manner of test and experiment to bear a healthy child. Donor sperm, a passing boyfriend, or a borrowed womb from a sympathetic sibling.

'I see how much they go through, these women . . . and their partners, too, if they have any. Then sometimes, I feel it would be easier to remove the desire for children from their minds. Easier than implanting the reality in their bodies!'

I asked about her interest in immunology. She looked slightly embarrassed, but recovered quickly.

'Not enough, actually. I was invited partly because my, er, special friend, Dr Michael Frampton is one of the chief organizers.' From the sparkle in her eyes, I figured he was a recent special friend. I love the spirit of Americans in that direction. I'm sure the Europeans have it too. I just hope, at fifty-five, I'll be at least sexually active, if not running through my fifty-fifth affair. Dr Ferraro continued, 'and of course, I do a lot of consultancy work for America Aid, which, you know, supports family planning activities around the world.' Which led us easily into the subject of contraceptive vaccines. I asked her if she knew of any product that was market-ready in the US.

She hesitated, even though she had no clue of my personal interest. Then she shrugged.

'It will be out on the Internet soon anyway, I suppose. It's not like it's a big secret.'

I tensed. My swimsuit caved in at the waist.

'There is a conglomerate of companies in the US that have supported the development of a contraceptive vaccine for women. I believe the team in New York are at a crucial stage. They have isolated an antigen, but I don't know very much more.'

I expressed an avid interest in her information and explained my background in health reporting. She was genuinely curious, and I answered most of her questions honestly.

'Is there anyone here, at the conference, by any chance, who could tell me more? It seems to me that contraceptive vaccines will have the world's biggest markets in India and China. It makes a good story.'

She thought it over. 'I think Dr Kerring is a good bet. But as Director of the Institute of Reproductive Immunology, he is not personally involved in the research. I know that the research teams do have the support of America Aid, maybe even the WHO. But you could ask him for more information.'

We parted ways at the showers, promising to catch up at dinner. I said I would love to meet Dr Frampton. She was pleased.

Delegates returned to the afternoon session with reduced enthusiasm. Cocktails before lunch, then a swim or a snooze. Everyone had opted for a little break which now seemed difficult to break out of.

Dr Anshul Hiremath, the first speaker at the slumber session, had a tough task ahead. But then, he had conquered 'the final frontier' already. A few sleepy listeners were easy.

Personally, I was very alert. I had chosen to sit in the middle rows, so I could watch Anshul as well as Surabhi, who was in the first. I was also keeping an eye on Dr Kerring, the man who knew so much and would tell me so little. He was at the very end of the third row. Not far from the front exit.

With all my brand new knowledge, I could almost follow Anshul. His hypnotic intensity made up for the rest. Here was a man in love. In passion. Slowly, but surely, his charisma woke up the sleepyheads. People began to sit upright, bend forward, pull out their pens.

'Now you may well ask, why is the zona pellucida, or the ZP, the final frontier in the battle for fertility control. Well, for many years, researchers have realized that the ZP is possibly the most ideal site to look for an immunogen for a contraceptive vaccine.

'Now, after years of mapping every molecule on the ZP, we at India Biotech believe that we have found the perfect candidate for an antigen. At last. We have called it FRP-41. Instead of boring you with details, I will refer you to the sheets in front of you, which may be read at your own convenience.

'So, are we ready to set up a parenteral unit for our vaccine? Well, no. But, and I can smell it, we are getting there. Thanks to the giant strides in molecular biology, it has become possible for us to manufacture in bulk even the range of proteins which are infrequent in the body, such as the molecules of the ZP.

'Having said that, allow me now to share a secret with you.'

Anshul dropped his voice, looked intimately at his audience. He should have been in Bollywood. I flexed my fingers, stiff with taking rapid notes. Anshul had them all listening all right.

'I am now going one step further. Into the future of immunology. India Biotech is developing a synthetic antigen for its vaccine. If we succeed, and I have no doubt that with the skill and dedication of my team, we shall get there soon, it will revolutionize the whole idea of tissue-based immunogens. Imagine. An antigen that can be synthetically created, which need not be harvested from human tissue. Which will be tinkered with endlessly. Which can be safe, stable, easy to transport, easy to store. And, in the long run, cheap.'

I had not been able to resume my frantic note taking. It was lucky my fingers had gone numb. I caught the sudden movement in the third row. Dr Kerring was stealthily moving to the nearest exit. His frame was bent over, so as not to come in the line of vision of others. As he whispered his excuses, he was already pulling out a gleaming instrument from his coat pocket. A mobile phone, I guessed.

My brain synapses started high jumps immediately. What had agitated Dr Kerring? Something about Anshul's 'secret'? Or something else? I decided to follow him out.

It was much clumsier from where I sat. As I smiled apologetically, pushing quickly at comfortably ensconced delegates, I heard Anshul continue, his voice pitched higher than usual.

'My vision is to deliver an antigen that will make worries over contraception a thing of the past, not just in the developed world, but also in the populations whose resources cannot match their growth rates. If it is a dream, ladies and gentlemen, I am sure all of those gathered here share it too.'

I did not wait to find out if there was general assent. Moving swiftly towards the lobby area, I just barely caught a glimpse of Dr Kerring's bearded face turn behind a huge pillar. He settled down on a strategic couch, and started to dial immediately.

This, I thought happily, is the stuff investigative reporting is made of. Slipping a little self-consciously into the role, I casually walked over to sit as close as I dared to the suddenly verbose American. He could not see me. Not that he seemed worried. His entire attention was focussed on his conversation.

'Yes, he did. Not five minutes ago. I was there. There was no mention of a synthetic antigen in his notes. I thought you had said . . .' That is approximately what I heard. Perhaps I was filling in the less audible gaps myself.

So. It was the synthetic antigen that was bothering Dr Kerring. Why? It made no sense to me. I strained to hear more.

'Maybe you should make an announcement. I hope you are in touch with Washington.' Again, I wondered if I was imagining some of the words. I tried moving closer still. Just around the pillar.

To my horror, Dr Kerring was walking right towards me, his lean body angled comically forward. He was still talking and listening, one hand on the tiny phone, the other clutching at his beard.

He actually looked right through me. I was trying to be invisible. I must have succeeded. He just moved right on, straight to the elevators, scraped through closing steel doors and disappeared.

I stood there indecisively for a while. Then I returned to the conference hall. Anshul had obviously finished. He was at the moment engulfed by curious scientists, possibly questioning him further. I saw Surabhi at the fringe. She was glowing, candle-like.

TWENTY-SIX

As I dressed for dinner, I could feel Rohil's touch on my body, making me shiver with renewed anticipation. I had brought along another skirt. But I decided to wear an aquamarine sari in chiffon silk. It's the world's lightest material. It makes you feel as though you have worn very little. It also clings to any curves along the way. Since the accident, I think I had filled out mine. I clipped on long silver earrings, minakari bangles. I felt great about myself. It was so long since I had made such an effort to look good.

There was a knock. Rohil had promised to escort me down. 'Because I need my appetizers!' he had said. I opened the door a crack. He caught at my hair. I pulled him in. His eyes told me I had not wasted my time. 'Dynamite,' he said, very, very softly, his lips descending to mine.

Dr Frampton and Judith Ferraro, walking with their arms linked, looked happy together. Dr Kerring was nowhere to be seen. Surely that meant something. Wish I could figure out what. The rest of us sat down for the lavish Indian à la carte dinner. Rohil, who had thankfully dressed casually, took centre stage with his impassioned conversation on organ transplants. I watched him with open adoration. Since Dr Frampton was a senior immunologist, he listened attentively and gave Rohil many useful suggestions on proceeding with his work. That left Judith and myself to crack a few jokes, observe the sartorial displays around the ballroom, and talk, while eating rasgullas bathed in basundi. We discussed her trip to Bangalore the following week. I urged her to come visit my family, to which she readily agreed.

I caught Anshul and Surabhi after dinner. I thought they looked as if they were about to retire. Surabhi had gone ultra Western that day, in a very sleek mauve suit. She smiled at me and asked if I was enjoying myself. I looked across to Rohil, and my face said the rest. 'May I have a word with you both?' I asked. It was a gamble. But she smiled in assent.

We sat at a small table not far from the band which was preparing for after-dinner dancing. The tentative music covered our conversation but did not drown it.

'Anshul, I believe you are having some problems with the vaccine research? I met Ketamma.'

'Oh my God!' Anshul looked at Surabhi. I saw panic flash through her eyes. Then she steadied, covered his hand. 'This woman has been . . . has gone . . . too far,' he exclaimed. Then he returned to me. 'Look, I can explain.'

'That's what I'm here for, Anshul. Go ahead.'

He looked around, suddenly weary. He ran his hands through his mop of hair. He seemed to crumple in front of my eyes.

'Look . . . I am still trying to figure out the Keti angle. It just makes no sense. There is no way she could have got pregnant right after the vaccine was given. I myself checked and rechecked the antibody level reports. They were more than adequate. Unless . . . unless she was pregnant already . . .'

'Wouldn't they have checked that first?'

'Of course, of course. But mistakes happen. Although . . . Anyway, yes, if she were pregnant already, FRP would play havoc.' His voice tapered off.

Surabhi spoke. 'Anshul has had some unusual things happen at the end of this phase of the trials. Yes, it is very disturbing. But he has been looking desperately for the answer to the mysteries. Phase one went off so smoothly. There must be a reasonable explanation, to the, er, problem that has come up. He will find it.' Her eyes softened. I couldn't decide whether to feel sympathetic.

'What will you do now? Will you stop the trials in the meanwhile?' Somewhere deep inside me, I did register that we were talking impersonally about it all, as though the players (or was it victims?) were all dolls, unreal.

They looked at each other. I was a common enemy. They bound tight against me.

'I do not know,' said Surabhi, enunciating carefully, 'exactly what right you have to ask all these questions. You are a journalist, yes. But we do not have to answer.'

I have faced this sort of situation before. I knew what to say.

'Yes, of course that is true.' I measured each word, but dropped my voice. Both had to lean forward. 'You do not have to answer. I can get my information any which way, and I can write that you refused to comment. What I have found out is gory enough. It will make an eye-grabbing headline.' I saw the instantaneous reaction rushing to Anshul's mouth and spoke before he could. 'No, I am not threatening you. I am just offering you a very reasonable choice. If you choose to co-operate with me, if you give me the information that is necessary before this story can be told, you will have a chance to present your side of the picture. As it stands now, India Biotech comes out looking very, very bad.'

There was an eloquent silence. The band struck up a waltz. Still practising. I waited patiently, my eyes on Anshul.

Of course, it was Surabhi who answered eventually. 'My husband and I will think over what you have just said, Ms Pandit. Whatever you may call it, it appears to me to be a distinct threat. Still, there is a price that will have to be paid. By us, in our silence. By you, in writing anything remotely libellous. Maybe we should all sleep over it. Good night.'

As if Anshul was a young child, she took him by his slackened arms. He got up. They walked together past the dance floor, out of the wide double doors. I watched them go, feeling completely ashamed, completely miserable.

Rohil found me a little later. 'What is it, gonya?' he asked, using a Konkani endearment.

Poor Rohil. We should have been talking about his presentation and his work. After all, I had come to the conference as an afterthought. But I had become so self-absorbed, I could not stand outside myself at all. I did find out later, through news reports on the conference, that Rohil's presentation had been passionate and fiery. Like his 'other' self. He had challenged the government to use the resources of doctors such as himself to create a national organ donor network. The health ministry had actually invited him to Delhi in response. That day, however, he did not mention himself once. I did not realize then how much I was already taking him for granted.

I told him a little of what had happened. He sat with me for a while, rubbing my neck. Then he pulled me to my reluctant feet. 'Come along. I know just the place for you.'

Within minutes, my inappropriate attire notwithstanding, we were in the real Goan paradise. On the beach. Last night's storm had washed the sky clean. It was about two days to full moon. Stars hung close to the horizon towards the north. Ahead, to the west, the black and white ocean tumbled forward to greet us, its tide on the rise.

Cool fingers of breeze picked up the folds of my whispery sari. It billowed around me, teasing, kissing. I was transformed into a creature of the elements. The sky, the water, the fire was inside me. The earth was beneath me, the air about me. And Rohil was by my side.

I healed as we walked. The soft sand parted as we touched it. Rohil took my arm, just let me be. I breathed in the salt, the spice. When I felt ready, I sat down on the cold sand. He dropped down beside me.

I really cannot remember what we said to each other. But they were binding things. Long-term things. We shared perspectives. Of life and injustice. Of work and family. I cried for Ketamma. I cried for Amma, who would miss Shweta the most. He told me about his parents, his younger brother in the US, who was already a successful software engineer. He spoke, reluctantly, of a favourite aunt who had died of leukemia recently. Death seemed benign, here in the open night.

When we got back to my room, we slept without making love. It was only towards dawn that we reached for each other. Our bodies danced a still new ballet, graceful and wordless. The sun rose.

TWENTY-SEVEN

'Funnily enough, I have always thought of it as a "moral" vaccine,' said Anshul, quietly. 'But now it seems as though there are internal contradictions which are inescapable.'

We were sitting on an open deck, facing the sea which was calm. Anshul and I, at a small table for two. Surabhi had decided not to come. Whatever decision they had reached in the night, she did not want to witness the next act. The smell of eggs, dosas, tea and orange juice rumbled through my stomach. So far, we only had a couple of dewy roses in front of us.

'How can it be a moral vaccine, Anshul, when it has done so much damage already?'

He removed his glasses to wipe them. His eyes startled me. They were really big. Very soft brown. The eyelashes looked faintly ridiculous. For some reason, he did not put back his spectacles. Maybe he didn't want to see things . . . or me, very clearly.

'Because, unlike all the other vaccines, it does not allow conception to happen. You know, I totally stand by a woman's right to abortion. But show me one woman who can be genuinely casual about it. My vaccine seemed . . . seems,' he corrected himself fiercely, 'so perfect. Other contraceptive methods are so invasive, they mess around with hormones, one way or the other. You never know when the body will react to that sort of interference . . .'

'What if the body reacts to your antigen also, Anshul? Much later?'

'Look, Poorva, there is no way anybody can guarantee anything. No medical research would be possible with such a caveat. The element of chance will always remain. But you have to take this chance consciously and take all precautions. Keep yourself informed so you can intervene quickly at the first sign of trouble.'

'And did you do all that, Anshul?' I was gentle. He looked at me, willing me to look inside his soul. I pictured a mottled grey pond with sunlight bouncing off its surface.

'I think I tried. Harder in the beginning. Then . . . I guess I got very involved with the business side of things. I have Rita after all. She is so efficient. She shares my vision. She also has the trust of the tribal women, from what I can tell. That's really important.' His American accent became stronger. 'I have been very happy with the way things have been going so far. Thing is, I guess it does need my complete hands-on attention. But unless I can fix the money part . . . it would make no difference.'

'Some problems on the financial front as well?'

Anshul banged manicured hands on the flimsy table. The roses jumped. 'Damn it. Biogene Research Foundation has got wind of the pregnancies. I cannot understand how! That Kakodia couldn't have . . . I made sure. Besides, Rita and I had not . . .' he realized, I guess, what he was saying. So soon after the moral bit.

'Given out all the information?'

'Yes. We suppressed it.' He looked different, puffier. As though he was trying to look bigger to ward off threats. 'I deserve a chance to make corrections if things go wrong. We have not created any life-threatening situations for anybody. We had a few conceptions in the early stages. That is natural. In-vivo trials were important to determine antibody level requirements. We did careful MTPs. Dr Padma, our doctor from Maddur, is a good gynaecologist.'

Medical termination of pregnancy. MTP. Usually through vacuum suction. Or DNC. Dilation and curetting. If done properly, very simple procedures. Scars more psychological than physical.

'What about Madhamma?'

'Madhamma? Oh shit, that woman with the stillborn baby. You know about that too? I guess you would.' He sounded jaded. 'Though how you got them to talk, I don't know. That Dr Gopinath of yours, he hasn't succeeded, even with all his wily methods.'

'Madhamma is lucky that her baby died.' I remembered the description of the foetus. Goosepimples erupted on my forearms. 'What would you have done, otherwise?'

'That should never have happened, of course. But she went away. I pored over her file for days. She went away, left the camp, just like that. They . . . we . . . tried to find her. But the Banigas, they . . .' his tone turned bitter. 'It's so hard to keep them, er, steady. In one place. You know. They get so many ideas.'

If only all our little experiments could be performed under completely controlled conditions. Like loving. Like raising children. Like developing the perfect vaccine.

'Why was the baby so deformed in the first place?'

'We spent hours over that, too. Believe me! We reached the conclusion that it was not because of the vaccine. In the records, the antibodies showed consistent ranges, suitable for contraception. We looked at epidemiological studies—there was only one incomplete one, way back from British times—to see if there were patterns. Nothing. So why was the baby deformed?' He seemed to be asking *me* that. I felt compelled to shrug.

'Something,' he said slowly, more to himself, 'something went terribly, terribly wrong. And we narrowed it down to the administration of the vaccine. Rita is very, very meticulous in her record keeping. That's why I can trust her.' I remembered the careful movements, the file cabinets, not one paper out of place. I believed him.

'Finally, I began to think the problem had something to do with the quality of the antigen itself. As it is, we have a hell of a time keeping it stable and active. If there was some original problem in the kinetic action of the . . .' he realized who he was speaking to. 'We have now sent out some samples to the US for independent analysis.' He looked at me significantly. But I did not feel illuminated at all. He sighed.

'It's not feasible to mass produce the peptide for the antigen here. It's too sophisticated a technique and requires very high capital investments—even if it were possible to find qualified people who would bother to work with us. So I import it. From the Philippines, of all places.' I could sympathize with his bitterness. Third World-ers like us cannot understand when another so-called Third World country does such things. It feels like hope, but also like betrayal.

'They make it themselves?'

'Yes. No, actually. It's from the Transpharma subsidiary there. That's a US multinational. Oh yes, you know Jimmy, don't you?'

Thuk. It fell into place. Transpharma had a great deal of interest in the success of Anshul's vaccine. It was one of the donors to the agency that funded him. It had an earlier business relationship with him. And, on top of that, it also supplied him, from its Philippines operation, the key material for making his vaccine. Anshul had 'made sure' that Kakodia would not squeal on him. That he would keep from Transpharma or Biogene the little problems he was facing. No wonder Jimmy Kakodia had been so reluctant to talk to his old buddy, my father.

If not Kakodia, then, somebody else had informed Transpharma. Naturally, Transpharma must have been furious. Surely, it would also put Kakodia's position in jeopardy. But who could have a motive, a vested interest, in exposing Anshul? Could it be the same person or people who had caused the foetus to rematerialize at Vikram's? I was feeling a little overwhelmed. This was quite different from covering the annual general meeting of disgruntled shareholders.

'And now . . . they claim I have been duping them all along. So they want to back out. Now! Just at the end of the rainbow. They want to stop my money, my peptide. They want to strangle me.' I wondered if Anshul would look ugly, like most people, when he became apoplectic. He did not. His eyelashes merely fluttered a little faster. He spluttered. 'Not that I will allow it. We can make, er, alternative arrangements.'

I was curious. Were those tears? Or just the reflection from the sea?

'So what will you do now?'

'Believe me,' he looked suddenly different, not exactly menacing, but steely. 'I will do, I *am* doing . . . Everything . . . anything . . . in my power to make sure this project gets back on the rails.'

Just how far would he go, I wondered. Like Anshul, I was confused. I was no longer able to distinguish good from bad, perpetrator from victim. I would have to think. A good night's sleep would help too.

A waiter graced us with a five-star breakfast at last. We both tucked in at once, as though it were just ordinary fare. We were ensconced in our separate little worlds. Anshul had run out of words. I had run out of questions.

I did catch up with Dr Kerring again. He would not give me anything. He skimmed lightly over the subject, distracting me with little anecdotes. 'As you yourself said, young woman,' he said, his eyes paler than ever, 'it's a direct competition. And I can't tell whose side you are on.'

All I could do then was take his e-mail address. And give him my card.

TWENTY-EIGHT

Bangalore seemed unneccessarily chaotic after the single-lane slowness of South Goa. I tried to shut away the ugliness on my ride home. I hate holidays which end in a feeling of regret. I remembered just in time that I had not been on a holiday.

Shweta was not near the door to receive me. Laxmi let me in. Instantly, I knew something was wrong.

My little sister was in bed, looking ghastly. It was a virus, Amma said. She looked like she had not moved from that spot since I had left. Damn! And damn! Shweta is so susceptible. I looked down at her, my heart in my mouth. She opened her eyes and gave me a wan smile. Her fever was riding high. Amma and I sat beside her. I talked softly, filling them in. I described the beauty of the ocean rain, I shared anecdotes about Rohil. I took out the baubles I had picked up for Shweta. She clutched at my hand. Amma nodded to me, and gratefully went away to attend to her other chores. I just sat there. Once Shweta was asleep, still clutching my hand, but with no strength, I allowed myself to think. I fell asleep right there with the effort.

The morning was harsh. No birds, no ocean. I tried to adjust, to become a city girl once again. It was hard. I burrowed deep into my story. If I assumed that Anshul was telling me the truth, they were trying hard to stem further problems at MR Hills. Meanwhile, he was being starved of funds. And deprived of a crucial raw material. He would, I reckoned, have no choice but to make 'alternative arrangements' as he called them. But how?

This was a man who had willingly suppressed information, by his own admission, to his sponsors on a vital issue like malformed foetuses and unexpected conceptions in the clinical trials; who had possibly kept Kakodia happy in some way, to prevent him from spilling the beans too early. Now he was ready to justify himself. How much could I trust his information?

Perhaps Jimmy Kakodia had some answers. Leaving Shweta to her own devices, I called Anna at work and exchanged fond pleasantries. I got the Transpharma telephone numbers. Anna was not at all happy that I was betraying him by involving Kakodia. But I was adamant. I said I would fill him in at night.

I called at the office and left a message for CP, who mercifully was not in, that I was working from home that day. Then I got Kakodia.

'Jimmy Uncle, I am doing a story on India Biotech. I need some information from you.'

Now, over the phone, he did not sound like the jovial gentleman I had met at the Club. He was wary. He said he would call me back. I waited. The telephone bell jangled Shweta's nerves. I patted her down.

'Jimmy here. Look, I hope you are not involving Transpharma in this story.'

'Not particularly. I believe you are supplying India Biotech with a raw material for Dr Anshul's vaccine?'

'We were, yes. Right now, I believe some . . . negotiations . . . are going on. But this is all strictly confidential.'

'What is Transpharma's relationship with the Biogene Research Foundation?'

A short silence. 'We are one of the donors. That's all.'

'Does Transpharma have any interest in acquiring the rights to the vaccine when it is market ready?'

'I am sorry. I am not privy to that information. Even if I was, I would not have given it to you This is highly sensitive business information. People do not go to the press with it.'

'I understand. I hope I have not upset you, Jimmy Uncle. Thing is, I don't want to make any errors when I report this. I don't know if you are aware of this, but there is a woman in MR Hills right now, who is carrying a probably malformed baby inside her. I believe the antigen—FRP 41—that your company supplied to India Biotech was used in the vaccine that was administered to her. Transpharma is involved in this story, sir.'

A spluttering noise. A loud silence. 'All right. You have made your point. I will get back to you in a little while.' I had to be content with that.

Laxmi came in with some spicy rejuvenators. She also brought a long list of messages that had been left for me while I was away. I called Mr Shah, the retired Drug Controller, first. I imagined him sitting next to the cordless telephone, dressed in spotless white, sipping some herbal concoction.

'Ah, beti, I was trying to reach you,' said the old man. 'I spoke to some friends in the DC's office, the Drug Controller's office, that is, in Delhi. There is a lot of interest, actually, in the subject you have raised!'

Mr Shah went on to give me details, some of which I had already learnt in Goa. There was pressure on the DC's office all around. Anshul Hiremath's father, whom I had not brought into the equation at all, was a highly placed bureaucrat in the Prime Minister's office in Delhi. Chandrakant Hiremath. He was tipped to be the next cabinet secretary. That's big. Governments may come and go but the arches in the steel frame last for ever. I remembered that the medics who set me off on this chase had mentioned

162

that Dr Anshul's father is an IAS officer. So okay, he'd climbed the rungs rapidly.

Apparently, the India card was being played heavily. It had become clear that an international conglomerate was trying to get its vaccine, very similar to Anshul's, out into the market as quickly as possible. Two transnational pharmaceutical companies, Benden of the US and Merik Fromm of Europe had joined hands to support the final phase of production and proposed launch. The FDA was favourably inclined to allow phase three trials. USAID, WHO and the likes were also interested and were backing the vaccine, which had been code-named VAC 1998.

Anshul's product, which incidentally, the Indian government had initially refused to support financially, had suddenly become a pawn in an international race. India has been one of the biggest opponents to many of the GATT clauses. It would love to deliver a home-grown product that could sweep the world market before 2005 in spite of all the constricting clauses.

The Drug Controller's office was being asked to push clearances for phase two. It was known that some problems had cropped up, but even some of the DC officials were sympathetic to Anshul in this case. It was very likely that phase three would be launched shortly. Anshul was already preparing his product licence application. Various government institutes were now offering him financial aid. So far he had declined.

I was dazed. The story had suddenly taken on the proportions of an international thriller. Could this really be happening? Our world has become so interdependent that it is hard to tell which string will lead to which base! I thanked Mr Shah profusely, my words tumbling all over themselves.

'Not at all, beti. I am enjoying myself thoroughly. Promise you will keep me informed of all developments.' I did.

TWENTY-NINE

Shweta was getting a bit better. I promised her the moon and then some, and went across to the cybercafe once more. Pranay, the in-house Cyber-guru, gave me a red rose, and a prime place at a corner terminal. I walked into the parlour of the spider's World Wide Web. I looked up reproductive immunology. There it was. Only eighteen thousand and twelve entries. I persevered. Finally, I found press clippings from a company report.

Benden USA had gone on record on its interest in immuno-contraception with specific reference to a contraceptive vaccine for women. For Benden, said a quote from its in-house document, the vaccine would be an exciting addition to its product basket. The document, which had been released verbatim, went on to praise the company's performance, its strategy, the potential market for contraceptive vaccines, which it described as 'the most cost-effective vehicle for contraception worldwide'. It also mentioned, almost in passing, that Merik Fromm would be Benden's partners in this exciting venture.

I also looked up India Biotech. I got twenty-three entries, twenty-two of which were completely irrelevant. That's the major problem with the Internet. It has blinkers on it. India Biotech did not have a homepage. Why? I could not figure it out. With someone as cyber savvy as Anshul it had to be deliberate.

I needed to access more information about India Biotech. I had to find out why Anshul was now refusing financial aid from scientific institutions here. What did he have up his sleeve? If Transpharma stopped delivering his antigen, from where would he source it? Could he afford to stop or delay his trials? Now that the competition was hotting up so dramatically, he would have to move very quickly.

Pranay came by with a cup of coffee. Taking it gratefully, I asked him half in jest, 'Suppose you wanted to access some information from a company's in-house documents. Could you do it through the Internet?'

Pranay jumped as if scalded. He looked around furtively. 'I have never, ever done any such thing.'

'I know, silly.' I had not realized I had a detonation device in my armour. 'I'm not talking about you. I was just wondering if it was possible. Like all those hackers one reads about, who start nuclear war and stuff.'

He relaxed, but kept an eye out behind him. 'It takes time, but yeah, sure, it's possible. So long as a company has an Internet-enabled system. Then you can do almost anything.'

I thought of the giant receivers outside Anshul's office building. I thought of the blinking monitors at every desk. Sure, India Biotech was connected. But was that enough? 'I thought companies had become very conscious of security issues . . . they build firewalls everywhere,' I said.

'It makes the challenge more exciting, yes,' he said, a bit too casually.

I tried to be clever. I failed. 'Pranay, do you think you could tell me how these hackers would do it, you know, just for fun?'

He narrowed his eyes, which made him look even funkier. He looked me up and down. Surprisingly, it did not offend. He took his hair back and rolled a rubber band from his wrist onto it. 'I could, Beautiful, but sure as hell not in here. What say *you* treat *me* to a cup of tea, for a change?'

In the South, tea is looked upon as an inferior cousin. Nobody bothers to make it the way it should be made. We settled for Chinese herbal tea at the Chung-Wah.

Pranay belongs to that crazy, mixed-up generation that pooh-poohs academics fairly early. Then, surprisingly, after trying out many things, they find in themselves a craze for computer games. Somehow it hones their minds and they head straight to the software industry, quickly finding comfortable niches. They become universalized. Bohemian on the outside, they are straight and narrow on the inside. Eventually and inevitably, they register for some high-flown Ph.D course somewhere in the USA. Pranay soon told me all there is to know about breaking into people's personal computer systems. To tell the truth, I found it quite funny. For all their sophisticated security software, the industry has few defences against superbrats like Pranay.

'You make it sound really, really easy, Pranay. I feel very dubious.'

He admitted he'd sort of skipped a few of the problems involved. We laughed together. I decided to take him into my confidence. I told him a bit of the story, enough to tickle his conscience. I lingered over the bits about illiterate women being experimented upon. I described the stillborn baby. He looked very uneasy by the time I had finished.

'If I could take a look at some of the research papers, or some of the correspondence between India Biotech and Biogene . . . maybe I could at least figure out if Anshul has been lying. Some proof, and I have my story. What do you say? Can you help me?'

He took a toothpick and nonchalantly cleaned his molars. Luckily he had a sparkling white set of teeth.

'Maybe I could help you at that. But we would have to work after hours. It would have to be completely confidential.

If my name appeares anywhere, or if I am caught, Big Man will krrrk-!' He made a horizontal slashing gesture across his neck . . . 'finish me off.' Cybercafe was owned by TBN, a prominent software group in the city, led by the larger-than-life myth that was its chairman, T.B. Narasimhan. It had been much touted as a yeoman service to the have-nots of information technology.

We shook hands firmly. It was a pact made in sweat. He agreed to meet me at the cafe at eight o'clock the next evening.

THIRTY

Anna came home in a thunderous mood. It is so rare a happening that none of us recognized it at first. It was Shweta who whispered to me, after Anna had checked in on her, that in her opinion, something was bothering him greatly. She was still in bed, her fever down but a pale look over her that took away my cheer as well. I watched Anna carefully at dinner time. He was ominously quiet. He had only had one of two nightly pegs. Then he abruptly called me over to the family room.

'I thought you had promised to keep the Kakodia thing between you and me? So what happened?'

Damn. I had quite forgotten. That man must have called Anna to complain. I felt awful.

'I'm really sorry, Anna. I had to call Jimmy Unc . . .'

'Poorva,' he interrupted. 'I have always helped you in your work whenever it was possible for me. We have also understood, up until now, the limitations to that. Our fields overlap. There is a possible conflict of interest. I hardly need to spell it out to you. From now on, you may not come to me with any of your damn stories.' Cold, cold tone. Freezing icicle eyes.

'Anna, I'm sorry you feel this way. I really am. But I wish you would listen to me . . . This is not just a story for me any more, Anna! There are people, women . . . babies getting hurt. I don't know, it's a challenge . . . a sort of test of my beliefs. And these are values I have picked up from you and Amma. It sounds corny. But tell me, do you think I should now pull back from exposing India Biotech? And yes, Transpharma if neccessary? What would you have done?'

'First of all, I would not have taken such a crusade . . . as that's what it seems to have become for you, onto my frail shoulders. Secondly, I would inform parties who might be hurt, like myself, in advance of what I was going to do. Thirdly, I would not make so many assumptions about the role of players in the story I was building up.'

I was completely chastised. I moved closer, sat on the rug at Anna's feet. He seemed so remote.

'It was a mistake not to tell you first, Anna. You're right. I have become too full of myself on this crusade as you call it. Okay, you tell me, what should I do next?'

Anna relented a little and asked me a few questions. He began to see that Kakodia had been telling him only those things that suited him. Anna is, above all, a fair man. A decent man.

'I think I want you to proceed, Poorva,' he said finally, his eyes still cloudy. 'But with caution. In fact, I think I will help you. Perhaps I can find out, through other sources, whether Biogene has finally pulled out. Whether Anshul has found another sponsor. Maybe tomorrow.' He reached down to ruffle my hair. I nearly cried with happiness.

'If Anshul had really bribed Kakodia not to give information to Transpharma, won't Kakodia be in trouble too, Anna?'

'He certainly seems worried. You know what, maybe he suspects you of having, in some way, leaked information. He sounded quite bitter about you.'

Oh great. Now I was really into the act. As a suspected informant! Kakodia must be out of his mind. He deserved what was coming to him.

I left Anna that night still in his favourite armchair. I was in my own world and did not know, until later, that he had faced other, equally serious problems at work that day. The government had come down heavily on his company, accusing it of selling sub-standard drugs. Its best-sellers had been unceremoniously suspended from the market, pending enquiry. Anna, the spokesman, had borne the brunt of the media wrath. Only later was the vexatious issue resolved. One of the firm's contractors had been retrieving drugs assigned to the incinerator for not meeting stringent in-house quality standards and selling them as real issue. He was caught red-handed, but the bad publicity could not be reversed overnight. It depressed Anna for days, as I found out later, because the contractor had been hired as an energetic freshman by Anna himself.

Quite unknowing of my father's trauma, I took on CP the next day. He listened, in his usual way. I told him I could not do the story yet. I wanted some proof of malafide intentions on Anshul's part. I wanted proof that the DC's office was being pressured to give him clearances. I wanted to know if the Transpharma-supplied antigen was responsible for Madhamma's malformed baby. Had it been tampered with? I had to know for sure.

Besides, if I broke the story now, it would be incomplete. Anshul, or Transpharma, may go to court and bring a stay on further investigation. It could prove libellous.

CP quite clearly understood that I was roadrolling him. We had a little skirmish then. Since I was becoming so good at veiled threats, I suggested obliquely that I had no interest in doing any work right now, outside my story. Furious, he dismissed me for the day. I returned home gratefully.

Rohil dropped by in the evening. We sat in the garden with Shweta, who was quite rejuvenated in his company. He kept her well entertained through dinner, knowing instinctively that I was just not there. Then he carried her back to her bed. He told me she gave him the most dazzling smile he had ever seen on a human face.

We snatched a few private moments in the study. It was not Goa, but it would have to do. If good sex is a foundation for a good relationship we were off to a great start. In the balcony of my room later, I told Rohil about my upcoming rendezvous with Pranay.

If only I had known what would follow, I would have clammed up. To my great astonishment, Rohil became terribly angry. 'My goodness, Poorva! Now you are actually planning to break into someone's office. That's what it is virtually, you know. It's downright illegal, apart from being immoral. I'm, well, I'm shocked!'

So was I. I had just not looked at it in such black and white terms before. I had thought I was doing my job. And extraordinarily well. I had cleverly omitted to mention it to Anna last night. Otherwise I may have got a similar reaction sooner. I retreated from Rohil, stunned at the way his demeanour had changed. His good-natured, open face had shut down. His usual relaxed posture was strange, stiff. I had not seen him this way before. Perhaps, I later realized, I had not really looked at him before.

I stood for a minute in front of the full-length mirror. There was both darkness and light. Shweta always slept with the night bulb on. Something was bothering me. Something told me I used to have a conscience. Something asked me where it had gone.

I tried to argue with Rohil about the high morality of my intentions. But I sensed he would not yield. Rohil was easygoing enough to allow me to dominate the relationship. He did not mind taking a backseat to my work. But he was no pushover.

'Rubbish,' he said after about two and a half minutes of listening to my argument. 'That's what they all say: the end justifies the means. Just how does all this make you different from Anshul? You are a journalist. Your job is to report things as they are, as you find them. Not to suppress information for a later, larger picture, assuming it's really there!'

I heard him, but in a remote kind of way. Like Anshul, I wanted to keep aside my spectacles right now, not see things quite so clearly. I had nothing to say to Rohil just then. He looked quite shattered at my silence, my apparent lack of remorse. We stood there, inches away, miles apart. Muttering a goodbye, he turned away from me. And left. I did not stop him. I could not.

THIRTY-ONE

There was only one person besides Pranay and me at the cybercafe at 8.15 p.m. that night. Whoever he was, he looked like a respectable bureaucrat, maybe from the Bangalore City Corporation. He was small, even mouse-like. His spectacles glinted in the eerie light of the monitor before him. Pranay told me, rather reverentially, that he was the best brain in software systems design, ever. He was doing some complicated research for a project he was developing. He was the future, Pranay said, and he did not want to share his vision. Quite sold on such a fashionable idea, Pranay allowed him to sit there at night.

Although I was the driver of this whole murky enterprise, I am still not sure exactly how we finally got inside India Biotech's computer systems. I know it took us two hours. I know I had to supply strange information to Pranay like the spellings of Anshul and Surabhi's names, forwards, backwards, every which way. Apparently, we had found a user ID for Anshul. We needed a password. He told me, if we couldn't get in that night, I'd have to return armed with information like their birthdays, parent's names, dogs' names if any, car numbers and such like.

'Most people use some personal password which is actually very simple and very much related to their day-today life. Stands to reason. Otherwise they themselves may forget it, you see. By far the most common password is "password" itself but your Anshul is not quite so predictable.'

He was not my Anshul but I let it pass. Still, I doubted very much if I could just call up Surabhi and ask her the name of her dog! I might as well ask for her password! But I held my tongue. On a hunch, I suggested we look for another user within India Biotech. Tushar! His name naturally followed the idea. Financial whiz-kid and my school classmate. I even knew his sister's name!

We got lucky. Tushar, no doubt quite innocent of our— I mean my—intentions, had not bothered to keep a very difficult password. Sridhar was his father's name. He called himself S Tushar. On the third try, we got in.

I was suddenly staring at Tushar's personal directory. I scrolled down the file names. 'Biogene.doc' jumped out at me. I double clicked. Pranay, after doing a little victory dance, had gone downstairs to get us coffee.

I sucked in my breath when the document came up. It was a letter to the Fund Manager at Biogene expressing deep regret that he had refused India Biotech's request for continued funds as per the original contract.

> We seriously ask you to reconsider your decision. We have not violated any of the conditions of our contract. We have enclosed all the relevant documents for your perusal. Also included are explanations of the three clinical cases which you had brought up in our previous correspondence.

The letter was signed by Tushar himself, as Director, Finance, India Biotech Pvt Ltd.

That information was not new. But seeing it on paper made me feel uneasy. I kept looking around, as though someone would pop up behind me. Maybe club me on the head. I couldn't remember the last time I had felt so guilty.

Except when I had realized that Shweta had received the hand-me-down gene, and not I.

I exited the file. Scrolled down the directory again. I opened a few irrelevant files and closed them quickly. One was a really personal letter from Tushar to what must have been a female interest. I started to read it without really registering anything. Once I did, I closed it. It was hot stuff. Funny. Some people, I guessed, could write better than they spoke. Otherwise, I thought, remembering Rohil, there would be no need for those words. Towards the end, I found an entry which said 'sushruta.doc'. I remembered Anshul's anecdote about the ancient group of roving doctors. Maybe India Biotech had chanced upon some fusty old secret herbal remedy! I casually opened the file, still a little embarrassed by my previous gaffe. It was a letter.

To
Mr Sanjay Kumar
Managing Director
Sushruta Healthcare India Ltd
Ref 110 05468

Dear Mr Kumar,
    We are very happy to note that your Board of Directors has approved the proposal to fund our FRP-41 contraceptive vaccine project. The additional information you had requested, giving details of cost analysis and funding flows, are included with this letter.
    There is some concern that your company has expressed about Clause B (ii) in the initial draft of the contract on royalties. We have made a note of your suggestion.

There was more. But my jaw had dropped so far that I could not see beyond those lines. 'Prannnaaayyyyy!' I yelled, making the software expert leap. I had to calm him with an inane smile. Pranay came tearing back. I showed him the screen tremulously.

'Good,' he said. I don't think he got the full impact. But he was concerned about something else. 'Hurry up and get out quickly now, for God's sake. You can't dawdle in there. Someone may trace you. It's dangerous.'

Sobering, I made quick notes. I wanted to print out the document. But Pranay said no. He pointed to the other man. I nodded in impatient understanding.

We quickly exited the India Biotech system. I thanked my partner in crime before disappearing into the night. Pranay had warned me that he would only risk doing this sort of thing one more time.

THIRTY-TWO

I was up bright and early the next morning, ready to perform an edited version of my yoga routine. I bugged Laxmi to give me an instant breakfast and left for work even before Shweta was up. I had pushed Rohil resolutely out of my mind. It left a yawning space which I plugged with a different passion—work. I felt strangely energized. Sushruta Healthcare India Ltd. It sounded familiar. But I could not pin down why it had been in the news recently.

I waved cheerfully at CP, who himself was in on time, for a change. He looked at me frostily. I caught Mrs Guntur as she was on her way in to the library.

'My goodness, we are in a great hurry today,' she tinkled. I egged her on. Within minutes, I was looking at newspaper clippings on Sushruta. Then I remembered. Less than a year ago, Sushruta had created advertising history with a big splash over their initial public offering. It was the first time television had been used for raising public money. Sushruta had been pictured as nothing short of representing the culled wisdom of ancient Indian medicine. In newspaper ads, on TV, on hoardings, its founder, old man TK Kumar was seen draped in rishi garb as he exhorted investors to help India bring back its glorious past, at least in healthcare.

It must have worked. The newspapers informed me that

Sushruta had collected rupees sixty-two crore, and that the issue had been oversubscribed ten times! Apparently, the old man himself was only functioning as Chairman Emeritus of the publicly held company. His two sons, Sanjay Kumar—of the letter I had read—and Sunil Kumar held the reins. Of the two, economic editors seemed to suggest that Sanjay Kumar, a graduate of the Kellogg Management School in Chicago, was more mature. He was the Managing Director of the company.

Well then, I would have to meet him. But first, I had to go to my favourite source for business backgrounders.

Samir Narayan, Harvard MBA, thinks, walks and eats finance. It has made him fat. Both in the flesh and in his pocket. He used to work for Peregrine, then figured he would create the next Peregrine himself. Right here in India. So he set up Integral Finance. Turns out he was just in time. Peregrine got into fatal trouble soon after he left. I am told his company has six branches in India and a couple in Europe and America. He is giving the bigger financial services firms an allergy to Integral. I love success stories like that.

'Long time, long time,' he reached out two plump hands to enclose mine. It was difficult, since he had one of the largest desks I had ever seen. I was almost pulled off my feet.

As soon as I had settled, a discreet lady brought in fresh lemon juice and salted pistas in a silver bowl. Samir does things in style.

I asked after his six-month-old baby girl, Namrata. 'Complete' men in the nineties have developed an obsession for doting fatherhood. He launched into an account of crawling prowess, gurgling abilities and nutritional problems. It is the one and only time I have ever seen him animated about anything other than money transactions. I listened haplessly, till he had worn himself down.

'Sushruta Healthcare,' I said when he asked who I wanted to pry on this time.

'Ah! TKK! Old man belonged to the old school. Good company, solid product base, excellent results, profitability averaging twenty per cent, which is very high for the industry. Terrific investments in R&D. Pity he retired. Had health problems, I believe. It was not publicized. Bad for the image, you see.'

It took me a while to digest that. I almost forgot what I wanted to know.

'On what grounds, exactly, did Sushruta raise rupees sixty-two crore last year?'

'Let me think.' He lit a cigarette. Smokers always claim it jogs their brain cells.

'Haan, yes,' he said, arriving at instant nirvana. 'You see, they already have two or three best-sellers which have kept them going for many years. Over-the-counter stuff. You know . . . Shakti pain balm, Shakti vaporub and I think, Super Shakti skin cream. But the way the industry is going, it was not going to be enough. The products had matured. You know, TKK's two boys have taken over. I think they realized they had to think big. They sold the idea to the public that they needed the money to invest in R&D. Primarily to develop some revolutionary ayurvedic product that they were planning to introduce . . .'

'But that's vapourware, Samir! Do people invest money in just an idea?'

'My dear girl, you can raise a golden edifice on a successful idea. I call it idea equity. It has to be developed, like brand equity. Over the years, Sushruta has regularly brought out new—and successful—products. There's no reason for people to mistrust them, though the mettle of the sons is untested.'

'Is there so much money out there, then?'

'Well, the primary markets have taken a beating recently, with all the scams that have surfaced. Come to think of it, Sushruta was among the last big issues that were so well received before all the scandals scared away the investors.'

179

'Okay. So what have they done with all the money?'

'Wait a sec. Let me check.' He swivelled around to his blinking computer cursor.

His fat fingers fairly flew over the keyboard. In a trice, he had the information he needed. 'H'mm!' he frowned, deep vertical lines appearing across his broad forehead. 'My fact file says that actually, nothing much. As yet. Apparently, that great ayurvedic product they had touted—a migraine remedy—has been denied patents. Some IPR, er, intellectual property rights case is in the courts. They have not announced anything more to the public.'

'Then would they be looking to invest in a near-ready product with a small start-up company?'

'Oh, that would be ideal. Several pharmaceutical companies are using those stategies around the world. They have themselves become so humungous, so sluggish, they need the infusion of fresh ideas from maverick companies. Just as it happened in the computer industry, in Silicon Valley in the eighties. I guess it's still happening. You should just see the M&A, I mean mergers and acquisitions in the industry.'

The problem with Samir was that he gave you so much strategic information, it left you too dazzled to keep your focus. His mind was just like his computer. Always on-line.

Still, I had what I needed. Samir and I have a pact. He never asks me exactly what I need the information for. In exchange, I give him little pieces of information as they come my way. Once in a while, he comes home for dinner with his lively wife, Varuni, to eat crabs Mangalore style. It's a good deal for me, since I don't have to cook them.

THIRTY-THREE

Sushruta Healthcare Ltd was on Bellary Road. Thankfully, Samir's office had been in the same general direction. Without making any appointments, I just took an autorickshaw and went across. A few damaged vertebrae in the potholed ride were not too high a price for a good cause.

I handed over my card to the smiling receptionist. She made me wait amidst fresh flowers of all hues. A few quick, though muted conversations later, she told me, still smiling, that Mr Sanjay Kumar was very busy today. Could I please make an appointment for next week? He would be happy to see me then.

I asked if I could send in a note. I said it was something Mr Sanjay Kumar would be very interested in. Ms Smiley hesitated, her facial expression changing. Then she spoke into the telephone again. Her smile came back, as though it was too much of a strain to withold it. I took the paper she gave me and scribbled a few words. 'Exactly how much money are you going to put into India Biotech?'

They escorted me down a short hallway to the MD's office. Sanjay Kumar was at his desk, on the telephone. I noticed the gold pen clipped onto the pocket of his button-down light blue Oxford shirt. He had a red tie on. His jacket rested behind him on a swivel chair. As I walked into the room, he looked me up and down insolently. Men do that if they want an advantage. Actually, men do that anyway. I was wearing a simple white churidar-kurta with a large orange dupatta. Nothing much to see.

'I'll call you back,' he said to whoever. Then he stared at me. I stared back. I did not have much to lose. Finally, he blinked.

'Please sit down, Ms . . .' he looked at my card, 'Poorva Pandit.'

'Thank you.'

'I was just speaking to Dr Anshul Hiremath. He told me quite a lot about you.'

'Good things, I hope. Since he knows me so well.' Coy, that was me.

He looked displeased. 'I'm sure you know exactly what he said. Tell me, how did you find out about Sushruta's interest in India Biotech? Anshul said he certainly hadn't told you.'

Journalists get to ask questions. They are not bound to answer them. I know my rights.

'Strategically speaking, Mr Kumar, it makes good business sense for Sushruta Healthcare to fund India Biotech. Especially after the IPR problems you had to face recently. Do you feel confident that the contraceptive vaccine they are developing will be market-ready soon?'

He stared at me again. What could I do? I stared back. This interview, I thought inwardly, was going to take a long time.

Just then, a gentleman burst through the door. He was short, dark, his straight black hair flopped around his face. But there was a strong family resemblance to the curly-haired man in front of me.

'Sanjay, this information has just come in . . .' he was saying as he rushed up.

He saw me, looked at his brother, question-marked his

eyebrows. His brother's glance contained some elaborate messages. He hid the papers he was holding behind his back. It was quite amusing.

'Sunil, this is Poorva Pandit of *Deadline* magazine. Apparently, she has been at Anshul Hiremath's heels for a long time. She appears to know about our involvement with him.'

'Great!' said the brother quite confusingly. 'We need to have the press on our side. Especially such a charming representative.'

He took a seat, closer to my side of the table than his brother's. 'What do you want to know, Ms . . . was it Poorva?'

Sanjay may be the 'mature' MD of Sushruta, but I thought the brains were with this younger brother. I respected his attitude.

'How much money will you be investing in the company, Mr Sunil? How confident are you that the vaccine will get all the clearances required before it can go to the market?'

'We're negotiating the exact sum, but it is at least rupees ten crore. As far as the vaccine is concerned,' and he glanced at a stone-like Sanjay Kumar, 'we have every reason to believe it will receive clearances shortly.'

'How will Sushruta benefit financially from investing in the vaccine?'

'Come on, Ms Pandit,' smiled Mr Sunil, warmly. 'Surely you don't expect me to provide you with details of our contract. Rest assured, we hope to recover our money. We see it as a sound investment obviously, an early edge into a new technology with a huge market.'

It seemed like a high-risk strategy. But the rewards would be higher. If there were any. Nothing ventured . . . said my conscience.

'Why have Dr Hiremath's previous sponsors dropped out at this stage?'

'Oh, I think we can answer that. I believe the project

went way over budget and time allocations. India Biotech's previous sponsors are bound by certain rules and laws that apply to their funding activities. They had to refuse an extension.'

No mention of any irregularities. Either Anshul was a competent liar, or Sunil was. Maybe Anshul had convinced Sushruta that the problems would soon go away.

'Would Biogene gift away a potential golden goose?'

'No, not at all. They are very clever.' Did he sound bitter? 'They have retained certain privileges on the product on account of their initial support. They are also well linked to some drug companies in the US. They plan to come even in the deal.'

'Are you aware of the problems that have arisen during the clinical trials at MR Hills?'

'Naturally, Ms Pandit. We have gone over every detail with a fine-tooth comb, I assure you. We see no insurmountable problem at all.' My God, the man was smooth. Even Mr Sanjay Kumar seemed impressed.

I, on the other hand, was disarmed. I thanked him for his time. I should have asked a million questions more, aired many suspicions. That was mere hindsight though.

'Not at all. Please feel free to call me anytime.' Another card, another interviewee, just another day.

I called Anna at work from an STD booth.

'My God, Poorva. You were right. It seems Jimmy Kakodia has gone on long leave suddenly. Out of the country. Rumours are flying thick and fast this morning. The latest one I heard was about a FERA violation investigation!'

'Then Anshul will be in trouble, too!'

'Maybe, maybe not. I doubt if he would leave a trail.'

So that left only the question of *who* had ratted on Kakodia.

THIRTY-FOUR

CP was hopping up and down impatiently by the time I got to the office. He gets like that when things are not going his way. But this time he was worse than usual.

'What on earth have you been up to? You sure have ruffled a lot of fine feathers this time.'

He sounded Dickensian. Comes of reading literature at Indian universities. Of course, I had no clue what he was talking about. So my innocent look was real.

'Avaru called me. He wants to see us. Apparently, he's been getting calls from people, yes, about your using threats to extract information. Have you gone out of your mind?'

I did feel a little out of it then. Who could bother to put pressure on the old man about me? Anshul? Kakodia? Or . . . Ah yes! I felt elated—Anshul's daddy!

I told CP of my suspicions, mixing up all the chronological details on my story, leaving him rather confused. He cut me off. 'Give me the details later. Avaru wants to see us both right now. Let's get that over with.' And with very curious eyes following all the way, we took the lift to Mr Heggade's seventh-floor offices.

I had been there once before. But it had obviously been renovated since then. Even so, it still looked large, old-fashioned and spartan. Only one incongruous feature struck the visitor immediately. The inescapable picture of his grandfather, usually garlanded, seemed to have recently yielded the prime spot behind his desk. To an original Hussain! It was a colourful impression from the artist of film star Madhuri Dixit. I gaped. Who would have suspected it? Mr Heggade, editor-in-chief, Heggade publications, a secret fan of La Dixit? Or just of Hussain? *Dil to Pagal Hai*. Avaru drew himself up in his chair, drawing my attention back to him. He looked much the same since I'd last seen him, a timeless sixty-eight.

'Sit down, CP,' he said, and indicated for me the chair alongside. 'Coffee?' I couldn't remember when I'd last eaten anything. 'Yes, please,' I said, quickly. Three cups of steaming steel came even more quickly. Fragrance. And copper bases. Quite chic.

The old man got right down to it. 'CP had told me about the leads you had got on the story about India Biotech. I believe he has given you extra time for this special assignment, leaving you to your own devices, for what, more than a month now? I would not have interfered, normally. Your work has been satisfactory.' I felt like a ninth grader in front of a principal. I adjusted my body language, to get back some control.

'However, it has been brought to my notice that you, er, are using, how to say it, extremely . . . unconventional methods to get your information. At this rate, Poorva, I may have to request you to drop your investigation. I do not want this publishing house to be facing the wrath of the courts.'

'But sir, I was only . . .'

He held up his hands. 'Let me finish,' he said, stentoriously. I quietened.

'I don't know if you are aware of this, Poorva. I believe the vaccine being developed by India Biotech is competing with an international product which is very similar. My source said the two were neck and neck. I also believe that if successful, this vaccine will make a significant contribution to India's market share in pharmaceutical goods. At this juncture, if anything unsavoury comes out without good cause, maybe as speculation, it will irreparably damage the prospects of the Indian vaccine.'

I thought rapidly. It was no use challenging the pseudo-nationalist argument. Indian businessmen are so used to being protected by the government, they feel very, very indignant when competition is allowed in. They cry for level playing fields. They form clubby groups to influence the government. GD Heggade, our Avaru, is nothing if not an Indian businessman.

It was even less use trying to convince Avaru that I was not speculating, that I had enough evidence about malpractice in the clinical trials. He had obviously been well tutored on the subject by some influential informant. There was only one way out.

'Precisely, sir. With due respect, I am very much aware that an improperly researched story could cause unnecessary harm to some potentially innocent people. That is why I have been asking CP to give me more time on this assignment, sir. There may be much more to this than meets the eye.' I leaned forward over the desk, my eyes almost pooling. 'Especially now that there are international players involved.'

CP looked at me with such cynicism on his face that I had to quickly look away. But Mr Heggade looked rather pleased. He had warded off any immediate article on the subject. He could return to his informant with ease, maybe even chalk up an obligation against him.

We then spoke in very general terms about the India Biotech vaccine. CP agreed that I should be left alone a little longer. I agreed that I would not use any underhand means to get information. Avaru agreed that I could publish the story once it was wrapped up. And once he had okayed it.

CP gave me several pieces of his mind on the way back. He said he objected to being manipulated. He suggested my brain had become addled in the accident. He added, rather sarcastically, that when my great work was finally published, he hoped it was worth all that I had put my conscience to.

I satisfied Meenal's curiosity partly before I left for the day. I saw something very genuine in her eyes. 'Be careful, Poo,' she said.

On my way out of the building, I saw one of the boys in the printing section. He has lovely brown hair. That day, it reminded me of someone else. A shaft of pain flashed through me. A whole elevator of memories and regrets rode up and down, leaving me transfixed. Maybe Rohil had been right. I was losing my perspective. Maybe I should call him, beg forgiveness, promise to be good forever. Because it did not seem as if Rohil had any plans to call me.

THIRTY-FIVE

Shweta was miffed with me. She felt left out of my life. And she was frank enough to admit it. I told her about my research. She showed me her poem for Keti. It was very touching.

> When the hills will not speak
> And the wind will not leave
> When the clouds will not rain
> And the women will not grieve
> Then I shall walk, in pain and in hope.
> Then I shall talk, of chains and of ropes.
> —Shweta Pandit.

I took a copy of the precocious piece. I decided, there and then, that I would make my next trip to the MR Hills in a couple of days. I put balm over Shweta's wounds, asked her to pray for me. She felt better at the end of it, I think. But only a little.

Anna brought home the news about Sushruta soon enough. He said industry rumours put the MD of the company, Sanjay, down as highly motivated. 'There was a suggestion that he would look the other way if it suited the company's interest. One of the reasons, apparently, why he has been dragged to court by a competitor.'

That would explain, I thought, why India Biotech and Sushruta Healthcare were so quickly drawn to each other in a crisis largely of Anshul's making.

I filled Anna in on what I had learnt. He said he had never seen me so focussed on a story before. Amma was with us when he said that. She raised her head and caught my eye. 'Poorva, I want you to examine your motives carefully. There's something here which is worrying me.' I gave her a rare hug. 'I'll do that, Amma. Please don't worry.'

Vikram, over the phone, told me that the India Biotech team had confirmed that the foetus he had found was Shaivi's baby. She was one of the early volunteers for India Biotech. They had told her that the pregnancy was a mistake, nothing to worry about. She had been compensated financially. She had continued in the programme and was not unhappy.

'But who planted the foetus in your office? And why?'

'Unfortunately, we haven't found out yet.'

I told him I was hoping to come over in a couple of days. He said it would be no problem.

Dr Judith Ferraro called from Bangalore. It took a while to place her. Then I was genuinely glad to hear her cheerful voice. She said she had been left to her own devices by her friend, Dr Michael Frampton, who was involved in some dealings with the government and NGOs on AIDS matters. I invited her home to lunch.

Shweta had a holiday. It was Janmashtami. My life had become so unreal that I had not noticed. We were vegetarian that day, as I had to explain to Judith who came armed with books for the whole family. When she met Laxmi, she gave her a 14 kt gold chain. Laxmi, ever graceful, accepted it with dignity and joy.

'My digestive tract needs a break anyway,' she laughed. When she saw the spread on the table, fluffy rice preparations, buttery sweets for the birthday celebration of Krishna, curries in coconut milk, sprouts, she exclaimed in mock horror. Shweta found her very funny.

After lunch, I took her shopping to the old parts of Bangalore, where the silk trade still flourishes. She gripped the sides of her seat and applied imaginary brakes all along the small bylanes that we rumbled through. Her face was the picture of frozen terror you see on roller coaster rides. Safe in the shop, we revived her with coffee. We selected scarves and handbags, cushion covers and quilts. She was like a teenager, all excited when choosing a silk tie for Michael. I enjoyed the break from my routine of the past few days.

We talked, on the way back to her hotel, of my work. I figured it would do no harm to tell her what I was researching at the moment.

'That reminds me,' she said. 'Michael shed more light on the vaccine that's being developed. It uses an antigen raised from the human egg lining. Trials are still on. In Venezuela and Costa Rica.' Not in Venice or Copenhagen. Naturally, I thought to myself, but I thought I saw a flicker of recognition in her eyes.

'Their most recent breakthrough, Michael says, and one of his good friends is actually working on the project in New York, is that they have arrived at a formula to make a synthetic antigen.' Something began to nag at me. There was an old connection here. It look long seconds to recognize information. Anshul's presentation in Goa! The so-called secret he'd shared with the audience—that India Biotech had developed a synthetic antigen. It was then that Dr Kerring had rushed out to make a call.

No wonder! His New York team was also in the same race.

I remembered Anshul telling me how difficult and expensive it was to mass produce the peptide for his vaccine. If a synthetic version replaced it, would it reduce costs? Crunch the time required to bring out the vaccine? Make the vaccine more reliable? He had said the natural antigen was difficult to breed, difficult to predict. Would the synthetic replacement improve his chances in the market? I asked Judith about it.

'Oh, dramatically, I should think,' she said. 'Also, the synthetic antigen, I assume, would be more stable, less prone to damage and destruction with small variables of temperature. It would be a tremendous breakthrough.' Dr Kerring's agitation now seemed justified. The competition was hotting up.

I asked her if she would please, please find out the name and telephone number of Michael's friend in New York. She looked surprised at my greedy fervour, but agreed. We exchanged fond goodbyes, both promising to look each other up again, somewhere.

I fixed up to meet Tushar Sridhar, Finance Director, India Biotech, at 7.30 p.m. at the Black Stallion, arguably the pubcity's most popular evening hangout.

He was dressed very nattily, checked shirt, slim-cut trousers and suspenders! I love them on men, they define a good backside so well. I did not have much of an opportunity to examine Tushar's that night. He was there before me, and we were face-to-face throughout.

I was able to determine quickly that he had not been warned off me. I thought it a little sloppy on Anshul's part. More so on Surabhi's. But maybe I was not as much of an obsession, or even a threat to them as I imagined.

We had to talk of schooldays, of course. As the draught beer loosened him up, Tushar recounted hilarious stories about the boys in our class. He told me, rather slyly, that I was the object of many a fantasy. I was sipping very slowly, so I didn't believe him.

After a pitcher had been downed, I brought up India Biotech. Tushar told me he'd been with the firm since the beginning, two and a half years ago, when they were looking for a place to set up. 'Can't say I've regretted it. But maybe I could move on, soon.'

I asked whether there was enough challenge for him, in a small firm like that.

'Oh, it has its plus points. I have complete freedom. I feel part of a successful enterprise. I get to manage a fair amount of money.'

'The Biogene Research Foundation grant was quite a substantial sum, I'm told.' Nobody had told me, actually.

'The project required it. Our set-up costs were very high.'

'Anshul said BRF's pulled out. Lucky you found a new sponsor.'

'Yes. That fellow moves like lightning, you've got to hand it to him.'

'For Sushruta, it seems a perfect opportunity to fulfil their ambitious projections for the next few years.'

'You bet. They've got Anshul into a fair corner. Great deal they have for themselves. Exclusive marketing rights, split royalties, the works. That Sunil-Sanjay duo can be dynamite. They're also pushing the government hard.'

He showed no surprise that I knew so much. This was the company's whiz-kid?

'How on earth did Anshul find Sushruta in the nick of time?' I interjected, trying to sound admiring.

'Actually, it was they who found him. I believe they approached him with a business proposition. Something different, not about the vaccine. That's how it came about.'

What a coincidence, I thought. Or maybe it was not. Maybe Sushruta had known about BRF pulling out of India Biotech. Certainly Sunil-Sanjay sounded as if they had an ear to the ground.

Thinking back over the conversation, I wondered whether Sushruta, desperate for a market opportunity, had actually spied on Anshul. Could they have been the ones to have leaked information about Kakodia, and in fact, about Anshul's problems, to BRF?

Industrial espionage. Was I getting too fanciful? But why not? In the annals of business, no intrigue has been left untried. I decided to do some spying myself.

I changed track, temporarily.

'Anshul has lots of clout too. That helps.'

'You bet. Chandrakant Hiremath, his father, is in the cabinet secretariat. Sharp as a needle, I hear.' He chuckled. 'Clever fellows. They're promoting the vaccine as India's answer to everything short of the space shuttle.' Chandrakant Hiremath. Sometime, I would have to follow this new angle. But later. First, I still had to know how much Tushar knew about the problems in the vaccine's field trials.

'But is the product itself foolproof? Unless its efficacy and safety are quite established, it may backfire badly.'

Maybe Tushar realized he had gone far enough already. He started to back off. 'Of course, you are right. But Anshul has been very confident all these months. There have been some setbacks, especially recently. But that's to be expected.'

I thought of setbacks like Madhamma and Ketamma and Shaivi. The 'you can't make an omelette without breaking a few eggs' theorists would surely disregard them.

THIRTY-SIX

Judith had left a message for me. 'Dr Stephen Jacowski. Fellow, Columbia College of Medicine. Tel: 212 568 4035. Good luck!' God bless her. May she have more romances than she can handle.

Calling the US would be expensive. I could hardly bill it to CP. I asked Anna if he felt like footing the bill. He said yes, in lieu of my next birthday present. He also told me, incidentally, that my car would be delivered in a day or two. My car! I had quite forgotten about it. Maybe I could take it to MR Hills.

Then, my fingers shaking, I dialled Rohil. He was cool. Polite.

'How's it going?' he asked.

'Slow. Frustrating.'

'Dr Shaila, you know, my HOD? She finally brought up the Anshul subject. She said she has been hired to do some cross-checking of medical reports from his first phase trials. I have asked her to keep me informed. She doesn't know about you.'

I was awfully grateful. A powerful surge of feeling for him coursed through me.

'I appreciate it, Rohil. And Rohil, I miss you very badly.'

A few seconds passed. 'I miss you too, Poorva. But I

have to sort out a couple of things, okay? In my own mind. But I'll call you soon.'

Slightly relieved, I turned to my next task. I had to activate ISD on my telephone. I looked at the clock. It would be night time in New York. I did not know if the number was residential. No harm in giving it a try.

I think I got his wife. She yelled, 'Stephen!' over a muffled receiver. Precious seconds passed. 'Dr Jacowski here.'

I told him I was a journalist doing a story on international developments in contraception for a national newsmagazine. I told him I had met Dr Frampton. That he had given me the number. I mentioned Judith. I think that helped a lot. Like me, he was obviously very fond of her. I asked about the vaccine. And then I asked him about the synthetic peptide. He confirmed Judith's report just like that.

'It sounds like an important breakthrough, Dr Jacowski,' I said.

'Yes, we are really excited. I believe we can put out the product sooner than we expected.'

I asked him if he could send me some details that I could write about. He said it should not be a problem. It would also be posted on the Net soon. Not the exact details, of course. But enough. I marvelled at his openness. In India, no scientist will talk to you about anything, not even his latest foldable umbrella design, over the telephone. Americans thrive on publicity, manipulating the media to their benefit. And they are not afraid to make mistakes. He asked me if I was on the Internet. I regretfully said I did not have a personal ID yet. But he gave me his e-mail address. I told him I'd be in touch, thanked him and signed off. I would have to bother Pranay again soon.

I called CP at home. He must have been cursing his poor judgement in hiring me, four years ago. He asked, 'Now what?' in a voice reserved for fledgling trainees. I told him I was calling him to say goodbye. That I was returning to the hills. 'We'll send out the warning to Murugan,' he said. I don't think he was being sarcastic.

My car did not arrive before I left for MR Hills the next morning. I had to rent a taxi. It's lucky I have some savings tucked away. It helps to live in your parents' home at twenty-eight. They sort of pay your food bills. Still, maybe I could collect the money from *Deadline* later. If it all worked out.

I had touched base with Anshul. He was scheduled to return from MR Hills the previous night. So I called him early in the morning. His residence number was listed. He sounded sleepy and then shocked that I could intrude on his home life. I told him I knew about the Benden-Fromm vaccine and about the synthetic antigen. I don't know if he registered the news. His irritation with me was paramount.

'What the hell is your interest in all this, Poorva? Is it just for an article? That's really hard to believe.' I tried to convince him, but with little success.

'Anyway, did you get the analysis of your previous stock of antigen from Transpharma?'

He got quite distracted. 'Yes, now that you ask. There were no irregularities. The potency and stability were all right. Which means the problem lies somewhere else altogether. It's quite unsettling.'

'Have you developed your synthetic antigen yet?' I asked, changing the subject.

His voice got testier, 'No, that's dead-ended. For now.'

Advantage: New York team. 'We have been unlucky. Though we came damn close. Now you say they have confirmed that they have done it? Benden-Fromm?' He cursed large bits of the universe.

It was ironic. I was supplying information to Anshul about his competitors. If it helped me to ensnare him, so much the better. The word 'ensnare' sounded a bit much, even to me. When I hung up, I could hear the gears in Anshul's mind shifting, clanking. I did not bother to tell him that I was going to pay a quick and dirty visit to his precious research station at MR Hills.

On the way up to the hills, I remembered my promise to Amma. Five hours was plenty for soul-searching. What did I want? Fame? Glory? Justice? Answer, I told myself sternly.

I wanted a little bit of all three, I guessed. But somehow, I felt more like a child determined to finish a jigsaw puzzle. Shweta's illness has had a dramatic impact on my life. I feel impotent about it. If I could somehow string all the threads of this story together and coil it into a knot, maybe, maybe, I would get some peace. Or, said a very, very small whisper, revenge.

THIRTY-SEVEN

In spite of everything, it felt good to be back at the Baniga Kalyan Kendra. The air was like fresh, pure ghee, soft and fragrant. Familiar faces smiled at me. I grinned back. Dr Vikram was in his clinic. I decided not to disturb him. Chamla found out I was there. He managed to escape his duties to come talk to me. I gave him the T-shirts I had brought for him. He grinned shyly.

I asked him about the mood at the Baniga Shakti Sanghatana camp. He said his cousins had told him that things were a bit tense. Ketamma's pregnancy was making people uneasy. The police had been snooping around too, trying to find out about the foetus. I asked if the trials were continuing. He didn't know about that. I asked him if he would accompany me to the research station again. He was rather excited and scuttled off to inform Dr Vikram that we were leaving.

I went directly to the research station. There would be time later for Keti.

If anything, India Biotech looked even less occupied than before. This time, it took even longer for the door to be answered. There was good reason. Dr Rita was not around. That was a great pity. I had hoped to pump her for a whole lot of information about her boss and mentor. I had also brought along a gift for the Running Doctor. It was a jogger's water bottle, shaped, rather fortuitously, like a syringe.

Hiding my disappointment, I asked to see Sadanand, the friendly microbiologist. I was taken to his lab. He was at a desk, making notations of some kind. His long legs emerged from the other side, the mud-packed slippers probably a size eleven. Behind him, the laboratory looked as if it was very much in use. Maybe the trials had not stopped after all.

He was not his earlier smiling self. He barely looked up at me. I asked him how Anshul's visit had gone. He gave a monosyllabic answer. I asked if Dr Rita had returned to Bangalore. He said no, she was in the USA, because her sister who lived there had taken critically ill. He seemed to suggest people should time their sicknesses better.

I changed direction, began to ask him about himself. Whether he had to be away from his family, up here at the station. Whether the work was satisfying. Just things that we all love to pour into a sympathetic ear. He said his wife and his newborn baby, 'a boy, nine pounds', were in Mysore. With her parents. I congratulated him, asked when he'd been there last. He would have been there right now, he replied wistfully. Except that Dr Rita had been called away to New York. For the second time, he said, in less than two months. Her sister had advanced cancer, it seemed.

That explained why Sadanand could not get his smile in place. We talked a bit about his family. Only later, I gently brought up the baby-in-a-jar business. He shook his head, looking into the distance.

'It made no sense at all. First, when it disappeared from our lab. We were doing a routine examination, you know. Looking for the presence of the antigen, to see if it had synthesized with some protein in the baby's body somehow, leading to a problem with the formation of the embryo. Crazily enough, it disappeared before we could make the final tests. Even worse, it appeared at Dr Vikram's office!

And now the police have been acting as if we are murderers.'
He lifted his arm to his head, scratching his hair in a clumsy
way.

I pictured the situation. A local policeman, completely
unappreciative of scientific methodologies. A non-local
scientist, using jargon. A local baby, dead, bottled. Not
conducive to happy endings.

I asked about Dr Rita. I praised her efficiency, her
apparent dedication. I asked if he had worked on all the
reports with her. I did not tell him that I wanted to know
if he was aware that Anshul and Rita had conspired to
keep information from BRF.

He did not answer immediately. 'Dr Rita, she is a
perfectionist. She does not like to delegate. She prefers to
do it all herself. She often works all night, long after we
have gone.'

I knew the type. Workaholics. They couldn't trust
anybody but themselves. It made juniors feel redundant.
Poor Sadanand.

I asked about Rita's qualifications, her educational
background.

'She is extremely professional. Brilliant, even. She has
an enormous capacity to learn and tremendous patience.'

His face had come alive in admiration. If there were to
be an election for President, Dr Rita Fan Club, it would be
a no-contest!

'She was trained in the US, you know. She has an MD
in clinical pharmacology. She was working there at a biotech
laboratory. That's where Dr Hiremath met her.'

I asked Sadanand why Dr Rita had not married. For the
first time, the corners of his mouth lifted a little.

'It is hard to imagine her married. "I'm wedded to my
research," she says.'

I marvelled at Anshul's ability to get people to slave for
him! But how much did the brilliant Dr Rita know about
his doings?

I asked about the tribal women. Whether they were suspicious of the researchers, especially after Keti's refusal to abort. He exclaimed in surprise that I knew about it.

After that he really relaxed with me, I could feel the change. Must have thought, hell, what difference does it make?

'For the first time since we came here,' he confessed, 'I am feeling a little nervous. Everyone is looking for a scapegoat. Because of that . . . that er, conceptus. Because of that mad Keti and her baby. You know, that baby should have been rejected. There should have been a spontaneous abortion. We had a couple of those. But this damn baby is growing as though it has every intention of living a long life. Dr Padma, the visiting gynaecologist from Maddur, does not know what to do.'

I thought over his words. 'That mad Keti.' So typical of his ilk. Turning victims into perpetrators, especially if they were women.

'Maybe it will come out normal after all.'

He looked at me pityingly. 'The amniocentesis test, the one and only one we could get that lunatic to do, reveals severe brain damage. The physical damage is irrelevant in comparison.'

I felt panicky, light-headed. I asked for water.

'Is it because the vaccine, the antigen is faulty, Sadanand?'

He considered my question carefully. His loyalties were in conflict. Anshul, I thought idly, at work again.

'But that's it,' he said finally, literally wringing his hands. 'There is no clear pattern to suggest that the vaccine does not work.'

'How do you mean?'

'Well, our antibody levels in ninety-four per cent of the women showed contraceptive adequacy. Consistently. Month after month. We have raised our antibody efficacy to six months in our third batch of vaccines. There are forty-eight women right here,' he pointed in the direction of the tribal settlement, 'who are enjoying carefree contraception. Who have had almost no adverse reactions. Our tabulations would have looked excellent. Except . . .'

'But isn't that precisely the point? That adverse reactions can show up in only one out of ten thousand cases?'

'Yes, but Dr Rita and I struggled over the reports. We juggled the statistics every way we could think of. We found no pattern, no causative indicators. We looked at inherited traits in the three women here who conceived malformed foetuses. There is nothing in their history. The antigen dosages we gave have been meticulously recorded. Now even the Xyler test, which we got done on the antigen to see if the batch was sub-standard, has come out clean.'

He proceeded to inundate me with technical data about why his clinical trials should have been without incident. To me, it looked rather simple. India Biotech was starting out with the assumption that their product was sound. They were now trying to build a hypothesis based on entirely extraneous factors to prove their point. I may be a graduate of literature, but I know my basics.

There was still an important question mark though. I asked Sadanand how the Drug Controller's office was about to give clearance for phase three when this very important mystery was yet to be solved. He had the grace to look ashamed.

'Actually, we, er, Dr Rita, er, we didn't think the er, three, er, case studies, were relevant to the er, tabulations.'

To er is human, but he was going too far. So, I thought, Dr Anshul, Dr Rita, Mr Sadanand and God alone knows who else, had a neat little operation going. Laundering the statistics on one end, leveraging the Drug Controller's office on the other, and a whole string of lies and pressure tactics in between. Why had Sadanand made the admission so easily? Perhaps he had classified me as 'us'. After all, I knew Anshul and Dr Rita. I knew all about Madhamma and Keti. Obviously, I was sympathetic to the cause.

'But haven't the Drug Inspectors come here? Surely they know about the deformed babies?'

'What do you mean babies? There has been only one.' He mustered up a whole lot of indignation.

Excuuusse ME! The four-month foetus, of course, doesn't count as a baby. And Keti's hadn't come yet.

Sure, the Drug Inspectors came on a regular basis, said Sadanand. They were treated royally by Anshul. They were very sympathetic to the cause of the vaccine. They quite agreed that the question of the abnormal pregnancies was due to an unrelated problem. They knew how hard Anshul was working at resolving the anomaly. They had also interviewed many of the women who were successfully using the vaccine. And at the end of it, they had been entirely satisfied. So there!

My internal temperature was rising. As journalists, we see ourselves as keepers of the nation's conscience. It is easy to get us on our high horses. Mine was whinnying tall and loud.

I asked to be shown around. I asked if I could see the consent forms signed by the tribal women. It was a measure of Sadanand's innocence that he instantly agreed. But he discovered, to his chagrin, that everything was neatly locked. And no, he did not have spare keys to those cabinets.

I had precious little to ask after that. I would have dearly liked to break into all of those cabinets, to see for myself how Anshul's records were maintained. Perhaps there were two sets of every document. One for internal use, one for the Drug Controller! Well, short of breaking and entering, I could do nothing. Rohil would have been proud that I dismissed the idea quickly. Then I remembered the synthetic antigen.

'Have you been working on developing a synthetic version of FRP-41?' I asked. The more you show you know, the more people tell you. I don't know if the journalism textbooks have incorporated that yet, but any good reporter will corroborate it.

Sadanand was not really with me anymore. Perhaps he was shaking a rattle at his two-month-old, enjoying the baby smile. In any case, I waited till he returned.

'My God, at one time we almost did not eat or drink or breathe for days, when we thought we had cracked the formula. But it turned out to be a dud. It worked only in highly specific environments.'

Pity, I thought. Otherwise, maybe they could have really raised the Indian flag.

I left Sadanand to his thoughts and his work then. He said he was just doing routine haemotological analysis of the trial samples. Double-checking computer calculations. I was impressed.

THIRTY-EIGHT

Keti looked bigger. More radiant. Didn't her hormones understand that disaster awaited? I wondered at her stoic acceptance, her cheerfulness with her children. She welcomed me into her fold, offered my raging gastric juices a calming meal of ragi mudde and saaru. I showed her Shweta's poem, translating the idea for her. I told her Shweta thought she was very brave. Keti laughed.

'Your sister, she is the one who is brave. I have seen that kind of illness-face. It cannot get well. But she smiles all the time.'

I was touched. Her husband came by just then. His name was Shiva. He sported the typical features of his kinsmen. He wore shorts and a T-shirt. He told me he made good money collecting herbs, roots and all manner of plants that grew in the forests.

'Who do you sell them to?'

'Many people come to the Sanghatana office. There are some regulars. Some of them are from abroad. Some from government institutions.'

'Do you know what they want to do with the plants?'

He shrugged. His ancestors couldn't have come from any medical vocation.

'They want to study the plants. Our soil has curative properties. Everything that grows has some use for human health. They say they will make medicines that will cure many sicknesses.'

'Are you worried that they may make a lot of money with your knowledge of plants, and your hard work?'

He shrugged again. I liked his attitude. I began to respect this man, who had become sad, not violent, about his wife's strange decision to keep an abnormal baby.

'Let them make money. We have what we need.' He cuddled his baby, giving her a smacking kiss before leaving again for work.

I asked Keti if she felt, ever, like changing her mind about the baby.

'Only once,' she said, after a long pause, while she vigorously cleaned our lunch plates. 'When they told me about the baby who had been kept in a bottle.' She looked up at me, calm as the morning sea. 'My baby will not be kept in a bottle.'

No, but her baby would probably need incubators, drips, bubble environments just to breathe. Then, special institutions to look after its growth. Sadanand had said it was a girl. I didn't dare ask if she knew that.

It was likely, of course, that her baby would come out stillborn, like Madhamma's. If it did not, it would be a colossal disaster. Here, I assumed, among these ancient, centred people, different or special human beings would be absorbed into the community. Maybe not with fairness, but certainly with compassion. But with the attention of the outside world, or representatives of it, like (I had to admit) myself . . . it would not be a natural process. It would become warped, unhappy.

But how could I offload all this on Keti? I just let it be.

I met Madhamma, who was better. She had settled with the idea that the deformity in her baby boy was not of her making. She now rested the blame squarely on the shoulders of the clinic doctors. She told me she had decided to start a crusade to stop the trials.

'It's our men who have turned the minds of the women. The investigators, they pay money if we sign our names. They give clothes, they give rations. Our people have become lazy. They want easy money. They think, somehow, that these doctors will take them to the cities. So they tell the women, go, take the injections. Why should they bother what happens inside our bodies?'

I was quite taken aback. It was a radical change from the listless woman I had met the last time around. We all need to find a purpose. I did not know whether Madhamma's new righteousness would affect India Biotech.

I also met Shaivi, who had miscarried the foetus that had become so notorious. She was remote. I did not have the heart to question her. After offloading the Santa Claus bag of goodies I had brought with me onto the children, I returned to base camp.

Dr Vikram Gopinath looked extremely tired. There had been an outbreak of amoebic dysentery. They had worried it was gastroenteritis. Even here, visitors could bring in disease. I tried to make his evening easier. I said it was make or break time for India Biotech.

'Are you, personally, against the idea of the contraceptive vaccine?'

'No, not at all.' He was surprised. 'It is a radically new concept, yes. And like all emerging concepts, it will have a turbulent period before it is accepted. Look at the IUD, the diaphragm, the pill. Every manner of danger was attributed to the use of each of them. But today, each product has found its own market, its own comfort level. No product is perfect. No product has claimed to be. The vaccine will find its place also.'

'If it gets to the market before the Benden-Fromm vaccine.'

'What?'

I realized how tangential I had become. I updated him. He wasn't overly impressed.

'An Indian product can easily tap the reserve of goodwill here, if it plays its cards well. In this era of hamburger chains, Pepsi and Coke, the time is right.'

It was such a refreshing idea, I could only blink at him.

On the spur of the moment, I decided to stop by at the police station on my way back from the hills.

It was a good fifteen kilometres away from the nearest Baniga hutments, in an emerging town called Chikkooru. After being totally misled about distance and direction, we finally drew up in front of a little bungalow that housed the lawkeepers.

The ASI was on his rounds. Only two policemen could be seen. And a couple of rifle-burdened guards.

I identified myself, flashed my press card.

'I need to see the . . .' I said, and stalled badly. I had forgotten the word for foetus in Kannada. The man in front of me looked positively mischievous as he waited for my tongue to sort itself out. The he made some officious noises about needing permission from his superiors. Since I was quite sure that the whole community had seen the specimen by now, I had no qualms in persuading him to let me do the same. He furtively gestured me into the back room.

It was suspended in a wide mouthed, dusty glass bottle with an aluminium seal. Next to some files, a couple of plaques and an ink-pad. On a wooden table which had seen sturdier days.

Neglected, vulnerable, ashamed. A dead human being. A human non-being.

In the surreal setting, I felt more alienated than shocked. Still unsure of my next reaction, I inched forward to the table.

It was not obviously human. Not 'us'. It could have been any life form. I became clinical in my observation.

Disproportionate. Even for a four-month foetus. Very long neck. Only one arm formation. Sex not determinable, at least to me. Two leg stubs, almost enjoined. Translucent head, veins criss-crossing, dots for eyes. Stillborn.

I could not turn my back to walk out. I reversed slowly away, colliding into the policeman who was nonchalantly looking away. I muttered an exit line, almost ran to the taxi. My throat was inexplicably parched. I reached for the Bisleri and allowed warm, plastic-smelling water to run past my oesaphagus into my gullet. I drank and I drank until it overflowed out of my body and onto my clothes.

All the way down the winding hills, my mind kept pushing a question at me. Relentlessly. Ruthlessly. Is this not better than a deformed life? And because of Shweta, my heart kept sending back the answer. No, no, no.

THIRTY-NINE

I returned home to find Shweta not up to par. There was a pallor on her face that I had not seen before. The doctors had been called in and had put her on steroids. She said she felt weak. Her blood pressure was lower than usual. The heart, after all, is a muscle. When it starts to degenerate, little can be done. I hoped that stage was still far for my baby sister.

'My legs are giving up on me, Akka,' she said, trying to smile. 'Now I'll have to be carried around, like a bride in a palkhi!'

'Nonsense. It's just a passing phase. We'll just have to get you one of those fancy wheelchairs with brakes and gears! And then we'll need speed breakers in the living room.'

Shweta giggled. 'Have you seen your car yet, Akka? Such a jazzy blue!'

I was glad that she was looking outward. Sometimes she sinks into self-pity. God knows it's natural. I promised her a ride in my new wheels later. We shared a chocolate bar. So far, her sugar levels have been fine. Then I offered to share a secret if she promised not to tell anyone. Even Anna. Shweta loves a conspiracy. I told her about funky Pranay and my Internet adventures. I told her I was going back there to dig out more information on the vaccine. She was round-eyed at the end of it all.

'It's just like in the movies, Akka. You've become a hacker! Like all those private detective types. A high-tech Nancy Drew.' Right, I thought wryly. If nothing else came of all this, I could star in a crime blockbuster. *Internet Indira's New Adventure. The Suspect Syringe!*

I drove my new car to my rendezvous that night. It felt great to be mobile. It was a neat little thing, just my size.

Pranay was distinctly less enthusiastic the second time around. When I entered the cybercafe at nine o'clock, I looked around for Mr Software. He was absent. 'His wife's birthday,' said Pranay, rather regretfully.

We had the whole place to ourselves. I had to think up a really good reason for wasting Pranay's time. He had already confided to me that he had found a 'chick' who was 'really hot'. I asked him if the words he was using were not outdated. 'Still current,' he informed me.

I had already decided that I should explore the world of the alternative vaccine. I made Pranay try 'VAC 1998'. Nothing happened. We brought up WHO, America Aid, everything I could think of. There was volumes of material, but nothing that mattered. To me, anyway. Then, rather belatedly, like a 'tubelight' as Shweta would say, I flickered with the memory of the redoubtable Dr Stephen Jacowski. I had his e-mail address. The Columbia School of Medicine would have its Internet gateways.

Pranay nearly gave up when he realized what lay ahead. I pressured him mercilessly. My personal demons were on red alert. We hacked and we hacked and . . . we hacked.

By the grace of God, and the extraordinary grace of Pranay's lateral thinking, we got into Columbia School's internal systems. It was easier after that. We could not actually access Dr Jacowski's personal files. But the school's mail server had its log enabled. We read through the outpouring of mail from the school. I will never, ever do it again. Not for one hundred crore rupees.

As it turned out, it was the turning point. Among the dozens of names in that midnight, red-eye list, I found the most astonishing name of all. A name that was repeated several times. All dated in the last four weeks.

My feelings of shock and elation combined in a heady cocktail. I stood up, did a pirouette, my hair flying into Pranay's face. He put a finger to his head in an age-old gesture. Totally batty, he meant.

Maybe. But now I had found a key. A key with a room number on it. I only had to find the name of the hotel.

By 2 a.m., when I finally allowed him to sign off, poor Pranay had decided to go in for construction work as an easier and more rewarding career.

FORTY

It was late. Actually, it was early the next morning. I had tossed and I had turned. I had contemplated alcohol and sleeping pills. But I could not sleep. I seemed to have reached yet another turning point in my short span as a 'real' investigative journalist. I thought of the name which had cropped up in my Internet search. A name which had no reason to be there. A name which may mean its owner was up to something. Something risky. And wrong.

I needed proof. Documents. On-the-record quotes. Maybe from Dr Stephen Jacowski, Fellow, Columbia School of Medicine. He was the head of the New York team for the vaccine development project being spearheaded by Dr Kerring's Institute of Reproductive Immunology in Washington. A project being funded by Benden-Fromm. Quite, quite confusing. But still, at least and at last, I knew where this story was leading. I only had to find out where it would end. A small problem faced me. You cannot print confidential documents off the Net. It would probably land you in jail. So if I needed to dig further, there was only one place I could find the spade. Any which way I looked at it, I needed to be in New York.

Of course, as a mere journalist in the big business of journalism, it was like saying I would need to go to the moon. With a shudder, I remembered the trouble I'd had clearing the Goa idea with CP. And that had partly been a junket.

Now we were talking, what? At least one lakh of rupees? Even if I starved on my trip. With the ridiculously low prices of food in the US, that would hardly save anything. And for what? To topple a government? To give people a new messiah? No.

It was a lot of money, just to uncover a little secret of one little company that was working on one little tribal community. Just one more possible research fraud. So how was I going to justify the expense?

I could be straight. I could talk of the human interest angle. I could describe how the 'victims' of the research were suffering. I could write off my estimated expenses as a mere fraction of the amount spent by all the players in this story. I could hint at the fallout of the 'guinea pig' syndrome. I could get the feminist organizations to turn on heat. But hell, I did not even have a multinational to attack. And if we took a high moral ground early in this game, it could give us an easy but small victory. And I, said I to myself, wanted the big one this time. If my nostrils flared, there was no one to watch.

As the newly oiled wheels of my scheming mind went into higher RPM, an idea went centrifugal. The big man. I had to pocket Mr GD Heggade. Bother CP. I could make up to him later. Ask Meenal to be nice to him or something. What I needed first was sanction from Avaru.

To tackle him, there had to be a clear strategy, I decided, biting on my handmade razai. The weather was muggy. I jumped out of my mosquito net, hearing a yippee from the little suckers. I went to the window and looked at the sky, maybe for inspiration. But there was not much to see in that monsoon weather. I looked over to Shweta. She was under heavy sedation. In repose, her facial muscles were slack. I knew it would only be a matter of time before they became grotesque.

215

I sat on the cool stone floor, cross-legged, my back straight. A handy tube of Odomos had made me temporarily immune from winged attack. 'Om,Om,Om,' I intoned solemnly, trying to massage my inner organs with my breathing exercises. I failed.

So, I paced. Only one way to get Avaru. I had to convince him that it was in his best interests to send me to New York. Four or five working days should do the trick. And I could offer him a refund if my strategy backfired. I could always sell my new car.

Once I had decided what to do, the demons went away. I slept till 9 a.m. Late for work, again.

Avaru's eyebrows, which I had never noticed before rose till they disappeared into his hairline. And that was saying a lot.

'Not only have you seriously jeopardized the position of this newspaper by your unacceptable investigative methods,' he said, 'you now want me to fund your trip to the USA, so that you can continue to worry us all about your intentions.' He inhaled an urgent breath. It hit me that he always spoke in complex sentences. So rare these days.

I bravely kept silent. I had already given my pitch, finely balanced between a promise of the Pulitzer, and the government of India Bharat Ratna, for services rendered towards India's brand equity. I had suggested mildly that this somewhat non-political story was just what the nation needed to 'be proud to be Indian'. Fifty years of Independence, I implied, and not a vaccine to show for it. Until now.

I found out much later that it was not my argument but 'my sheer audacity' that won him over. In any case, by the time I left the office, with Avaru now switching his attention to the golf clubs in the corner of the room, I was feeling blessed. I had twice been served coffee, once in porcelain china. And I had been given a cautious go-ahead. I walked out jauntily, benignly supervised by a symbolic, faceless

Madhuri Dixit. Gulf Airways or nothing, I had been warned, in case I had visions of first-class Atlantic airlines, and an intercom button had been pressed, informing my editor. Of whose reaction there is nothing to be said.

FORTY-ONE

A maniacal three days later, I was on a flight to New York via places best left unmentioned. If there had been standing room only, expectations would have been more realistic. Luckily, I'd had so little sleep in the seventy-two hours preceding the journey, that a cocktail and a polyester pillow had seemed like a miracle. My three neighbours should have been so lucky.

International travel brochures never tell you about queues and surly immigration officials at JFK. The young white rookie whom I had the misfortune to encounter asked me everything short of my sexual preferences. And from the way he was looking at my tired bust, it seemed he wanted to. Still, I survived, while he showed off how the Immigration and Naturalization Service had computerized its records, pointing out to me that I had been in the US and Canada two years ago on a holiday. I had agreed, visibly marvelling at the advancement of technology, almost promising never to come back if he would only get this over with.

And now, here I was, stuck with some unfortunate and unfamiliar relatives in New Jersey on account of the fact that I had to save money for the big boss. With the whole household asleep, I was left to negotiate the jet-lagged night by myself.

Stillborn

I looked through my bags. They were full of material on the story. I had managed to squeeze in about eighty hours of work—with parallel processing—in forty-eight. I had called on old debts, making some lawyer friends tell me trade secrets. I had read up as much as I could on US patent laws trying to understand how they were different from Indian laws. I had also asked for direct access to Avaru's corporate lawyers to help me sort out some sticky ethico-legal issues I was facing. Would such and such questions that I planned to ask amount to blackmail? I asked innocently. The two men and one woman sitting in front of me turned visibly nervous. Fidgety. They also knew that no media baron ever became one by being squeamish. So they did their best.

I must admit everybody in the office had swung into full gear, getting me names, addresses and e-mail numbers of anybody and everybody in NY and the rest of the USA I could possibly need. I could sense the muted excitement rising like vapour in the corridors. Even sworn enemies knew it was hands-off time.

With all that, I had almost forgotten to pack clothes. Luckily, it was high summer. My skirts and blouses and shorts would do just fine. Hopefully, my jet lag would also be lighter, not like winter hibernation.

So what was my grand plan for the five days I had been given in the world's most glamorous city?

I actually had only three appointments. Our office had contacted its representatives in the US and got me an appointment with the patent lawyers' firm I had asked for. Ditto for some promised fifteen minutes with the Dean of the Columbia School of Medicine, with a special request for Dr Jacowski to be in attendance. I could get used to the office handling such things for me! Somebody called Venkataiah had called to curse me, saying it was almost impossible to get that particular appointment and did I have a solid reason? I had smiled politely into the handset.

219

Then I had given him a few facts to use. The third meeting was with Rajni Gupta. It had been arranged for me at Avaru's insistence. It was a familiar name, often quoted in newsmagazines across the world. Rajni Gupta was probably India's best known expatriate businesswoman. She had recently been named a director in McDonell Associates, the world's largest management consultancy.

Avaru had attached a post-it note to a clipping from the *Wall Street Journal.* 'Rajni is my wife's cousin. By marriage. Now divorced. Her special interest: pharmaceutical multinationals. Meet her. It will be an education.'

Obviously, he thought I needed educating. I did not mind. I would love to meet Avaru's wife's cousin. By divorce. It was good to belong to a race to which every sixth person in the world belonged. It would soon be every fifth, especially if Anshul and others could not get their act together.

Monday was quite wasted. I read the *Wall Street Journal.* Nothing much was happening in the financial world. A few mergers, a few acquisitions and Bill Gates managed the rest. Once more, I spent the night awake, poring over my notes. The next morning, I glugged glassfuls of '100% orange juice, not from concentrate' and imbibed soothing cereal with cold milk. The flakes were interspersed with nut-coated raisins. The Americans, I thought wistfully, think of everything. Even contraceptive vaccines, which they do not particularly need. I sharpened up at the thought and rushed back to my wonderful guest room, paisley comforters, matching bath towels and all, to plan my day.

The appointments with the lawyers and Columbia School of Medicine were scheduled for Wednesday morning. Which left me with all of Tuesday. I conquered my jet lag with determination and last-minute homeopathic medicines sent by Meenal, of all people, just before I left India. Two pills, every three hours. But no coffee, and no alcohol. I took the footnote in the right spirit. Feeling almost evolved, I volunteered to take my little third-cousins, Sammy (for Sameer) and Trip (for Trupti) to the Bronx zoo. Honestly, it was a wonderful experience—the polar bears, the ice cream and the bus ride. Completely unrelated to my work, but equally demanding. Especially since Trupti, all of four years, had an adult's mischief in her.

I met Rajni Gupta at her McDonnell Associates office in the afternoon. It was a New York address overlooking Central Park. I was dressed in a black-and-mauve skirt suit, my eyes expertly painted, my stockings in place. The cabbie, mistaking me for a New Yorker, actually abused me when I hailed him suddenly; he was Lithuanian, not Pakistani. He also shared anecdotes about 'these bloody summer visitors'.

Rajni Gupta was small, maybe five feet and a couple of inches. But not an inch was wasted. Feeling much too tall in my block heels, I smiled down at the powerhouse in front of me, finding little to say. But she was used to uneducated visitors from the East. She led me through the early formalities, even setting the agenda for our talk. I wondered why so few women like her thrive at home. Maybe they do, we just do not get to know them.

We talked of generalities, then surprisingly, of recent Indian pop music, heatedly arguing over the musical genius of Ilayaraja and the Colonial Cousins.

Finally, we got down to business. Avaru's recommendation was good enough. I could trust her. I briefed her about the vaccine. About what I was here to achieve. Then I asked her to clarify something that had been bothering me for a long time.

'Rajni, if both Columbia School in New York and the Institute of Reproductive Immunology in Washington are developing the vaccine, why do they not also fund it? Would it not make more sense in the long run, to completely own the rights to the product? Why bring in Benden-Fromm? Why so many agencies?'

'Well, collaborative research is quite the done thing now, you know. Ivory-tower scientists don't really exist anymore. Plus, the capital cost involved is just so high. Few educational institutions, even in this country, can fund such open-ended projects. Usually, a venture capital firm or the ultimate client for the researcher—in this case a pharmaceutical company—will raise the money required. Benden-Fromm, in spite of their very recent merger, has been very aggressive in the market. It has acquired several smaller companies with best-selling chemicals. This project you are telling me about, if successful, would fit right into its strategic plan.'

It was beginning to make some sense. I thought of Sushruta, India's answer to Benden-Fromm in the Anshul project. Well, maybe we could still win the war, even if we lost some battles.

I asked Rajni for some advice on how to handle my meeting with the Columbia School doctors.

'Oh, just go for it,' she said, smiling. 'Americans love gutsy women. You have enough aces up your sleeves. Use them well. Remember, timing is critical.'

I repeated the phrase as though it were a mantra being conferred on me.

'I know the Dean, Dr Rudolph Perry, socially,' she added as an afterthought. I imagined chandelier parties, low-cut evening gowns and liqueur. 'Maybe I can probe a little on your behalf.'

'Please don't tell him about . . .' I started, rather unused to international sophistication.

'Of course not. I do understand your position.' She reached across a carved wooden table, probably ordered from India, and shook my hand warmly. 'Please call me tomorrow after your meeting. I'd like to know how your work is progressing.'

I walked out of her plush, silent building, feeling right as rain. The sun was out in all its glory, beating down on joggers and skaters, drunkards and businessmen, each apparently in his own world. In Manhattan, children are a rare sight. It is almost an unwritten rule—Thou shalt not raise babies in the Big Apple. As I was thinking that, I sighted a determined black woman in office clothes, most unexpectedly pushing a pram. I surreptitiously peeked inside, half expecting to see a stack of papers. The cherub inside was licking an ice cream cone. She seemed to suddenly have enough and cast off its gooey remains onto the pavement.

Footpaths here are often cleaner than some Indian bathrooms. I felt acutely the shame of the NRI as he walks into his childhood toilet, only too aware of the smells, the wetness and the probability of disease.

But here, in these Clinton years, the only greys on the horizon came from sexcapades and Saddam. Small problems. For New Yorkers, the real threat remained the down-on-luck car-jacker, the subway marauder or the serial stalker. I walked lightly past pavement sellers of baubles brought in from every corner of the world. One black lady with ringlets and an attitude tried to sell me Mysore Sandal soap! I fingered it, but shook my head, laughing at the absurdity of global trade.

I ate, with some disappointment, over-salted pretzels and unsalted popcorn. Then I went into a Jewish dive and tipped the scales with a corned beef sandwich, falafel and a salad dressed in olive oil. I had ice cream at a Baskin Robbins, but only because it was there. In India, it would have to be an outing. As I licked the chocolate, I thought longingly and irrationally of Nani's Corner and the city's best fudge sundae, not far from my home.

Tomorrow would be the clincher, I thought, as I dimmed the analog light switch over my bed. No mosquito nets here, thank God. Even the cockroach, an American native, had emigrated to less hostile countries. The air-conditioning was turned to a comfortable low. I had set the radio alarm to wake me up with *Randy the Ripper* on 101 FM.

That night, I knew sleep would come.

Wednesday rose bright and warm. Television news anchors chirped like sunbirds. I tried to tune in to the worries of a stay-at-home dad concerned about the nutritional value of packaged cereal. Luckily, Sammy switched to *Sesame Street*.

In spite of my new sandals, I walked to my first appointment. I had prematurely ejected myself from the subway that brought me into Manhattan. It was just twenty blocks away, if my *Manhattan Guide* was correct. At eighty degrees Fahrenheit outdoors, this would have been just another day in Bangalore. Here, extra anti-perspirant kept me odour free. Polycot kept me almost wrinkle free. Life was a breeze.

The offices of Laneman, Schizowich, Michaelson and Golmoden (LSPG) were in what was definitely intended to be projected as the most ancient building in Manhattan. Its Corinthian columns solemnly bore the weight of baskets of flowers etched in exquisite detail. If they had been around today, the building's grandiose commissioners could have insisted on artificial fragrance as well. Upper floors with discreet balconies were sealed off from the inquisitive eye with blinds or air-conditioning equipment. The stone facing in yellowing grey was old enough to demand free medical treatment.

I tiptoed delicately past a black security guard in livery, quite awed by my surroundings. As I studied the nameboard, looking quite raw, he came by and offered to help. Before I could complete 'Laneman, Schizowich . . .' he interrupted. 'Fourth floor, miss,' he said, with a smile. I almost bowed.

I had prepared myself well. After all, have you ever read any crime fiction where the lawyer does not make his appearance in a dark, book-lined office, his accent impeccable but his spectacles slightly off the bridge of his nose?

I lost my lines when I realized it was mahogany. I was, daftly enough, envisioning teak. The receptionist, a handsome young male in a dark suit, offered me a glass of water. He used the high-tech devices at his fingertips to find out that I would have to wait a mere five minutes. Under such tender loving care, I became myself again.

The two gentlemen who finally met me were David Knopf and Paul Tabbott. Nobody called Laneman, Michaelson, Schizowich or Golmoden showed up. So, these were mere junior partners in a forbiddingly ancient firm. I breathed a sigh of relief. The suits in front of me were thirty-somethings. I could handle that. Even if they were specialists in the regime of patents.

'Thank you for meeting me at such short notice. As you know, I have come to speak to you about not one, but two of your clients—Columbia School of Medicine, and . . .' I paused for effect, 'Benden-Fromm.'

They seemed amused. Maybe because they already knew that, considering that the appointment had been made from halfway across the world. Maybe because I sounded like a marionette. A sleepy one at that. Not too bright, what?

'Yes, hi! I'm David,' said one, reaching across the mahogany table to shake my hand. 'I'm Paul,' said the other, doing the same. I almost said, 'I'm Bobby, *mere saath dosti karoge?*'

I looked at myself from across the table, from where they were. I could understand their scepticism. A journalist from a developmentally challenged country, expecting easy answers from the most unlikely-to-reveal-anything professionals, top-notch lawyers. I put my chin up, pointing it accusingly.

Outide the tall stained-glass windows, New York did its Hollywood backdrop routine. Helmeted cyclists cut lanes and flouted rules to deliver flowers. Cabs inched along. Buses squealed in alarm everytime they had to brake. Trees. People walked with cellphones earnestly at their ears. Joggers jogged.

I spent half an hour in the hallowed room. The two young men were patient and cordial. Even when I requested that I should be allowed to switch on a micro cassette recorder. I guess they knew they would not reveal much, anyway. Lawyers do not. I made sure they became wary and interested.

All my practice with Avaru's lawyers paid off. I told them exactly who I was. I sketched my interest in the subject. I said I had some information about a contract that their clients were about to enter into. A contract which could be worth millions—unless the information I was about to volunteer was completely accurate. The contract was to be with an Indian national. 'Timing,' Rajni had said. I then named the Indian national. I got their attention at that. Like me, they had done their homework. When the phone buzzed, they cut it off, asking not to be disturbed. I felt a post-colonial satisfaction.

FORTY-TWO

Dr Stephen Jacowski was the tallest man I had ever met. I'd always thought of New York Jews as small, bespectacled and witty. Dr Jacowski must have a German or Dutch mother. I nearly had to raise my arm over my head to accommodate his handshake. His boss, Dr Rudolph Perry, Dean, Columbia School of Medicine, was more average looking. But from the way he looked at me, I knew he was not average at all.

He took charge right away. 'Go ahead then, Ms Pandit, what has brought you to us from so far?' My surname came out with Pan as in Peter. I would have liked to correct him. Maybe I should be spelling it with a 'u'? I launched into my spiel, hoping against hope that the lawyers had not yet reached Dr Perry.

'As you know, I have already been in touch with Dr Jacowski on this. When I met Dr Michael Frampton and Dr Judith Ferraro at a conference in India recently, we had occasion to speak at length about the vaccine that his team has developed.' I gave the giant doctor a brilliant smile. His mousy moustache moved, suggesting reciprocity.

I then asked politely if I could switch on my recorder. They looked at each other, and I thought they were about to refuse. Bother ethics, I thought. I should never have asked.

To my surprise, however, Dr Perry smiled. 'I was going to ask you the same thing,' he said. Suspiciously quick, he took out a sleek little machine of his own. It was smaller, newer than mine. Sony. I would have to be careful with what I said. I checked if my batteries were in order and pressed down the red 'record' button.

'I have, for the last few weeks, been researching the development of contraceptive vaccines in the world. Family planning, after a major setback in the seventies, is returning to the national agenda in India, as I am sure you are aware. I thought it would make a good story for my magazine, which is one of the leading publications in my country, with a readership more than that of the *New York Times*.'

So far, so good. Watching and waiting.

I addressed myself solely to Dr Perry. 'The reason I am here is because, in the course of my research, I have discovered several alarming things that could once again set back our family planning programme in India. It could also cause major international embarrassment for the players involved, particularly, er, yourselves. Considering that Dr Jacowski is part of your institution.'

My turn to wait and watch. No reaction, even after six seconds. So I continued.

'I understand that Dr Jacowski works partly under the aegis of the Institution for Reproductive Immunology with Dr Kerring on this project. Still, Columbia School of Medicine would certainly figure in a news story.'

The bigger man shifted uncomfortably in his chair. I felt a twinge of guilt. I also felt a lilliputian power.

Dr Perry cleared his throat, like in the movies. I had a tangential thought about how cine aesthetics mould social mannerisms.

'Young lady,' he began, and retracted, suddenly afflicted with political correctness, 'if you do not mind my calling you that. I hope you have some very specific information to give me on this subject. When we received a call from your office fixing up this interview, we were most reluctant. But your, er, representatives were rather blunt and definitely persuasive. We had to reschedule many meetings.' He fiddled with his watch. Humbug, I thought. How many meetings can you schedule in fifteen minutes?

'I do very much appreciate the time you have given me, Dr Perry,' I said. 'Yes, I have some very specific information for the two of you. I believe you are in the process of finalizing a contract with . . .' Once more, I used the name that was guaranteed to get me a reaction.

They looked at each other again. This time with eyebrows knitted, lips curling.

'There is only one problem. It will, I am told, involve some clauses in the very latest version of the US patents act under Section 271, on infringement of patent. I believe the latest legislation includes inventions *outside the United States* under its ambit. I also believe that new laws, still unchallenged, allow that those who did not participate in the conception of an invention cannot be inventors. Given that the contract you would like to enter into . . .'

There was a suppressed splutter. Dr Perry stood up. He became equal in height to Dr Jacowski, who was still seated.

'We, I mean they,' he pointed to the gentle giant, 'have not signed anything yet. We are involved in very preliminary consultations in this matter. I am sure our lawyers are perfectly capable of protecting us from any malafide intentions. So unless you can add anything above and beyond these generalities . . .'

Tsk.Tsk. So much impatience. I went into a role-playing that would have landed me in a schizophrenic's ward if a competent psychiatrist had witnessed it.

'Excuse me, Dr Perry, perhaps I have been meandering.' Then I whipped out a little notepad in which I had jotted down the points I had to convey. 'What I want to say is that you may be dealing with a person who is, perhaps, completely unauthorized to sell you anything. If in fact you were to enter into a contract, it may not hold any water in a patents litigation.' I proceeded to fill the two gentlemen in. Then I snapped my notepad shut and turned down the tip of my Parker micro-point.

Jotting points copiously, in spite of two recorders, Dr Jacowski's body had frozen in bulk. Only the fingers flew. Dr Perry kept looking at the notepad, then at me. I recited information, rehearsed grittily at three airports. Time presumed wasted is often time retrieved.

A theatrical silence ensued. Thank God for the performing arts. We know what to do, how to act in any given situation.

Just then the telephone rang. From the changing expressions on Dr Perry's face, I gathered it was the lawyers, David and Paul. He listened quietly, hardly interrupting. 'Yes, she's sitting here right now. I will talk to you later.' Slamming down the phone, he conveyed the gist of the conversation to Dr Jacowski.

'You are quite sure, are you not?' were the almost pleading first words from Dr Jacowski. I thought I heard a dream burst.

'I am,' I said, giving him a sympathetic look.

'Well then, back to the drawing board,' he said resignedly. 'Though we should have known . . .' Dr Perry was definitely frowning.

'Well, Kerring did raise some doubts. But we had . . . Anyway, we shall do some verifications. Perhaps we can, still . . .' he looked at me fiercely. 'If you print anything about this, I should tell you that we may be forced to protect ourselves. I will not . . .'

I cut him off. He was surprised. People don't do that to the Dr Perrys of this world. I was not being impolite, just overexcited.

'Dr Perry, please. I promise you my story will not be unleashed until you have verified my information. Until I have your considered quotes on the subject. However, in addition to this interview, of which I will only use statements that you have agreed to let me use—I do need some authentication from your side. Could you possibly give me something, maybe a letter, to at least confirm that you have met me in connection with your ongoing negotiations on the vaccine project? It will help me tide over the time until you give me the green signal.'

He actually agreed. His mind seemed to be several jumps ahead of mine. I felt a bit nervous. Patent laws are constantly evolving in the United States. There are many loopholes, many untested grey areas. Perhaps Dr Perry was already charting a course.

On the Columbia School of Medicine letterhead, the Dean wrote a brief note to whomsoever it may concern. It was brilliant in that it said almost nothing. But it would serve my purpose. I thanked him, promising once again to hold off on the story till I had spoken to them. I said I would call before I left New York on Friday night.

Dr Perry took down my numbers. Both in the US and in India. I had just got a new hotmail account, thanks to Vijay Anna, my New Jersey uncle. I proudly gave him my e-mail address. He gave me his. Very clearly, he then dismissed me, which was fine. I had an admission on tape that my information was not inaccurate. I had a letter to prove I had met the Dean of Columbia School of Medicine. I had used blackmail, traded temporary silence for temporary information. Rohil would have disapproved severely.

Carefully gathering my papers and my excitement, I walked out of the door, my long hair stunning them, I hoped, in my retreat.

FORTY-THREE

I had promised that I would let Rajni Gupta know what had transpired. I bought a phone card and called her, but she was busy. Her secretary promised to get back to me. Fifteen minutes later, she did. At the telephone booth. America works. Could Ms Pandit meet Ms Gupta at Brazil restaurant, between 37th and Broadway at 8 p.m.? Ms Pandit certainly could!

I decided not to call Dr Kerring. Dr Perry would certainly keep him in the loop. The way he had stonewalled me in Goa, it was unlikely he would tell me anything now, at this juncture. Especially since it appeared as if Dr Kerring's precious team in New York might just fall flat on its face.

I had a few numbers for one of the key players in this imbroglio. Benden-Fromm. But the names from my list were faceless. I had not built up any contacts with anybody there. There was little likelihood of them telling me anything useful. Multinational companies are notorious for transferring all press persons to the ubiquitous PRO, who then proceeds to say a lot and tell you nothing. So I left the telephone numbers unused. I would call in on Messrs Benden-Fromm later.

I made a call to Dr Judith Ferraro. There would be no time to meet her, since she lived in Washington DC, but at least I could fill her in. After all, if she had not given me the crucial lead about the synthetic antigen and Dr Jacowski's work, I would not be here. She was not at home. In fact, she was out of the country. I could hardly call her friend, Dr Frampton, even though I had dropped his name so casually earlier that day. He would not to be able to place me, even with assisted flashback. I left a complicated message for Judith at her office.

Since there now seemed to be nobody else to call, I began to look forward to my evening. Vijay and Mangala, my uncle and aunt, had briefed me well about Brazil. It was a casual restaurant, with a single-minded devotion to Brazilian food. Mangala had refused to serve me an evening snack, saying she did not want to be responsible for spoiling my dinner. I wore an embroidered T-shirt in the palest of blues and hip-hugging stretch jeans. My belt had a turquoise stone embedded in oxidized silver. My hair was loose, but a matching motif hairband framed my face. My long earrings in silver and blue completed my ensemble.

Rajni had obviously come straight from work. Her formal suit and her crumpled neckline told the story. She glanced enviously at my freshly bathed look and consoled herself with a frozen marguerita, ditto for me, from a handsome young waiter in red, white and black.

I do not know if the margueritas did it or just the sumptuous food. The salad bar with its never-ending variety of beans and greens would have been enough. But we also had to contend with good-looking young men armed, quite literally, with long skewers of succulent grilled meat—beef and pork and chicken—which they offered with the most tempting smiles. They appeared to move in a sinuous rhythm along with the samba music playing in the background. I took in the visual treat and left it to the connoisseur to choose the treat for my palate.

It was a short meal but a long evening. Rajni, on her third marguerita became expansive. She congratulated me for being in a terrific bargaining position with these 'self-propelled academics'. She spoke of her increasing longing for a culture she thought she had left behind. She spoke of a bitter divorce. She spoke of the inexpressible joys of having breached the glass ceiling.

I was too fascinated to send up thanks for one of the top ten meals of my life. I think the success of the Mardi Gras must have more to do with the food than the nudity. But listening to Rajni Gupta, arguably the most conventionally successful of expatriates, sent me into a private tizzy. I watched the forty-five year old, her expressions, her frankness, her quick intelligence. What would I be like at her age? Would I be loved? A shaft of pure pain ran through my innards, nearly aborting my digestion. Dr Rohil Kamath. You of the passionate eyes and the honeyed smile and the quick fingers. Where are you?

I asked her how it felt to be a pioneer of sorts. She looked at me piercingly, her soft brown eyes suddenly hard. A small lift of her hand brought a waiter. I had thought only men of a particular persuasion could do that. 'I'm a regular,' she explained. I felt my world-view slipping back into place. She ordered coffee, 'the usual', two cups.

'I did not expect to arrive where I have reached,' she said, twirling her multicoloured table napkin into intricate designs. 'I lost a lot along the way. Now I am looking at alternatives, at impossible dreams. I think of merging my yesterdays and my tomorrows in the colours of today.' Marguerita madness, I thought. I was wrong.

'I can see the beginnings of a . . . of an almost compulsive co-operation between like-minded people across the globe,' she said, her eyes sort of leaving our space. I thought of the long-reigning Jyoti Basu at home and the Communist Party of India. Then I remembered that he'd visited America often enough recently. That he had invited foreign participation in the greening of West Bengal, and made a success of the idea.

She read my mind. 'I don't just mean of people with a certain political perspective. I'm thinking of people beyond history, really.'

She proceeded to count examples on manicured but blunt-nailed fingers. She spoke of conservationists and space scientists, implying that they had common goals. 'Forging the future,' she called it. It was a new idea to me. Dreamily, she added that she was thinking of 'doing a book' about her theory.

I swallowed my hot Brazilian coffee, which tasted rather like Mysore coffee except that it had been served in ceramic mugs by a clean waiter. I was more used to stainless steel glasses housed in unwashed bowls.

Rajni seemed to have worn herself down. 'God, I have a long day tomorrow,' she said, her weariness making her seem vulnerable for the first time. We got up to go and I half bowed my head, in deference to the modern miracle in front of me.

I spent Thursday with Mangala and the kids. By then we had become comfortable with each other. She insisted I call a friend of hers who was a pediatrician specializing in neuromuscular disorders. I did so and was glad later. Dr Sheila gave me some hope about emerging work in neurosurgery. She promised to keep me posted and asked for a detailed medical report on Shweta.

We had a barbecue dinner on the patio with some neighbourhood friends. The NRI community is like a quiet suburb of main city America. A world within a world. I noticed an ennui though, among its citizens.

My last day in New York. I visited MOMA, the Museum of Modern Art. There was a section called post-deconstruction. I marvelled at the jargon, educating myself about current trends in art. As a teenager, I used to think I could sketch. Nobody else thought so, so I diverted my frustrations by writing occasionally about art and artists. At the MOMA store I bought some prints for myself and one very dark

235

painting full of women for CP. I also found a strange, newfangled bed light I thought would be perfect for Anna. I did some more shopping for the family, using rusty mental math for currency conversion. Amma, Laxmi, Meenal and Shweta, Shweta and Shweta. I found a collection of Sufi poetry, with translations and a critique for in-case-I-ever-met-him-again Rohil. Then I called Dr Stephen Jacowski's office.

He seemed very subdued. 'I'm sure Rudolph, I mean Dr Perry, will inform you himself. We have been speaking with our lawyers. Preliminary investigations of your information have begun. It appears you are certainly correct in some of your apprehensions. But we see no cause for worry, as we have not made any commitments yet.'

So how about thanking me for my early warning system, doctor? He heard me thinking.

'I guess once this is all confirmed, we may have to, I mean we will be grateful to you for sharing your information with us. We would have caught on, of course, but certainly this has saved us a lot of time.'

Oh well. That's what happens to messengers of bad news.

By the time I left for the airport after cheerful goodbyes and sticky kisses from Sammy and Trip, Dr Perry had called me with the same details. He agreed that I could now publish anything from our interview. Like me, he must have listened to the recording and heard me talking far more than they had. Still, he was surprisingly courteous and wished me a safe journey home.

FORTY-FOUR

Back in Bangalore, I skittered out of a familiar bed on Sunday afternoon. Shweta was reading in hers, looking smaller in just one week. I had been given a rousing welcome when I arrived at seven in the morning. After a magnificent breakfast of neer dose and coffee and malgoba mangoes served in cubes, I just about made it to my room before I fell asleep. Rain clouds were darkening the window when I woke, disorienting me completely. But it was not even noon. The monsoon gods are very courteous here. It usually showers only in the evenings and nights. I stretched and yawned theatrically, feeling groggy but overexcited. My jigsaw puzzle was taking shape. And now I knew where to look for the last missing pieces.

I reached for the telephone.

First call to CP. I sounded, I'm sure, as triumphant as I felt. I asked him to call Avaru. To repeat the gist of what I had just finished telling him. I had never called the big man at his residence and did not want to start.

Second call to Dr Anshul Hiremath. Surabhi picked up on the other end. Her Sunday voice was husky. It was hard to make it sound cold and disapproving, as she no doubt felt towards me. No, Anshul was not in. No, she did not know when he would be back.

'I have some very important information for him. I have to meet him personally. Soon.' I remembered my earlier use of the word 'ensnare' to describe what I wanted to do to Anshul. Surabhi said I could try at the office later. But it was a Sunday. There would be no telephone operators around, she warned me.

I decided to gamble on Anshul's being at the office. I told Shweta to be good, and left in my new Maruti. There was no need to readjust myself to the idea of left-sided traffic. In Bangalore, people drive on both sides anyway. In my reverse jet-lagged state, I took one whole hour to reach India Biotech. The traffic was heavy and shrill—on a Sunday morning. No hope for Bangalore at all.

The security guard was watching cricket on a small black and white television in his cabin. India vs Pakistan. He barely registered who I was. He told me that Dr Saab had not come. His eyes kept straying back to the TV. Rahul Dravid at the crease. I gabbled, asking him the score, egging on the batsman. Then I told him how I had just spoken to Surabhi Madam, who had asked me to come here. She had told me Anshul was on his way. I was a reporter for Star TV doing my initial interviews. Did he remember I had come in previously?

I irritated him thoroughly. He let me in. I didn't look very harmful, anyway. The gates closed behind me. Cricket nut went back to his screen. I drove nonchalantly past the rolling lawns. The skies had turned darker in that sudden Bangalore way. It would rain very soon. I parked, walked up to the graceful white building. The doors were only partially open. Nobody was in sight. I walked in as though I belonged there. No one to stop me. At the atrium I took the leftmost corridor. Just as my eyes alighted on the rosewood door, it opened.

Dr Rita emerged with some papers in her hand. God, I had quite forgotten that she might be there. She was looking down as she shut the door carefully behind her and did not notice me.

I did not know whether I was pleased or irritated at meeting her there. It was too late to do anything about it, in either case.

'Dr Rita, hello! I thought you were with your sister in the US!' I said cheerfully.

The poor woman did a little leap, the first uncontrolled movement I had seen in her.

'Oh! You really surprised me, Poorva Pandit. Are you here to meet Anshul? He's not around.'

'I know. I'll wait for him. Can I have a word with you till then?'

She hesitated. Looked down at her papers. I guessed she had work to do.

'Oh, just for a few minutes. I won't keep you long.' I put on a soft expression.

'Okay then, come.' She led me back to the atrium, into the next wing and opened a door marked in her name. The keys, I noticed, hung on a Biogene key chain.

Her office was about half the size of Anshul's. So was her desk. No Ansel Adams, no thick carpet. Just some sensible office furniture in metal and plywood. It came as a bit of a surprise. Dr Rita George, it would appear, was really a very simple woman.

I continued to observe the room. Again, the same meticulous tidiness as at the research station office in MR Hills. No papers askew. Her computer was on, a screen saver design of molecule chains repeating itself endlessly. She sat down, carefully put the papers she had in her arms into the topmost drawer of her desk and waved me to a chair opposite.

'How is your sister?' I asked solicitously.

'She, er, she is not well, she's dying. Maybe another month, maybe three.'

I said I was sorry. 'Where does she live? Your sister?' I asked, quite stupidly.

'She's in New York.' Abrupt.

'Oh yes, of course. Dr Jacowski told me.'

'You know Stephen . . . Dr Jacowski?' Genuine surprise at that.

'Yes, indirectly, through a friend. Do you know they are ahead of you people in the vaccine race now? They have the synthetic antigen.'

'I believe so, yes.'

'Does that feel very frustrating, after all your hard work?'

'Believe me, it does. Now maybe I should get back to it. There is a lot more to do.'

I made my excuses and left. When I looked back, she was pulling open the drawer.

FORTY-FIVE

I marched at a brisk pace back towards Anshul's office. I nearly bumped into his tall, lean frame as I reached the door. He was coming out, looking absolutely furious. It took him a second to understand that I had materialized.

'My God! Poorva Pandit! You have absolutely gone too far.' He pretty much yanked me into his room. Then he slammed the door shut. The sound made an alarming echo in my head.

'I should have guessed all along. No journalist ever acts like you have been. When the watchman told me you were here, I suspected the worst. That idiot will be sacked. And then, I just spoke to Rita.' Ominous, he made it sound.

I found myself just standing there, my head raised to look into his darkened, raging eyes. His fists were clenched. In Goa, he had looked almost menacing. Now, he looked deadly. He took a step closer to me.

'Damn you, Poorva, you will never get away with this. If I have my way, you won't even get out of this room! Not without handcuffs! I am going to . . .'

I did not wait to find out what he was going to. I shouted as loudly as I could. It came out as a valiant croak.

'What on earth are you talking about?'

'Don't play innocent with me!' he shouted back, his teeth

clenched, his arm rising as if to hit me. I shrank back. 'You bloody little spy. Going behind our backs, wheedling all sorts of information . . . And daring, daring to go to our competitors . . . You think I don't know? Dr Jacowski. That, that big twerp. Oh I know all about his work, his incompetent little brain. You take ten years of my life and sell them to him? Never, I will never allow . . .'

His hand, almost of its own volition, came down cracking on my shoulder. I winced and moved back very quickly. He looked at his hand, dazed. I couldn't decide whether he had liked the power my fear gave him. He might try it again, just to make sure he did.

I picked up the nearest thing. It was a sleek tall pedestal lamp. I wasted a few seconds jerking it out of the socket. I held it in front of me, defensively. It was heavy. Hopefully I wouldn't have to keep it up for long.

'Wrong. You've got it wrong, Anshul.' I slid out the words on adrenaline power, giving him a quick account of what I actually thought had happened. I enunciated loud and clear the name of the real villain. He listened incredulously.

'Are you stark staring mad? You expect me to believe that?'

His arm came swerving down at me again. I pushed the brass head of the lamp forward. Metal thudded against knuckle bone. He withdrew involuntarily. I understood that his heart was not in exterminating me. But the way my own heart was hammering, I may not have needed his help.

'Rita? Rita is the spy? Dr Rita George? My right hand for three years? You fool! You think you can get away with an accusation like that?'

I began to panic. This was not at all how I had pictured my Sunday would go. Anshul was rapidly losing self-control. The months of tension had found a target for instant release.

'Where are they? Where are my papers?'

I did not know what papers he was talking about. Behind him, I suddenly noticed drawers and cabinets had been flung open. Anshul had been looking for something. Which was obviously missing. Papers. Maybe like the ones Dr Rita George was carrying when she left this room some time ago?

'She has them. In the drawer of her desk. Go see for yourself.' It was a gamble I had to take.

His eyes were still blazing. He looked very much as though he would hit me yet again. The shoulder was throbbing already. Anshul is a big man.

'Dr Rita has no sister in New York, dying or alive. She went there to meet Dr Jacowski.'

'What?' There was a small flicker in his eyes, the voltage fluctuated, then dropped a notch.

'Yes. I met him myself. In New York. And his boss, Dr Perry. And their lawyers. Look, I'll give you their cards. And this letter.' I let go of the lamp, swung my handbag around, rummaged for my pocketbook. All the while, I kept an eye on him. He still appeared unstable.

I handed him the letter given to me by Dr Rudolph Perry. The letterhead alone should have convinced him. He took it, looked at it and tossed it aside.

'How does that prove anything?'

He was right. It didn't. I took a very deep, very painful breath.

'Anshul,' I said, deliberately quiet. It automatically makes people listen harder when you do that. 'I am trying to tell you something. I think the formula for the synthetic peptide that Benden-Fromm and the New York team now have was developed right here! In India! At MR Hills. By Dr Rita herself.'

It sank in. Slowly. It was like watching a schooner go down. Just as he had in Goa, I watched Anshul slump, crumble. His clothes became baggy. He closed his eyes. But there was no Surabhi to prop him up. Would I have to do the needful?

243

'If you want any proof, you will have to go to Dr Rita now. She was in your office when I came here earlier. She had some papers with her. What are they?'

Anshul removed his glasses, wiped them, stared at me myopically, then put them on again. His eyelashes made a grazing sound in the silence. Honestly. He began to mutter in disjointed sentences.

'Sunil of Sushruta, he has managed to find out something about the synthetic peptide. Don't ask me how. You had already mentioned it to me. He gave me some papers which had fractions of formula identification. He asked me to compare that with the original work we had done. He wanted me to see if I could get some leads. To do some cloning, some reverse engineering.' Anshul sounded sad, as though he had lost one of his pet morals.

'When he gave me those papers, I pulled out our own work on it, to check for differences. I came in here early this morning. Then . . . then I went to get Surabhi, once I had discovered that some of the mathematical phrases, even the wording, was just the same. When I called her along the way, she said you might have come here looking for me. So I turned around and came back.'

I felt less frightened, my heartbeat slowed a little. 'Are you convinced that the extract you got is from the India Biotech work?' I put the question in a neutral, non-threatening tone.

'Damn it. Yes. Yes. And yes.' His colour was rising again. He paced a little, like a boxer preparing for the ring. 'Of course, there are some differences. From what I can tell— Sunil gave me only fragments of information—it uses a different base protein. From the lining of the egg. But the damn formula is bloody versatile. It has been altered to fit. A neat tailoring job. Damn and damn.'

He came at me, but like a middleweight in the last round. 'Come on. I'm not leaving you here. You better come with me to Rita.' He pulled me along, none too gently. I let my body go slack.

FORTY-SIX

Dr Rita was on the phone. She was definitely agitated, her movements were jittery. It looked uncharacteristic. Her fingers drummed on the table; she was bobbing her head. Sweat stood shining on her forehead and upper lip. We entered the room without knocking. Anshul dragged me in behind him.

She hurriedly put down the phone when she saw us. She must have noticed Anshul's grip on my arm.

'Good. You found her. I was just trying to make a few calls. To find out what she has been up to.'

'Rita,' said Anshul, sounding totally exasperated. 'This crazy woman says she was offered ten thousand dollars to give Benden-Fromm information about our vaccine. She has been supplying them with every kind of information. It seems she bribed one of our research station boys to give her access to the computer. The little sneak.'

I gaped at him, my jaw working like a tic. Had he gone out of his mind?

He turned his head backwards to look at me. I picked up a signal, flashed back one of my own. The doctor was a genius. 'He moves fast,' Tushar had said.

Rita's expression would have been comical in the right context. Now it looked like moulding clay as it moved from one emotion to another. It settled in my direction, with a look of utter astonishment.

'Can you believe that?' An outraged Anshul shook me a little. Just for effect? Or was his subliminal irritation of me surfacing?

'She says she gave them the formulae for the synthetic peptide we had formulated! The one your team—*you* had worked on so hard. Wasted so much time on! The one which did not respond in the final in-vivo tests. She is actually boasting, the fool, that they tinkered with the equations and created a successful imitation antigen. She got paid extra, she says.' He happily shook me some more.

Dr Rita took one step forward, bumping against her desk. Her voice was mutant. 'Little liar.' Suddenly, there was a heavy accent. The 'l' rolled. 'I know she is lying.'

Anshul continued to make a bid for an Oscar. 'What do you mean she is lying, Rita? She herself admitted it. Look, she has this letter from Columbia School of Medicine.'

It was then that Dr Rita tripped. A look of pure anger, then pure hatred, passed across her face. At the same time, there was a loud clap of thunder directly above. It startled us all. Rain pelted down at the window.

'Show me that,' she said, grabbing at the paper. 'She is trying to fool you. I should know. After all, I myself gave Stephen the . . .' Dr Rita stopped. She looked at me. My face must have relaxed. She looked at Anshul. His lip had begun to curl with disgust. He suddenly let go of me. My centre of gravity shifted. I clutched at the edge of a chair.

Dr Rita moved back a little from her desk. She flipped open a leather purse which had been draped over the back of her chair. The next thing I knew, a small black pistol was pointed at Anshul. He took one step back, bumped into me. Trained by Hollywood for decades, we both started to raise our arms.

The shock followed. My pupils dilated. Little beads of sweat broke out on my face. The room dimmed and brightened in rapid succession. This was a doctor in front of us, for heaven's sake. I risked a glance at Anshul. He looked like a fish that had come close to the edge of its glass bowl.

My investigative instincts rose to the surface soon enough. I wondered whether the gun was real. Scientists are not supposed to carry guns. Then, with startling clarity, I remembered the Running Doctor telling me how scared she used to be in the hills by herself at first. How she had got herself some 'protection'. I vividly remembered her mock shooting actions. The gun must be real!

Anshul spoke then, as though nothing had happened. His first reaction was of pique, of injury. With his elbows jutting out defensively, he looked like a young boy.

'Yes, Rita. Continue. What did you yourself give Stephen?'

'Dr Hiremath,' mocked the woman standing in front of us. In a plain brown sari. With a gun. 'I gave Stephen the successful formula for the new antigen. Don't worry, I didn't quite waste my time, all those nights in the lab. I had found it right back then. But I did not want to give it to you!'

'But why?' Anshul sounded confused, deprived.

'Because, Dr Hiremath, I got tired of playing second fiddle to you.' Her hand wavered a little along with her voice. I hissed in alarm. But she steadied it.

'For three years, I have devoted my life to the vaccine. It was a good deal for you, wasn't it? Dr Rita, no husband, no kids to distract her. Work, work, work. Phase one, so successful. Why? *Why*? Because of *me*!' She had raised her voice, her words were firing rapidly. I hoped her pistol wouldn't.

'Because of me, you understand? Because of me. While you and your glamorous wife toured the world, published your papers, flirted with the government. Used the money from Biogene to build yourself this . . .' She moved the black weapon in a little circle, 'this palace. How much did you invest in our station, in the hills?'

Anshul was looking terribly surprised. He obviously had had no clue of the existence of this resentment now pouring over him. 'But Rita . . .' he said mildly.

'"Don't worry, Rita," you said.' The doctor did a poor imitation of Anshul's voice. '"It's only for a short time. Our next trials can be conducted right out of Bangalore!" So we lived there! For a whole year, in that godforsaken little place, cut off from the world, buttering up those stupid, illiterate tribal women.'

Anshul was thinking back, his eyes remote. He seemed completely unaware of Rita's finger on the trigger. I, on the other hand, had broken out into a fine trembling. I missed my mother.

'Rita, you know very well that if we had not had those abnormal pregnancies, you could have left sooner.'

'For what? So that you could get all the glory? And the money? Dr Anshul Hiremath, inventor of the world's first contraceptive vaccine. Hero number one.' She said it without any humour whatsoever.

Anshul's eyes were glittering now. 'Yes! *Yes*! It was . . . it *is* my vaccine. Don't fool yourself. I picked you out of that insignificant lab you were working in all those years ago. Believe me, you would still have been working on mice and monkeys if you had stayed.'

I cowered. It was not a smart strategy on the part of the resident genius to challenge the gun-toting biochemist.

'Fool myself? You are the fool. You didn't know what was going on right under your nose, did you? Your trips to MR Hills were becoming so rare, I could have walked off with the whole lab. Dr Rita can manage! Well, I did.'

A crafty, triumphant glaze came over her eyes. It was like watching my garden geckos stalking a butterfly.

'How do you think those two women got pregnant?'

A silence crept over Anshul. I could feel him stiffening next to me.

'I tampered with the dosages of your precious antigen.

I altered the amplification frequency in the peptide PCR. Instead of 100,000 times, I made it 10,000. Only one little zero! The antigen dosage we injected in those women was not enough to raise adequate antibodies for contraception. The fertilized eggs were partially hatched. It caused the foetal abnormality. I kept double records of everything. It was easy. That half-educated Sadanand didn't have a clue!'

Anshul's body had straightened up. His eyes had rounded like his open mouth.

Rita suddenly gripped the pistol with both hands. 'And it would have been all right. Except for that fool Keti. She kept her baby. I got a call from Padma this morning. She delivered a four pounder. Girl, eight weeks premature. Face structure okay, except for forehead. Some brain damage. Breathing with support. Apgar scale four. Lower body deformity.'

I thought of Keti, her family. Her cheerfulness. A loud sob came from me, startling Rita. Her aim moved towards me. I trembled like unset jelly.

'Idiot woman,' she said venomously. I felt keenly that all my good luck on this story had just run out.

But she was talking of Keti. 'She could have aborted the foetus. But no, she wanted some glory as well. Anyway, it's all right. My time was up. The truth would have come out sooner or later.' Her voice had become almost reflective.

Anshul is a completely crazy man. There was a look of pure happiness on his face. I kept looking from him to the gun, from the gun to him.

'Are you saying that the problems we had, those deformed . . . that they are not endemic to the vaccine?'

'Oh, I wouldn't say that, Dr Hiremath. Your precious vaccine may still not work as well as you hope. The peptide you are raising is unstable. You need my peptide.' Dr Rita smiled. Pure triumph. 'But you cannot have it, doctor! I've sold it to the higher bidder. They have promised to file a provisional patent in my name. I get to be on the team for future royalty payments. I get to be a star too!'

249

Anshul refused to face the reality of death, or severe injury, that faced him squarely in the form of gleaming black metal. He was floating serenely. Mad. Quite mad.

'Dr Rita, don't worry. You should have told me! It's not too late. We'll rework your contract. I give you my word.' Stupid, ineffectual words. I reworked my new opinion of him.

Rita seemed to agree with me. She took careful aim, just like in the movies. 'Your word, doctor,' she said, suddenly calm, 'is not worth its weight in boiled rice.'

I thought, then, that it was time for me to speak. 'Er, hold it for one second, Dr Rita.'

They had forgotten that I was around. I felt a small rush of triumphant adrenaline to have got their attention.

'Dr Stephen and I had a long chat this past week. Dr Perry was there too. So were their lawyers. I wonder if you've met them? They have a lot of information on your work. They have put a trace on you. They are worried about your proposed contract with them. Something about IPR. Changing patent laws. About you having worked at India Biotech's expense, on India Biotech's time. That sort of thing. Won't hold water, it seems.'

I cannot describe the change that came over the woman in front of us. I only remember thinking that I must have a suicidal streak in me. As comprehension sunk in, she went from disbelief to grief to utter rage. Against me. I really should avoid being the bearer of bad news.

The pistol moved slowly. Unsteadily. It kept rhythm with her words.

'You . . . bloody . . . little . . . bitch . . . you . . . are . . . lying. I . . . worked . . . *on my own time*. There was no limiting contract between me and India Biotech. My research is . . . and will . . . remain *mine*.' Snarling, she took aim, pulled back the cock.

At that moment, the door burst open. Somebody had the script after all. The gun went off. I screamed. So did

250

somebody else. But something was wrong. There was no spark. It was a rubber bullet. It made a loud report anyway. I feel now as if I saw the bullet leave the barrel and head at me. I actually remember seeing it thud against my chest. Trying to shield my body from the impact, I moved back in reflex, and hit a large metal shelf. One of its drawers was open. Pain was instant but unreal. I saw the world's biggest eyes peer into mine. They were the wrong colour, though. For some reason, I was on the floor. And there was warm liquid running down my neck, ruining my blue salwar kameez with an unseemly red. Then the two colours merged into the deepest purple.

FORTY-SEVEN

Purple and red began to blur and re-focus. They turned golden-brown. Honey eyes dripped anxious warmth on me. 'Poo, baby, sweetheart,' Rohil's voice, repeating endlessly. I told him later how irritating it had been. He answered that it had served the purpose. That my eyes flew open and I said, '*Arre*, what?'

I was back at St Paul's. I could tell even without looking at hospital issue linen. This time there was not even an instant of amnesia. I remembered the fake gun, the real terror. But how had I got there, so far away from India Biotech? Our local institutions are rather wary of taking in accident or crime victims. Too much police and legal protocol. Funnily enough, it was not the rubber bullet that had wounded me. I had hit the lower part of my head on the sharp drawer, and my left arm had crumpled up when I hit the floor. I hurt myself at the same spot as I had in the accident, and the pain had sent me into shock. I'd been carted, bleeding and unconscious, to St Paul's. And to Dr Kamath.

The medical reports seemed to suggest I was strong as a cow. My head injury was less serious than it had appeared with all the blood. I was bandaged up, my poor hair had to be snipped at one place. The imitation bullet, of course, had done me little harm. All my fear and panic for almost nothing! Still, I think that little powerpack of rubber felled Rohil instead. He has been excusing me all my excesses ever since. Except for one. He is very upset that, as soon as I could focus again, I asked after Anshul. Even before enquiring about Shweta.

Luckily, it was not my right arm that was fractured. I had turned reflexively towards the door when it opened. It was Surabhi who had come in, to protect her husband from me. She must have been astounded to find a new villainess. Hearing her enter, Rita's reflexes had also worked overtime. The pistol had gone off, almost by itself. The rubber bullet had made her look stupid and that had made her angry. A MAD magazine scenario had ensued. Rita had picked up a heavy glass paperweight and had flung it at Anshul, who was bent over me. Someone up there had decided to add more injury to my injuries. The glass paperweight fell on my prostrate body, bouncing off my stomach onto my unhappy leg. At least it did not shatter and leave me draped in shards. We must always, strictly, thank God for small mercies. It is now a rule in our house.

They released me from the hospital the next day without the fuss I had endured earlier. Goes to show that buses are more harmful than guns. Anyway, with Dr Kamath around this time we did not even have to do the paperwork ourselves!

That evening, we all sat in the living room. Shweta was draped immodestly all over me. Rohil sat close, resenting Shweta a little for the first time. Amma hovered, Anna listened. I had to tell the story, even though I was tired.

They oohed and they aahed when I talked about the gun pointed at me. Shweta went into round-eyed, what-a-great-story mode. Life is not very real for her, anyway.

I was admonished by my parents. I was told I had no need whatsoever to play God. What if the bullet had been real, and had damaged me forever? What if Rita had thrown something else, a knife maybe? The look in their eyes suggested I should understand that they already had one cross to bear. I swore I would never allow myself to be shot at again. Even by a child's imaginary gun.

I was chastized by Shweta too. I should not have put myself in danger. Nobody, but nobody accepted that I had had no premonition of any such danger. Who could imagine physical injury in corporate warfare?

Much later, Rohil and I sat in my room, waiting for dinner. I was ravenously hungry. Again. Laxmi had begun war-like preparations in the kitchen. He gave me a look that started my healing. He kissed my wounded arm reverentially, making me feel very woozy. He followed up, in his best bedside manner, with some soothing ministrations to unrelated parts of my anatomy. Then he checked my pulse. To make sure my tachycardia was not for medical reasons. Slowly, he began to unload his mind.

'We have to speak of many things, Poo. But first I must tell you this. It may be rather late. Maybe even redundant. But Shaila and I met for lunch yesterday.' Ah, the mysterious Dr Shaila whom I had not yet encountered. I felt something green and slimy, like jealousy. He held my hand.

'Actually, I kind of used the fact that she has this crush on me.' Oh, she did, did she? My lover-boy flushed appealingly. My own crush on him got squashier. 'I gave her some background. She said she was called in as a consultant, like I told you, on some follow-ups on the women who had participated in phase one of your Anshul's vaccine trials.'

My Anshul. I guess I did own Anshul, a little bit, now. 'She said there is bad news. Two of the women in that trial—out of thirty-eight, I think—have developed systemic lupus.'

I was completely blank. My reactions were delayed.

'Lupus is an auto-immune disease,' said the ever-patient counterfoil to my impulsive self. 'It is devastating. The body's immune system reacts against its own tissue. It starts off when some tissue reaches a part of the body in which it is not supposed to be. It is seen as enemy. Antibodies are created to destroy it. By then, it is too late. The antibodies go on a rampage.'

I was horrified. 'You mean the vaccine caused this lupus thing?'

Rohil shrugged. 'Shaila seemed to think so. Lupus is too rare for it to be put down to coincidence. She had concluded so in the report she is readying for India Biotech.'

It made sense, even to me! You try to fool the body into believing that some specific cells, out of its own millions, are actually the enemy. Destroy them, you command. The body obligingly starts to do so. Somewhere along the line, it gets confused. If these cells are enemy, these other ones, so similar, may be enemy too. Mutated, like those awful viruses! Why take a chance? Destroy, destroy.

'Does Anshul know yet?'

'Not yet, I guess. Shaila said she wanted to be very sure. She said lupus is so uncommon, she could hardly believe it herself. Two in thirty-eight! Ridiculous. Anyway, she was trying to reach him.'

But of course, Anshul had been away at MR Hills for a long time. Mentally, I turned away from Rohil. I had to think hard. Now there were more pieces than I could fit into my puzzle frame. Later, Rohil said he had been tempted to strangle me just then. Such violent times we live in! He had to forego his prepared speeches. I never let him have another word about us. I pumped him as much as I could on auto-immune diseases. Then I fell asleep, quite exhausted. Without Laxmi's mega-meal. There was still some string-collecting to be done on the story, it seemed.

FORTY-EIGHT

Tuesday morning. I was feeling worse in my body, in spite of anti-inflammatory, antipyretic, antibiotic medications. But I was clear in the head.

I called Vikram in MR Hills. I actually got through. He said things had taken a nasty turn. Chamla had reported that Keti's baby had caused the simmering anger and resentment to overflow. The doctors had let the midwife watch the delivery, it seemed. She had described it to the others as though the procedure had taken place in a small, dark room, without anaesthesia. The baby had become monstrous in the story. The India Biotech station had been attacked. Not too much damage had been done. It was more of a symbolic act. Sadanand and the others had managed to flee just in time.

I asked about Keti. 'Dr Padma, the gynaecologist, did contact me for some supplies. It was an emergency. They have transferred the woman and her baby to Maddur. I had sent the jeep. This morning, things are more stable. The driver has returned. He says Keti is cheerful.' I smiled. I wanted to rush off to see her right away. Better counsel, mostly medical, prevailed shortly.

I gave him an abbreviated account of developments in Bangalore. The good doctor seemed rather bewildered. He asked me if I had life insurance.

CP called. I had quite forgotten about him, quite forgotten who and what I was supposed to be. He sounded as though he was disgusted with me.

'I assume you got injured in the line of duty. We should pay your bills. Still, I have agency reports here from Maddur, of all places. I thought they only made vadas there. It seems there was some trouble in the hills. Some of the Banigas are agitating over a deformed baby. India Biotech has been mentioned. There has been some stone throwing.'

Damn. And damn! But I suppose I deserved it. I could hardly control information flows to suit my convenience. Now the wolf pack would descend on the hills.

'By any chance, Poorva,' said my much-tested friend and editor, 'does this have anything to do with the story you have been sitting on for weeks?'

If sarcasm was acidic, the telephone wires would have corroded. I had to think on my feet. Luckily, I was sitting down, my shoulder throbbing.

'CP. Relax. By midnight, you will have the first instalment of the story. It should ideally go into the newspaper tomorrow. We could do a magazine special later.'

He revived magically. We spent twenty minutes discussing the technicalities of making a huge splash in the media the next day. We spoke of Avaru. CP said Avaru had been informed of the New York discoveries and was not unhappy, except that he now thought the competition would have the story first. He was going to call me. But I should not worry. CP, without actually saying so, implied he would make sure there was no heat. I wondered at his change of heart. Of course, in keeping with his true self, he never asked me once if writing an article twelve hours after being out of hospital would hamper my style. He should be with CNN. They deserve him.

It's funny trying to type with one hand. Especially if another person is trying to use his non-'operational' hand to make up for yours. Romantic bliss is not founded on such togetherness, especially with Rohil's editorial comments. 'Are you sure you are not glorifying Keti?' he asked me once. Somewhere inside me, I knew I would have to deal with that later. Just then I decided to let it pass. My story came out stilted. But it came out. Let the subs deal with the typos. Even my spell-checker couldn't handle them all.

FORTY-NINE

Anna shook me awake, crushing the smell of fresh newspaper under my nose. 'Shabhash, gonu. Look at this!' I shot up, getting him under the chin.

We had made page one, three columns, top right. Best slot. Continued on page three. A little boxed note to readers, promising more, much more.

With a little dread, I registered the headline. ABUSE OF CLINICAL TRIALS ON VACCINE. DEFORMED BABY BORN AT MR HILLS.

Completely sensational. I cringed. But I forced myself to read. Just three typos. Not bad for an overworked night staff. The story itself was not sensational at all. I had underplayed it. It was full of journalese. 'It is alleged', 'sources said', 'unconfirmed reports suggest,' and so on. No libel, please. The reader had to read a lot between the lines. I got on the phone.

CP sounded like a hangover. 'What do you think?'

'Thank you,' I said.

'You bet you should thank me,' he growled. 'Avaru was wild. He says the *Times of India* has got wind of our little efforts. That they are starting full-scale investigations. He also reminded me that he was supposed to get the copy first. He says we disobeyed his orders. We should have given him the proofs to read. I have distracted him with details of follow-ups. I have also told him,' this was said in a careful tone, 'that Anshul Hiremath, son of Mr Chandrakant Hiremath, IAS, is not the biggest villain in the saga.'

'Thank you,' I said.

'Don't thank me,' he said, perversely. 'You have a lot of work ahead.'

Meenal called right after. I had called her the previous day to tell her about the 'shoot-out' and the ensuing chaos. She tried not to laugh at the images I conjured up for her. How I fell down, how I had panicked. She congratulated me on having actually filed my story. 'Very touching, Poo. Specially the Keti profile!'

Pranay called, sounding sleepy. 'Shit, man. Look what we achieved!' I thanked him for everything. If his high-powered hacking had not yielded the one name—Dr Rita George—that cleared the mist on this story—it would have been impossible for me to glimpse the truth. I promised him the world's biggest dinner.

'Do I have to go with you?' Petulant Pranay.

No, I laughed. With his current 'hot number' would be acceptable. He signed off, making me promise, again, never to reveal his role in the affair.

From then on, Anna fielded the calls. He handed me one, rolling his eyes suggestively.

It was the object of my obsession. Anshul was muted. 'I hope you are satisfied,' he said bitterly.

I wasn't. I asked him if Dr Shaila had contacted him.

'Yes. It's the nail, isn't it, on my coffin? You must be orgasmic about it!' I was shocked at his language. Must be the American in him. It occurred to me that maybe, just maybe, Dr Shaila had also hammered in the nails on the coffins of the two trial volunteers who had contracted lupus. I didn't bother to suggest it to him. He would have to reach his own hells himself.

Anshul had been so relieved when Dr Rita had yielded the possibility that the vaccine was clean. Now, he was despondent again. Back to the laboratory. Did he have the perseverance? The integrity? I could not have said, at that time.

I said I would have to meet him once again, and soon, to understand all the details. There was no point now in refusing me. We fixed up for the afternoon.

Shweta was extremely excited. She has always been my most devoted fan. She read the newspaper article aloud to Laxmi.

'Unfortunately, this is not a story about the tribal people of MR Hills. It should have been. But the history of events dictated that it become exactly the sort of potboiler you would expect from a NYT Top Ten Fiction list.'

FIFTY

Anna insisted on sending Mohan with me to India Biotech, to keep my appointment with Anshul. I was scared that I might see blood. Mine. Or scary paperweights. I didn't. Everything had been cleaned up. Disinfectant smells hung like static in the air.

Anshul's face was more hirsute than before. Men do not shave in a crisis. We sat in his office, both wary of each other. If I had any hope of meeting Surabhi, it was squashed. She was never going to forgive me for tearing down her husband's dream castle.

'Things started to go wrong as soon as you entered my life,' Anshul said, as soon as he saw me.

I thought he was being unfair. His troubles had started when he had become overconfident about his vaccine. I kept quiet. It's lucky I do not have a mobile face, like Shweta's.

'It was working, really. I was so, so . . . damn sure. So many years. Animal trials, struggling for money. Kowtowing to my father . . . then manipulating him. It was worth it.'

He removed his glasses, wiped them, set them down. I decided he did not like my face.

'The government came to me, as though all those babus were doing me a favour. I understood, without being prompted, that in the eyes of the civil service, it would allow me to belong to a fraternity. Of course, I would always owe somebody.' He shuddered. 'I said, *no*! I do not want your money. Biogene was there. They had seen my work.'

'Why did they pull out? Could you not have convinced them?'

'I tried.' He looked at me in that large, eyelashes-batting way that would have made lesser women weep. 'Of course it was a mistake to try and shut up that Kakodia man. It backfired on me. But I was desperate.' He shrugged.

'But,' he continued, not unduly disturbed at himself, 'I now think there must be some other factor involved. You know, these multinational pharma companies, they have such a network of contacts. And there are so many pressure points.'

We would never know the truth perhaps. Messrs Benden-Fromm wouldn't tell.

'But what about Transpharma? Why would they threaten to stop supplies of the antigen?'

'Well, to tell the truth, it was no big deal for them. Not a money-spinner. They obviously had their eye on the end product. And the marketing rights. I think they felt my product was not up to the mark.' He looked at me, his eyes milky. 'That was Dr Rita's great success.'

Of course! It had to be Dr Rita who put the cat among the pigeons at Biogene. Anything to stall Anshul, to put her own agenda in place. She must have also put in the foetus at Dr Vikram's, before final tests could reveal any of the truth. It just helped to delay Anshul.

I would have sympathized, I think, if not for Shaila's report.

'What will you do now?'

He looked like he would crumple again. I wanted out. But he straightened up.

'I think, mostly, that I will just have to start all over again. But I have no doubt that . . .'

'Will Sushruta stay with you?'

'I hope so. We could work something out. There are ways.'

To me, it looked as if the product was dead-ended with the news that lupus could be a direct result of its administration. But I kept quiet.

I realized I had never asked Anshul why he had named his antigen FRP-41. Now a macabre expansion of the acronym sprung to my mind. Forever Rest in Peace. I felt guilty and would not meet his eyes when we parted.

Later, Anna said that only one out of ten drugs under research makes it to the market, even after advanced trials. He also said, ruminatively, that people would realize, some day, that Anshul's contribution to immuno-contraceptives was seminal.

'He lost his long-term vision, his patience, somewhere. You see it all the time in a race, the best athletes sometimes don't time themselves. They lose, most often, to the strategists.'

I didn't know about all that. I knew something, though. I had started with the assumption that Anshul was a villain. That he did not care what harm his vaccine did, so long as he could peddle it. And himself with it.

Okay. So he was not the only villain. Not even the biggest one. But if there were a colour chart to be drawn, he would be firmly painted into the darker side.

I would have been tempted to become self-righteous, to feel serves-him-right-about-the-lupus. Except that, rather coincidentally, I was standing in front of a mirror.

I suppose my life may return to a new kind of normalcy. I hope so, mostly for Shweta's sake. The doctors are not too happy with her condition right now. There seems to have been an acceleration of her disease. But of course, as those of us who have read everything there is to read about it would know, it is only to be expected. Like children, diseases grow in spurts.

Amma, reaching outside herself in one big lunge, has started a Reiki course. It's a Tibetan healing system which taps into universal energy fields. We should not be sceptical of what we do not understand. I am glad for Amma.

Rohil has accepted that I am still looking for a purpose. I have finally understood that, like Amma, he is to be both the rock and the flower in my life. When I finally gave him the time for his speeches, he left me dazed with his romantic imagery. I hope I do not take him so much for granted again. He may just walk away, to pursue his big dream without me. The government has put him on a committee to bring out a feasibility study on a national on-line organ transplant network. Shweta is even more proud about it than I am.

I wrote the rest of my story in my own way. It got a cover and ten pages, with several related stories. I tried to protect those who I felt needed it, I tried to expose, instead, the capacity for evil that lurks in all of us. Which swims so cunningly to the surface when a quake begins. Like cream over milk.

The 'India vs the multinationals in a race' angle went across well. Readers and bureaucrats shook their heads, sorry that things had not worked out. The government issued statements of its new policy to support indigenous research. 'India Inc At Last?' asked a leading business magazine in a cover story.

Benden-Fromm and the Institute of Reproductive Immunology denied officially that they had promised Dr Rita George anything. Very preliminary consultations had begun, they declared. Naturally, they would have verified the origins of the research material in due course. Anshul was cynical about that. He said Rita had been foolish enough to show her formula to the New York team. They could probably develop something similar yet different now. The bitterness in his voice would have put a self-respecting karela to shame.

The question of who would now own the rights to Dr Rita's original synthetic antigen would be decided by the courts. It would be fought over bitterly for months.

I am probably the only person who came out clean from the entire tamasha. I know it is not fair. But right now, I am not complaining. They lionized me, especially the National Editors' Association. We need so hard to believe that we play a benevolent role. The prizes and awards are going to me, not to Keti. Or to Madhamma.

Dr Rita, who was quickly arrested that Sunday evening, was equally quickly released on bail. She is being prosecuted by the Health Department, and ironically, the Drug Controller. She has, however, appointed for herself a brilliant lawyer who is manipulating the media beautifully. Anshul's image is taking a public beating.

Mr Shah was imbibing gomutra when I caught up with him last. He said he feels a vicarious triumph in my victory. I think I have found a friend.

Dr Gayatri understood the real tragedy in the story, the human and social costs that had been paid for the development of the vaccine. She told me to keep up my good work and has since offered to start an action forum to raise ethics issues in medicine.

Dr Vikram Gopinath is quite unaffected by these neighbourly goings-on. Now that the bothersome mysteries have been solved and further damage to the people he loves has been contained, he has gone back to his work. His herb research centre has found many new, indigenous supporters, with all the cascading publicity.

At MR Hills, the research station has been temporarily shut down. The women have stopped taking the contraceptive vaccines. There have been some re-groupings among the tribals. Possibly the militant Baniga Shakti Sanghatana has lost some ground. People are once again questioning the alien world-view that has been brought to the hills. 'Progress without destruction', was the theme of a two-day seminar held last month at the Kendra. There was a record attendance.

I have been called to speak to Parliament sub-committees on 'Ethical Review of Drugs under Development'. I have asked for Anshul to be invited as well.

To be fair to Anshul, he understood that he was responsible for causing the trauma among the tribal women. Belatedly praising the courage and altruism of the volunteers, he admitted that he could not turn the clock back. Saying he was sorry, he has made a generous financial contribution to the Baniga community. A trust has been set up, governed exclusively by Baniga women, to utilize the funds.

Anna has initiated some highly overdue self-examination within the pharma companies. They have set up their own ethics committee. For the first time, it has outsiders to the medical profession on the panel.

'After all,' said Anna in an interview. 'We really did not need one journalist to tell us the truth about the industry. We knew it all along. But we are guilty, all of us, of a conspiracy of silence.'

Avaru compensated me handsomely for my troubles as well as my expenses. He is no longer worried about the competition. Especially since CP told him our magazine special was sold out and went into second print. People love to read, he says he told Avaru, about deformed babies. Their own, he thinks, seem less demon-like in comparison. I hope CP never gets married.

Some idiot reporter wrote that the backlash from this investigation would have an adverse impact on family planning in India. I had used the same argument in my interview with the Dean at Columbia. But these doubts must not be aired in public. What if they become self-fulfilling prophecies?

And then, finally, there was Keti. Rather I should say: 'In the beginning, in the middle and in the end, there was

Keti.' She was at the heart of this saga, it was she who had
tasted its rotten core. When the newshounds caught up with
me on the story, they played havoc among the tribal people
in the hills. They disrupted normal life, caused bitterness,
invaded their privacy. Keti would not receive messages from
me for days, would not agree to meet me, even when I
begged. It was a devastating indictment. Finally, I thought
of the expression in Keti's eyes when I had explained
Shweta's poem to her. So I wrote her a poem and asked
Shweta to edit it for me. I mailed it to her. She says she
laughed when her husband told her about it.

It was a warm, sunny afternoon when I finally caught
up with her at her home in the hills. Sitting in that clean
little hut, on a colourful cloth jhoola, she looked tired but
not unhappy. Her body had gone limp, like a deflated
balloon. But her eyes were still bright. I went and touched
her arm. She returned the gesture. For me, it felt like
absolution.

Keti's baby was sleeping in her lap. It was not easy to
watch her. She was a travesty. A constant reminder of the
costs that had been paid. But she was strong. Barely a month
old, and she could smile. I watched the pride in the mother's
eyes as she looked down at the twisted infant on her lap.
It was pure pride. Unmixed with any other emotion. I felt
an unmixed emotion myself. It was shame.

ACKNOWLEDGEMENTS

Writing is supposed to be a lonely business. As a home manager and a mother of two, it was hard to find the 'loneliness' which was my due. Besides which, I felt compelled to share ideas about the book with every friend and acquaintance. I'm glad I now have the proof.

My first thanks are to my husband Nandan for his support, his clarity of ideas and his gentle criticism.

Vir Sanghvi was subjected to my first draft. Thanks to him for his critical inputs and encouragement.

The medical research for this book was conducted over several months. I interviewed dozens of people, some unsuspecting of my motives. I thank them all, but name only a few.

Dr Firuza Parikh helped me construct the fictitious vaccine and introduced me to the zona pellucida. FRP-41 is named after her. Dr Bhavana Doshi spent hours explaining the intricacies of clinical trials for new drugs.

Dr H Sudarshan of the Vivekananda Girijana Kalyana Kendra, BR Hills offered his hospitality and shared his knowledge of the hills and its people. I met several people in the hills and I thank them for sharing so much.

KR Usha and MK Raghavendra spent a great deal of time and care over the manuscript.

Thanks to all those who readily gave information at St John's Hospital, Serum Institute, Recon India.

Thanks to Sudeshna Shome Ghosh and VK Karthika of Penguin Books, for working so well and so quickly on the editing.

Last, not least, many thanks to my literary agents, Jacaranda Press, of whom, Amrita Chak spent many months helping me edit the book and Jayapriya Vasudevan was all encouragement.